LULU MEETS GOD AND DOUBTS HIM

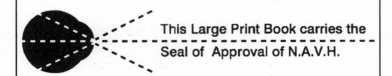

This Large Print Book carries the
Seal of Approval of N.A.V.H.

LULU MEETS GOD
AND DOUBTS HIM

DANIELLE GANEK

THORNDIKE PRESS

An imprint of Thomson Gale, a part of The Thomson Corporation

Detroit • New York • San Francisco • New Haven, Conn. • Waterville, Maine • London

Thorndike Press® Large Print Core.

The text of this Large Print edition is unabridged.

Other aspects of the book may vary from the original edition.

Set in 16 pt. Plantin.

LIBRARY OF CONGRESS CATALOGING-IN-PUBLICATION DATA

Ganek, Danielle.
    Lulu meets God and doubts him / by Danielle Ganek.
      p. cm. — (Thorndike Press large print core)
    ISBN-13: 978-0-7862-9863-1 (alk. paper)
    ISBN-10: 0-7862-9863-4 (alk. paper)
    1. Art — Collectors and collecting — Fiction. 2. Artists — Fiction. 3. New
York (N.Y.) — Fiction. 4. Large type books. I. Title.
    PS3607.A45L85 2007b
    813'.6—dc22   2007023506

Published in 2007 by arrangement with Viking, a member of Penguin Group (USA) Inc.

Printed in the United States of America on permanent paper
10 9 8 7 6 5 4 3 2 1

For David

ACKNOWLEDGMENTS

With gratitude to everyone at Viking who brought this book magically to life, with special thanks to the world's nicest editor, Kendra Harpster, and to Molly Stern, Clare Ferraro, Nancy Sheppard, Carolyn Coleburn, Ann Day, and Rakia Clark. With a big thank you to my agent and friend Leigh Feldman and her team, Mike Kelley, Ros Perotta, and Michele Mortimer. And with deep appreciation and love for Team Ganek, my favorite people, David, Harry, Nicky, and Zoe Ganek, who make sure every day includes at least one good laugh.

ONE:
FALL POSTWAR AND CONTEMPORARY SALE MONDAY, 7:00 P.M.

November

The auction starts — Ladies and Gentlemen, we begin this evening's sale of postwar and contemporary art with lot number 1, blah, blah, blah — and I hold myself still. It's a game I like to play at sales. I entertain myself with the implausible fear that if I so much as scratch my ear or push my glasses up on my nose, the auctioneer will perceive this as a bid and I will suddenly own a piece of art I can't possibly afford. That this is impossible only adds to the fun. I don't even have a paddle.

I stand at the back, squeezed in with the press and other observers. I take an elbow in the rib from a fat guy in a droopy overcoat scribbling names and paddle numbers in his notebook, but I hold my ground. I've chosen my spot in the sale room carefully. I figured I'd be invisible back here, in the standing section with the reporters and the

9

pretend collectors and other folks not too proud to watch an entire auction on their feet.

There is another whole room of people watching on a screen upstairs in an annex — talk about Siberia! But they miss seeing the bidders in action. From where I stand, I can see everything. And I hope no one can see me.

Especially not Simon. Except there he is, coming down the center aisle, clutching his ticket to his chest as though someone might snatch it away and he'd be banished to the back to stand.

Simon is late. The first piece, a smallish Richard Prince cowboy, always an easy sell, selected to set the mood — Buy! Buy! — has gone far above the asking price. There is just the slightest break in the tension in the crowded room. The bubble will not burst tonight.

I try to tuck myself in behind the fat man, so Simon can't see me. I don't think he'd bother looking in my direction; no one of interest to him would be standing. Or so I think. I'm wrong, as I often am when it comes to my former boss. He does look in my direction. And he sees me. He stops in the aisle and our eyes meet. He runs his hand through his hair. Surely this will be the extent of our exchange. This is already too much intimacy for Simon.

He continues down the aisle toward me. This is the most crowded sale room I've ever seen, the seats jammed up against each other like coach class on Continental. Simon has to step over legs in the aisle to get to me.

"Mia McMurray. What in bloody hell are you doing here?"

It's not like Simon to be so loud. The fat reporter immediately starts shushing. Heads turn in our direction as the auctioneer accepts bids on lot number 2.

"How'd you even get a ticket?" His voice gets louder. More heads turn.

The reporter waves a hand at Simon to get him out of the way. This doesn't work. Simon glares at each one of us in turn. He doesn't seem to know what else to say to me. I give him my friendliest smile. I haven't seen him since June. I wonder if he missed me a little.

"Take your seat," the fat guy growls. He makes a gesture toward the ticket Simon is still holding at his chest.

This works. Simon gives me one last withering look before he turns to find his spot in one of the rows of chairs. I step back. The fat guy edges over into the space

I just released, and I let him. "Thank you," I tell my new friend as he jostles into position. He doesn't respond.

Jeffrey Finelli's painting of Lulu is hanging in the sale room. It's on the right wall, above the bank of phones manned by a growing cadre of extraordinarily attractive salespeople employed by the auction house. He is flanked, not incongruously, by Ed Ruscha and Willem de Kooning, two of my favorites. From the far wall a Basquiat and a Hirst face the Finelli. There, the painting glows, imbued with the power of context.

The official title of the piece is *Lulu Meets God and Doubts Him.* Wordy, isn't it? Talk about awkward. Most people leave off the part about the doubting and call it *Lulu and God.* Or "the one with the girl and the paintbrush." Or just, "the big one." It certainly is big. A swirling riot of orange, pink, and yellow on a nine-by-twelve-foot unframed canvas. In the lower right corner is his signature, Finelli. A scrawl with an exaggerated *F* and a long tail on the *l* at the end.

It's an exquisitely composed portrait of a young girl holding a small canvas of her own in one perfectly detailed hand, a dripping paintbrush in the other. The use of light is remarkable, a clear golden light that evokes Florence. The scale gives the piece intensity, and the swirling colors give it Finelli's own unique style. But it's the look on the girl's face, wise and so clearly full of doubt that the explanatory title is unnecessary, that makes it difficult for the viewer to look away.

The Lulu in the painting has circular gray eyes. When they fix on yours, they lock in. You move before her and her eyes move with you, like Mona Lisa's eyes, only much bigger. She's riveting. From her spot above the audience gathered for tonight's sale, the nine-by-twelve-foot Lulu gazes down at the art world with a wry smile, as though amused by the spectacle before her. It is quite a spectacle.

There are three types of people crammed into the tightly packed rows of seats. First, of course, are the collectors. The big players peer down from their boxes above the action, like at the ballet. The others occupy seats as good or as bad as their recent buying history. There are passionate collectors, fueled by lust, and others, only mildly horny, looking to enjoy themselves without commitment. Within this category are a crop of new-moneyed thirty- and forty-year-olds with an air of being on a Saturday shopping spree.

Then there are the dealers, like Simon. They monitor the market carefully at auction, if they're good, sniffing the wind. There are young ones, scrappily negotiating arrangements that are only slightly unethical, and older ones, guarding their turf, knowing that in the contemporary world, new is always desirable. There are secondary market dealers. They're the ones who sell the works that come up for resale, unlike the gallerists who represent artists and sell art on what's called the primary market. That's the stuff you can buy, if you're lucky, when you walk into a gallery.

There are also lots and lots of art advisers, spending other people's money with a nice cut for themselves, sometimes a kickback from certain dealers. All of them trying to grab a piece of the pie, any way they can. Even the most jaded of them enjoy the spectacle.

I suppose I fall into the third category. The gawkers. We're here to watch. It *is* a thrill, seeing other people spend what feels like obscene and frivolous — or simply impossible — amounts of money on something as tenuously valuable as a piece of art. It's especially exciting when the numbers go crazy, way above the estimates in the catalog. This has been happening a lot. Apparently we're in the middle of a bubble.

In the gawker group are curators and art historians, elegant couples in smart suits who are cultured and speak many languages, ladies in long flowered coats they've brought back from Bali or large plastic earrings that are funky and awful, men in leather jackets they're too old or too bald to be wearing, the pretend collectors, and pretty young things in BCBG cocktail dresses and blown-out hair more interested in snagging a husband than a good deal on a Matthew Barney video piece.

"Fair warning," the auctioneer states in British English, slightly accented with Swiss German. There are a lot of wonderful accents in the international art world. The auctioneer's is a cocktail of European influences, but he is fully in control of his English. He wears a crisp Italian tuxedo and has noticeable sideburns and a very full head of hair. He's known for a penetrating stare that is famously effective at wrangling one or two more bids out of buyers. He stands at his little podium with supreme confidence, a preacher at his pulpit, commanding the room. Some of us have a small crush on him.

Above his head is an electronic board that posts the bids in different currencies. It's fun to watch the prices appear in yen and euro and British sterling. Lot number 7 has sold. A hundred thousand above the high estimate. There's a strain in the air you can almost taste, sweet and tart, a combination of anxiety and self-congratulatory glee at simply being here. The sale is going well, but I'm anxious for it to move more quickly. I'm interested in Jeffrey Finelli's painting of Lulu. Lot number 22.

"New bidder," cries the auctioneer, pointing toward the phalanx of well-dressed auction staff working the phones. His moves at the podium are graceful versions of traffic-cop gesticulations as he locates where the money is coming from on any given bid. "On the telephone."

The seller of the Finelli is a collector named Martin Better, although this is supposed to be a secret. Like many secrets, it's ill kept. Everyone who's anyone knows Martin Better is the seller. I see him now, in the eighth row, chewing gum with gusto, his wife, Lorette, at his side. Her precise blond bob catches the light as she stifles a yawn. I'm surprised to see her here — she's never been to auction before — but she does have a vested interest in tonight's sale. You can

16

buy a lot of jewelry for what they might make on the Finelli, even if it doesn't go above the low estimate.

In the last four years Martin Better has accumulated art the way some people throw groceries into a cart, dropping five, ten, even twenty or thirty million on a piece with the nonchalant air of a housewife grabbing a box of Honey Nut Cheerios at the Stop & Shop.

Martin Better is a real estate developer, although he is often erroneously referred to as a hedge fund manager because it's popular sport to disparage all new collectors as hedge fund speculators, implying that the only reason they're buying art is to — gasp — make money.

Marty Better is a notorious risk-taker — although the phrase, I believe, is "He's got balls the size of coconuts." Or something that sounds equally uncomfortable. He made a huge fortune for himself in the real estate market. Then he began buying art. Once he started, he couldn't stop.

Ironically, Dr. Kopp, one of the more vociferous of the older collectors denigrating the newer buyers in general, hedge funders, Russians — and Martin Better in particular — for what he perceives to be a lack of sensitivity to price, is seated right next to

Martin and Lorette. Maybe someone at the auction house was having a little fun. Poor Dr. Kopp. He's a world-renowned professor. And he can't afford the art on his walls.

We're on lot 14 when the energy in the room shifts. It's time for the celebrity socialite to make her entrance. Jenna Bain is the wife of prominent collector Robert Bain. Yes, you can read "prominent" as "wealthy." You're starting to speak the language.

Jenna Bain is spectacular. The dress clings in all the right places. The shiny blond hair bounces just so. She waves and kisses, kisses and waves, making an entrance down the center aisle although her seat next to her husband is more easily accessible from the side of the room. Her husband is already seated, and he sits up a little straighter now, knowing he's the envy of every man at the sale. Everyone sits up a little straighter, the shot of glamour reinforcing the feeling that here, now, is the place to be.

"I can sell it at four million dollars," intones the auctioneer. Then just one last query in the direction of the underbidder on lot 14. "Any more?"

And then, it's too funny. Almost immediately following Jenna Bain comes

Connie Kantor. One of the new collectors — no, not hedge fund money, her husband made his cash inventing some kind of toilet-paper dispenser — Connie in five-inch heels is a moving sight gag as she makes her way down the center aisle, although her seat too would be more easily reached from the side closest to the door.

She waves and kisses, kisses and waves, acknowledging anyone she happens to know. My shoulders hunch reflexively, although I know she won't even glance in the direction of the standing section. Her eyes dart this way and that with the acquisitive gleam of a collector in heat.

Hers is a lumpy body no amount of money can dress up, although she's trying, in what appears to be a mink sweatshirt with a hood. She has lank hair even the man known as the magician with the blow-dryer can't volumize and little eyes made smaller with too much makeup. She wears diamonds by the yard roped several times around her neck and a much larger one dangling from her ring finger. Off her arm swings an enormous Hermes Birkin bag in bright blue crocodile. That's one of those bags that cost ten grand at least, if you can get your name on the top of the wait list. The croc is more. This one is so big it looks fake, but Connie doesn't have the confidence to carry a fake.

Her husband Andrew, a troll-like creature slumped in a seat near the front of the room, does not turn around. He's on the crack, scrolling messages on the CrackBerry, his shoulders bobbing up and down. I've never seen him without that BlackBerry; he always looks very busy, but he could also just be playing BrickBreaker. Either way, he doesn't look up to see his wife come down the aisle. His are the only eyes in the room not on Connie right now. Even the auctioneer pauses slightly to take in the visual of her entrance.

The contrast between Connie and Jenna Bain is comical. Just as Connie gets to her row, blowing a kiss at Andrew, she trips on her heel. She goes all the way down to the floor, and from the blue bag spews makeup and cell phone and two tampons all over the aisle. It's all I can do not to guffaw. There are others in the room less restrained. The fat guy next to me snorts a loud laugh.

"Yard sale," he says, slapping his knee.

The suave auctioneer can hardly keep the focus of the crowd. He manages to do so with a quick sale of lot 15. "All done, then, at two hundred thousand dollars."

The sale is moving swiftly. Artists' records

are being made. So far, nothing has been bought in. Soon, we're at lot 21. This is a piece for which there was a lot of presale hype. When it sells, anticlimactically, for just over the low estimate, a few people get up to leave.

And then, the Finelli. The estimate is $950,000 to $1,150,000. Will it shock you to know Simon originally planned to price the painting at $75,000 at the opening in March of this same year, only nine months earlier? It should. I've never been good at math, but that's an increase of what? A lot.

The seller — yes, right, Martin Better — should make a tidy profit on a painting for which he paid $675,000. Six hundred seventy-five thousand dollars is where the price had gone for this piece by June, only four months after the opening. Sure, there's been plenty of vicious gossip and opinionated judgment about Marty selling the Finelli so soon after he bought it at the Basel art fair. And not just quietly offering it around through a secondary dealer, or giving it back to Simon to sell for him, but putting it up for auction. Auction is so public, so flashy, so, well, bold. Coconuts, hmm.

"Lulu meets God and doubts him," the auctioneer intones. He glances at the ceiling, knowing as he does how a piece of art that's generally been decreed to be the best of the artist's output can produce strange and exhilarating results at such sales. These kinds of results, wild excesses, are what keeps him in business, and what keeps all of us coming back, even suffering the humiliation of the standing section if necessary. Perhaps his glance at the ceiling is a little prayer.

The bidding starts strong, with multiple bids from around the room. The brisk action sparks the curiosity of some of the early leavers, who linger at the door to watch. There are phone bidders and lots of raised paddles, and the numbers go up steadily.

"Seven hundred thousand. Seven hundred and fifty. Eight hundred." The auctioneer hardly gets a chance to breathe between bids.

The price is quickly at nine hundred and fifty, the low estimate. The early buyers fall out as the price gets over a million. At a million four it settles down to three bidders.

One of them is a new collector I overheard at the preview loudly questioning the condition of the piece, probably because he had no idea what else to say. The condition? It was practically still wet.

The second bidder is, of course, Connie Kantor. She's recovered from her fall, relaced those mischievous sandals, and is waving her paddle as high as she can reach, as though the auctioneer might not spot it. Not for Connie the subtle nod or a discreet removal of glasses.

The third of these bidders is in the standing section, behind me. This person occupies an unusual blind area in the oddly shaped sale room, to the side of a pillar, blocked to the seated crowd. It's a spot visible to the auctioneer and the alluring salespeople lined up along the telephones and only a few people in the standing section. To most of the room this bidder is nothing but a paddle. A mystery bidder. The seated crowd loves a mystery bidder.

The bidding goes up steadily, paced evenly, with the three paddles alternating. The two million mark gets hit, much to the surprise and excitement of every person in the room. The currency board flips out the numbers: 1,565,195,000 euro. That's 223,359,084 Japanese yen. Even Lorette Better looks interested.

Then three million. A thrill takes over the quiet sale room. Talk about excess. Remember, this is Jeffrey Finelli, not Andy Warhol!

At three million two even the elegant auctioneer is having trouble restraining himself. "Three million three, three million four, three million five, three million six." He hardly pauses between the numbers, glee infusing his pronunciation of the words. His narrow hips swivel as he gestures first toward the back right corner of the room, then to the front left, then to the far right where Connie sits.

At three million seven hundred thousand the collector who was concerned about the condition of the painting drops out. He looks bewildered, as though he's just woken up from a trance.

It's down to Connie and the bidder in the back. The whole room seems to be playing my game, people holding themselves rigidly still, not even breathing, fearing the slightest misinterpretation of a tilted head or a loud sigh.

The mystery bidder seems to have the piece at four million dollars.

"Fair warning." The auctioneer practically dances at his podium. "Selling now at four million dollars."

There's not a sound in the room. Something in Connie's deer-in-the-headlights look causes the auctioneer to sense he might have another bid. He fixes his seductive gaze on her, now the underbidder.

"Will you give me four million one?" he asks, leaning way over the podium in Connie's direction.

Connie holds tight to the paddle in her lap. The other hand she has slipped under her thigh, as though to keep it from leaping up of its own accord and bidding without her. Her lips will be clenched with such determination they will have practically disappeared, only a smudge of lipgloss remaining to indicate that there once was a mouth in that region of her face.

"One more, madam?" the auctioneer queries.

The room is silent. Connie's husband refuses to catch her eye.

"Take your time," the auctioneer says, sounding gracious, although we all know what he really means.

Connie looks down at her paddle, then lifts her head and nods firmly at the auctioneer.

"Four million one hundred thousand dollars," he says with as much excitement as his Swiss manners will allow. "It's with you, madam, four million one against you at the very back of the room."

There's a slight pause.

"Do I have four million two?"

And the back-of-the-room bidder is right back in for four million two, so quickly, with a swift lifting of the paddle above heads, and then just as swiftly lowering it so it is almost missed by everyone except the auctioneer.

Connie turns her head once, quickly, toward the standing section. I slide behind my heavy friend, but Connie doesn't see me.

"Do I have four million three?" the auctioneer asks, ever so politely, of Connie. Connie looks like she could scream in frustration. But she clamps her lips together even more tightly and lifts her paddle in weary resignation.

"Four million three hundred thousand dollars," the auctioneer cries. "Thank you, madam."

I crane my neck, as we all do, to catch a glimpse of the mysterious bidder. It's considered extremely bad form to stand up, but one woman wearing a yellow-and-black-striped dress does a sort of crouch in her seat to try for a better view. None of them, not even crouching tiger lady, can see what the eagle-eyed auctioneer can spot from his perch above the action. The figure with the paddle at the back of the room has gone, probably slipped out the side door.

"Four million three," the auctioneer states, now matter-of-fact, as he knows he has to wrap things up quickly.

"Fair warning," he says, before Connie can change her mind. "Selling now at four million three hundred thousand dollars."

Whack goes the little smacker on the podium. There is enthusiastic clapping. Apparently this occurs only in America. According to Simon, no one in London would clap at an art sale. After all, he was fond of saying, after a gin and tonic or several, it's a sale, not a theater show.

I don't know about you, but I disagree with him. I suppose I disagree with just about everything that's ever come out of Simon's mouth. Except one thing he said at Jeffrey Finelli's opening back in March.

"Art is the new cocaine."

Two:
Jeffrey Finelli:
Simon Pryce
Gallery Opening:
Artist's Reception
6:00–8:00 p.m.

March

My story begins, as a good story often does, with a dead man. The dead man seems a fitting place to start. You might be disappointed to know the dead man wasn't murdered. No, there's no murder in my story. Not a lot of sex, either, if that's what you're after. If you want to call it a roman à clef, go ahead; I can't even pronounce that word.

This story starts toward the end of the previous winter when February starts to get old and spring seems far away. It's nine months before the auction that will become known — at least to me — as the Finelli sale. As February turns, finally, to March and our show of mixed media collages by emerging British artist Nigel Smith comes down, I'm still the receptionist at the Simon Pryce Gallery in Chelsea. At recent count there are over three hundred galleries in this part of New York alone — yes, we're in the middle of an art bubble, in case you didn't know — and Simon Pryce is one of the new galleries, so don't feel bad if you haven't heard of it.

I sit at a concrete desk just inside the front door, behind a stainless steel slab that serves as a counter. Steel and concrete; cozy it's not. There's a single calla lily in a vase on the counter as well as a white leather book. Visitors can use the book to jot down addresses and be added to our mailing list. We never mail them anything, but some people like to sign in with me. Makes it official, I suppose. I always try to smile, single-handedly attempting to dispel the myth of the nasty gallery girl.

They call us gallerinas. We're generally considered a loathsome breed, gallery receptionists. Aren't we represented almost universally as obnoxious, entitled, pretty girls in great clothes? Yes, yes, stock characters in miniature art-world dramas, we're pretentious creatures in intellectual fashion and high heels, dripping with attitude and sarcasm, rolling our eyes at visitors requesting something as mundane as the price list. God forbid you want to know where the bathroom is.

We know a lot of girls like that, rude attractive women hired to reinforce the exclusive, refined clubby atmosphere of most galleries. But I'm not one of them. For one thing, I don't think I'm pretty. And I suspect I'm not dramatically ugly either, at least not in a way that could be called jolie laide and become a signature. I could enjoy that, jolie laide, I think. It's a word I like, pretty-ugly, one I once heard a French collector use to describe his wife. But I'm somewhere in the middle, not jolie or laide either.

I have long straight hair, the kind of blond that is called "dirty." My hair has a disturbing tendency toward a middle part, although when I leave home in the mornings it is neatly brushed to one side. I smile a lot. People comment on how nice my smile is. Now a nice smile is all well and good, but it's a far cry from jolie laide.

My glasses are a necessity, not an affectation, and my clothes tend to be neutral. You could call it a minimalist look, or call it what it really is, a safe, if uninspired, lack of style.

I'm also the furthest thing from entitled. And I try to reserve what obnoxious behavior I can muster for only the rudest people who lean over my desk. The few times I've attempted an attitude, my efforts went completely unnoticed. So I'm not your typical gallery girl. I'm surprised Simon ever hired me. Even more surprised that I'm good at what I do, which, over the years, has come to be, well, everything that needs to get done in a gallery. Somehow, at the time that my story begins, I've worked at this, my starter job, for more than five years.

From my concrete-and-steel desk I have a view of both the entrance area, separated from the rest of the space by a plaster wall, and the large gallery. The whole front wall is glass, and I'm always cold in the winter. When the door opens, icy gusts of frigid air come swooshing at me. That may explain why I sometimes look less than thrilled to be receiving visitors, although I always smile. See, not typical.

The door to the gallery is an eleven-and-a-half-foot pane of the same thick glass as the street-side wall. It was designed, along with the whole gallery, by an architect with a recognizable name that can be dropped subtly into a conversation by Simon, like a tiny pebble plopped so gently into a pond it hardly creates a ripple. The door is dramatic and stylish but hardly functional. It suits the gallery in its temperamental nature. If you finesse it just so, you might make it in. But if you don't get your hips into it at the proper angle, no amount of pushing and cursing will cause it to open for you.

On this rainy afternoon Jeffrey Finelli swings the door open easily, even though he has only one arm. He comes to the gallery bearing cheese, which he hands me with a sweet, timid smile.

He's not stepped foot on American soil in twenty years. There was some discussion about whether he was even going to come from Florence, where he lives above a *salumeria.* That's Italian for butcher. I had to look it up. There Jeffrey paints in a sunny studio, he's told me via e-mail, and he's never come back. But here he is, offering up, with the demeanor of a lover bestowing a diamond bracelet, a wedge of cheese that makes the whole gallery stink like feet wrapped in wet wool.

"Mia," he says, bowing over my hand. He's rumored to be a count. His manner *is* aristocratic, although apparently there are a lot of counts and countesses in Italy. And Jeffrey is American. "You're the nicest gallery person I've ever met."

I fall a tiny bit in love with him. He's an unlikely romantic candidate, a short round figure at least thirty years older than I am in a pilling cardigan with one arm pinned neatly to his side, but I'm not as discerning as I should be.

He continues, in a rough voice half Brooklyn, half Continental European. "Not that I've met many of your ilk."

"My ilk," I repeat, smiling. "That's what we are, ilk."

"I come from a long line of failed artists," he says, fixing perfectly circular gray eyes on mine. I'm struck by the similarity of his eyes to the eyes in the Lulu painting on the wall. I wonder if it's intentional, his use of his own eyes in the painting, perhaps a self-reference of some sort.

"So do I," I say to his comment about the failed artists. I imagine it to be true, although as far as I know there were no failed artists in the McMurray clan. There was a failed liquor store salesman, a failed teacher, a failed fireman. But no artists.

Some might call Jeffrey Finelli, disparagingly, an aspiring artist, because he's never had a gallery show until now. But these could be the same people who claim their five-year-old could make better art than what's on the walls. That term, *aspiring,* implies a yearning — please, Art World, accept me! — that, at fifty-four, Jeffrey seems not to know.

Now aspiring artists are called emerging artists. Emerging artists' new work is what collectors want to buy. Dealers like Simon stalk graduate-school art shows for product, and everyone wants to know the names of the hot new artists. But they expect emerging artists to be young. The younger the better. High school age would be desirable, especially if they're photogenic, or have a good story. What people don't expect is a brand-new artist with his first gallery show to be fifty-eight years old.

By Jeffrey's age, most creative souls have listened to their inner censor and given up, the universe having failed to offer them the appropriate encouragement in the form of gallery representation and exchanges of money. But Process Not Product has always been Jeffrey's motto, or so he told me, in a series of e-mail exchanges I read as love letters.

Jeffrey hasn't seen his show. He instructed Simon to hang the paintings without him, although he also told him he would knock his lights out if he got too curatorial about it. At the time Jeffrey said he wasn't sure he could bear to return to America for the opening. But here he is.

"Let's take a look," he says now, jabbing one finger into the air and using it to wave me along. "I want to see what that lousy Brit did to me."

I step around from my desk, and he takes my arm in gallant fashion. "You've got a lovely smile," he says to me. See, I get that a lot.

The Finelli show consists of seven paintings. These are "the goods," as Simon likes to call them. Of course, Simon Pryce is a contemporary art dealer, and his attempt at being funny — the goods, ha ha! — falls into a category of humor that might be called dealer humor, if such a thing existed. I've never met an art dealer with a sense of humor.

Jeffrey and I move together into the gallery, and he gazes up at his own work with an awed grin, as though happy to see his paintings again. I've always wondered about this moment for an artist, the first shock of seeing one's private personal vision on canvas hung on the white walls of a public gallery space, displayed for all to bear witness. Terrifying, I imagine.

There are two interiors, one called *Studio at Dusk,* the other *Mona's Bedroom.* There is one self-portrait, *Portrait of the Artist as a Confused Young Man.* It's a younger version of Jeffrey. There are two rich landscapes of the hills above Florence, laden with religious iconography, fish, crosses, and burning bushes, that sort of thing. One is titled *Where Is God When We Need Him,* and the other *Yearning for Family.* There's a small portrait of a woman with auburn hair looking away, *Finding and Losing Faith.* Then there's the enormous portrait, *Lulu Meets God and Doubts Him.*

Simon told me not to print up a price list, but I know he wants $75,000 for *Lulu Meets God.* The others, smaller, are supposed to be $45,000. These are not earth-shattering high prices by today's standards, but Jeffrey is an unknown artist. Sorry, an emerging artist. The works are very strong, much better than Simon's usual stuff, and I think they could be priced higher.

Jeffrey and I pause in front of the large portrait of Lulu. It dominates the other six pieces, the young girl forcing the viewer's eyes to stay glued to hers. There's something aggressive about her, the way she commands us to look at her. She's an attention hog, the centerpiece of a show of smaller, more reticent paintings, those gray watchful eyes surrounded by hot colors.

I first saw this painting in the form of a computer image. It affected me right away. Even in that pixilated format, the power of the painting was evident. I knew immediately it was going to be somehow important to me. I just didn't know how.

Oh, sure, easy for me to say now. Now that we know the work will go on to sell for four point three million dollars at auction only nine months after being shown for the first time, of course I can claim to have predicted it all along. But really, I knew. *Lulu Meets God and Doubts Him.* The title bothered me. It's so wordy, so literal, so not cool somehow. It perplexed me. Annoyed me. And made me think.

"What's the story with this one?" I ask Jeffrey. It's a favorite question of mine. I point up at Lulu. Her image is etched on my brain by now, this beautiful fair girl who looked at me intently from the jpegs of the works I used to organize the materials for the show, from the proofs for the invitation and the ads, and then, once the paintings were hung, from the wall directly opposite my concrete-and-steel desk.

There's a hush to an empty gallery, like in church, and Jeffrey speaks in a whisper, although we're the only ones here.

"It's about the creative endeavor," he says. He beams proudly at Lulu. "It's about how we meet God through our creative acts."

"So you believe in God?" I ask. Religion does not agree with me, and I'd prefer it if he didn't ask me the same question. I'd have to tell him I'm — what's the term they use, lapsed — yes, I'm a lapsed Catholic. I just hope he's not one of those Jesus freaks. That would really do a number on my romantic illusions about him.

He puts his one arm around my shoulders. We're both still facing the huge canvas. "There are two types of people in this world. There are believers. And there are doubters."

He turns to peer at me, as though trying to figure out which one I am. I'd say doubter. Definitely a doubter. The count nods, as though he understands, although I haven't said anything. "I'm a believer," he says. "The transformative power of art is the only religion I know."

"And Lulu," I ask. "Your niece?"

"In this painting, she's all of us. Doubting ourselves, doubting our faith, doubting our ability to be artists, despite the yearning."

"We can't all be artists," I say.

"No," he says. "No, we can't. And for those of us who believe, this can be very painful."

Painful, yes. I'm obsessed with the creative process. It's confusing and mystifying and frustrating. And this little man seems to understand exactly that. Although I realize

this will sound ridiculously self-centered —
it is all about me, right? — I have to say I
feel suddenly that Jeffrey Finelli has created
this painting expressly for me. Or for people
like me.

"What most people want to know is how I
lost my arm," he says. "It's a good thing
I've got a story."

He pulls me close, and I breathe in the
smell of European cigarettes. Gitanes?
Gauloises? "It was an all-night race in
Madagascar. I was in the back of a pickup
truck with a goat and a Russian. We smoked
Turkish hash and ate the freshest plums I've
ever tasted. The Russian was not who I
thought he was. I woke up in a pool of the
goat's blood. And that's as much as I can
tell you, because the rest of it involves
prostitutes and guns and things that are not
appropriate for your lovely young ears."

"That's not much of a story," I tease him.

"The point to consider is this," he says.
"Why my left arm? I paint with my right."

I don't get a chance to ask him what he
means. We're interrupted by the sound of
Simon from the other side of the glass
exterior wall.

"Bloody door!" He's trying to push it
open without getting his hips into it. That
never works.

I go around the plaster interior wall to help, Jeffrey following me. Simon's at the door with a cup of tea in one hand and a striped umbrella in the other. He wears a navy raincoat and a pale green cashmere scarf knotted in jaunty insouciance around his thin neck. If nothing else, Simon understands the importance of a recognizable look.

How do I describe it? It's all about the hair. A leonine helmet that never, even in the worst heat or, as today, in a strong and steady rain, never shrinks or wilts or changes at all. It's about the hair and the colorful cashmere and a strategic pair of tortoiseshell glasses. They lend an air of studiousness.

"Bloody hell," Simon says as I open the door to let him in. He drops the umbrella on the floor. As he does so, he spills tea from the sippy cup in his hand over his wrist and the sharp white cuff of his Turnbull and Asser shirt.

Now, it is my personal opinion that Simon is no more British than I am, but he is resolute in his use of language. He goes home at night to what he unfailingly refers to as his "flat," he's always complaining about the marks left on the shiny concrete floors by the couples who roll children into the gallery in their "bloody prams," and every now and then he forgets his "trainers" so he can't take the jog along the river that keeps him in vain and slender shape.

"Mia, be a luv and fetch something."

I'm not fooled by the endearment. Simon is mercurial. Sometimes he acts positively infatuated with me. Other times, his contempt is a mushroom cloud, growing and spreading. He works many layers into our complicated and familiar working relationship. And I suppose I do too. We're like family, dysfunctional yet needy and stuck with each other.

I do as I'm told and fetch something to sop up the Earl Grey.

No one else ever seems to question the nationality of Simon's boyish charm. After all, he carries that brolly everywhere as though raised in a rainy climate, he's always sipping at endless cups of tea, and his conversation is peppered with unanswerable questions like "Why do American women have such large bums?"

It's late in the afternoon when the fight breaks out.

"I loathe the curatorial role to which you aspire," Jeffrey suddenly tells Simon, drawing out the word *loathe*. "Take them all down."

At first Simon seems unfazed. Artists are expected to act strangely just before their work is to be revealed to a potentially cruel and callous public. "The opening is in precisely one hour," he says.

"I've changed my mind," Jeffrey says. "They're not for sale."

"You've already sold them," Simon points out. This is true. While dealers in general, and Simon in particular, are notoriously uncomfortable parting with their cash, Simon wrote Jeffrey a check for one hundred and fifty thousand dollars to buy these seven paintings.

There was no contract, but there never is. There was no sixty-forty split arranged ahead of time, the way it is with other artists. Simon was so inspired by the work, or so he claimed, that he bought the paintings up front. At the time, this seemed only a bit odd. But Simon's behavior is almost always a bit odd, so I didn't think much of it. Yes, it's true; Jeffrey does not own these paintings. Simon does.

Jeffrey draws himself up to his full height of about five foot five and puts his face right up into Simon's. Did I mention already that Simon too is a short man? Or did you figure that out on your own?

Simon pulls himself up to his full height

of five foot eight. (Or so he says, but don't all short men claim to be five-eight?)

They each crouch into a fighting stance, facing off.

Jeffrey grabs hold of Simon's tie and pulls it tight. "I'll give you the money back."

"Don't be infantile. It's a cliché." Simon tries to pull his tie from Jeffrey's grasp.

Jeffrey won't let go. "The evil merchant dealer leeching off creative souls is a far worse cliché," he says. "You don't know anything about art. And even less about hanging it."

Now, there is absolutely nothing wrong with the way the show is hung. In fact, Simon's done a nice job placing the works, with the dominant Lulu painting enjoying pride of place opposite my desk. Jeffrey seems to be picking a fight.

Simon is used to this. The artist/dealer relationship is always complicated. Most of Simon's artists hate him. Oh, they all start out in love. At first, the artists are so appreciative. They're happy just to be there. They've been anointed, they're among the chosen. And they love Simon for it. But then, inevitably, little resentments build up, the relationships crumble, and the artists fall out of love. They often move on, to bigger galleries and other dealers who make them feel they'll finally reach their potential for genius.

"Why are you sweating the details?" Simon asks, now jerking the tie free. He attempts to smooth it down, but it's a wrinkled mess. He's going to want to change it. "Don't sweat the details," he mutters.

"Don't sweat the details?" Jeffrey spits out the words. "Art IS the details."

He balls his fist and swings hard at Simon.

Simon is agile. He ducks, so the punch goes nowhere.

Jeffrey swings again, but it's a halfhearted attempt. Simon has already moved away from him. He's pulled a pack of Smarties from his pocket and downed six or seven of them in one bite.

Jeffrey stands in the middle of the gallery as Simon paces around him. He looks deflated. But then he grins, like a mischievous child.

"Art IS the details," he repeats. He takes a cigarette and an expensive-looking lighter from the pocket of his cardigan and points at Simon. "You need to suspend your disbelief."

Simon simply looks at him. He's used to artists making proclamations. He usually doesn't try to make sense of them. Come to think of it, Simon's a doubter. He always doubts his shows will sell. Often he's right.

The cigarette goes between Jeffrey's lips, and he flips the silver lighter around to light it with a smooth, practiced move.

"You can't smoke in here," Simon says, as gently as he can manage, still catching his breath. Gentle is not a tone he manages well, however. Snide is his specialty. So that's how it comes out. Snide.

Jeffrey fixes his round gray eyes on Simon and lights the cigarette, taking a long drag. He blows the smoke directly at Simon.

"It's against the law," Simon warns, petulance seeping into the snide tone.

Jeffrey shifts his eyes to me for confirmation. "Against the law?"

I nod, a sheepish acknowledgment that Simon is being truthful.

"It is," Simon says, firm in his belief that he's doing the right thing. Simon likes to do the right thing.

Jeffrey shakes his head, but moves to the door.

Once Jeffrey steps out into the rain, I try to hide behind my stainless steel counter and lose myself in my work. On my desk is a pile of letters from the many, too many, earnest and talentless artists around the world seeking representation in, as they like to put it, "a New York institution such as

45

the Simon Pryce Gallery." But before I can bury myself in the letters, Simon looks at me, or in my general direction.

"So," he says, "what's the poop?"

Simon is always asking me for the poop. It's an Americanism he picked up somewhere. I think he thinks it brings him down to my level, rapping out with me. He has this idea that I yearn to have a gallery of my own, and often alludes to my unbridled ambition. He really seems to believe I'll have the poop. Actually, nothing could be further from the truth.

"It's been quiet this morning," I say, knowing this will disappoint on several levels. He seems to want to believe that I'm a girl in the know, working my access, networking, trading in information, because that's what ambitious gallerinas do.

It's disconcerting, to be misconstrued. But to change his view, I'd have to admit the truth. The truth is, I aspire to be an artist. There, I've said it.

Yup, that's the embarrassing reality. Just like all these yearning people whose letters clog my in-box, I have a dream. I went to art school and I came to New York, like so many before me, to seek my fame and fortune as a creative person. I don't simply aspire, I yearn. I yearn, I do, for the world to know this about me, to acknowledge me as the brilliant and talented artist I'd like to imagine I could be. But since I took this job I haven't told anyone my secret.

I'm a painter. Yes, I know what you're thinking: I'm really a receptionist. See, that's where it gets tricky. I came to the gallery thinking it was my entrée into the art world. Here I am, five years later, and Simon doesn't have any idea I'm still holding tight to my private identity as a painter. He acts like any day now I'm going to unfold my real plan: to take all his artists and move to my own white box down the street.

The only way to set him straight would be to tell him the truth. But the truth is so self-indulgent and humiliating — for I've not been blessed with talent, as far as I can tell — that I just let him go right on thinking I'm the next Marian Goodman.

"You better not take sides when he comes back in," Simon says.

I shake my head to indicate I have no intention of suggesting he rehang the show. I like where the Lulu painting sits, directly opposite my desk, the young girl peering down at me with that smirk, as though she and I are in on the same joke.

Simon wrinkles his nose suddenly.

"What's that vile smell?"

Jeffrey's illegal unpasteurized cheese is still on my desk. "A gift from the artist."

I glance outside at the rain coming down. Jeffrey is standing in the middle of the street looking back at the gallery, his head tilted to the sky as though the sun is shining. When he sees me looking at him, he waves his cigarette in my direction. It occurs to me to wonder at the wisdom of his position, in the middle of the road, but only for a second.

When he comes back in, there is no mention of the fight. Or of rehanging the show. Or canceling it.

This is Jeffrey Finelli's first opening. And his last. At the very least, he would have appreciated the irony.

Tonight we're serving white wine, the cheap kind, of course, and San Pellegrino in tall green bottles.

"Bad wine, another cliché," Jeffrey says to me after he sips. It's six o'clock, and people have started to trickle in.

"Sorry. Usually we don't serve anything. You've inspired this extravagance."

"Nice dress," he says. I've changed for the occasion into a light brown sheath dress I've come to think of as my "opening uniform."

"It suits your coloring," he adds. "You're like a caramel."

A caramel, huh? I'll take a compliment any way I can get it. But a caramel?

We stand together, watching Simon greet a couple with a baby. Babies are the new hot accessory. There are always at least three of them at openings, hanging around their parents' necks in navy blue BabyBjörns, gazing wide-eyed at the art and the colorful people. Simon bends down to coo at the fat infant staring up at him. Simon hates babies.

"What's for dinner?" Jeffrey wants to know. He sounds glum. I can see how it would be depressing for him. His first opening, and the only person talking to him is the receptionist.

"I think it's shepherd's pie," I say. "Just so you know, Simon's claiming it's your favorite. He always says the stuff is the artist's choice, but it's just because he's cheap."

By Jeffrey's look, I assume I've said too much. "Sorry."

"Don't be sorry," Jeffrey says. He points to the large painting. "She's coming, you know, the last of the Finellis."

"Lulu?" By now I'm on a familiar, first-name basis with her. But it hasn't occurred to me until this moment that she's a real person.

"I'm her only living relative. She said she was busy tonight." He shakes his head. "I had to promise her the painting to get her to come."

Which painting? I don't think to ask him. Later I will replay this exchange in my mind, wondering what he meant to say. For now I'm distracted; Simon is coming toward us with a new collector I should recognize. I scan my brain, searching for the guy's name. He's maybe thirty, thirty-five, wearing bright orange sneakers and the gleam of the potential addict in his eyes.

Oh, yeah, I remember him now. The Keeping-It-Real guy. He tried to pick me up once. Told me he was into yoga. "I'm practically a yogi," he'd said to me. "Art and yoga. Just keeping it real," he'd said, before he asked me out.

Thanks to a few high-profile affairs and second marriages, I've gotten the sense that gallery girls are becoming known as easy lays, kind of like I imagine stewardesses were back in the seventies.

What was his name again? Drake? Doug? I didn't go out with him. I'm not that into keeping it real.

There's been no advance buzz about the

Finelli show. Jeffrey's story hasn't gotten out there ahead of time, drawing the most avid collectors down to the gallery to see the work. None of the big junkies, Robert Bain or Martin Better or Dr. Kopp, who normally do business with better galleries, have been in early to place holds, seeking their next fix. Jeffrey Finelli's seven paintings have not generated any hunting fervor.

This is Simon's fault. The paintings are good. Very good. *Lulu Meets God* is a masterpiece, if you don't mind that overused term. But no one here tonight seems at all concerned that they might sell before they can get their hands on one. In fact, they hardly seem to be looking at the art. They're much more interested in the bar.

Yoga guy in his orange sneakers is all Simon's got. Simon works it hard. "Nice trainers," he says, complimenting the man's shoes.

Keeping-It-Real looks only mildly disinterested, and Simon is animated as he introduces him to Jeffrey, seeking a potential sale.

"Crowds make me grumpy," Jeffrey says to them after shaking the yogi's limp hand.

This comment allows Simon to deliver his line, one he's stolen from someone else who must have reworked it from, I think, Marcel

Duchamp, who once famously said that art is a habit-forming drug. Duchamp. Now he was a cool dude.

"Art is the new cocaine." Simon looks pleased that he was able to weave this in, as a way to explain the crowd in the gallery. He nurses this highly inaccurate fantasy version of himself as an erudite and witty commentator on the art world and America. Of course, who am I to pass judgment? I too nurse a highly inaccurate fantasy version of myself. I'm not really a gallery girl. I'm actually a talented, if undiscovered, painter. Ha!

"They're not even looking at the work. Just standing near it so it elevates their drinking experience," Jeffrey says.

"Welcome to Art World," Simon says to him. "Like Disney World. Only scarier and the tourists are skinnier."

The new collector turns to Simon. "Robert Hughes, right?"

"No, this is Jeffrey Finelli, the artist." Simon drags out the first syllable of the word *artist,* giving it weight.

"I mean your quote. That was Robert Hughes. The art critic."

"My quote?" Simon says, before he realizes he's been caught parroting someone else's witty and erudite commentary on the art world. Well, appropriation *is* an important concept in art history. "Certainly. Mr. Hughes said some very pertinent things about art."

The guy and his loud sneakers move on, and Simon follows, launching into his sales pitch about the Finelli paintings. It's obvious by his body language that Keeping-It-Real is not interested in adding any Finelli paintings to his new collection. He wants recognizable names, status artists and hot new emerging artists that he's heard more established collectors are buying. He wants large color photographs or sexy installations, stuff about death and sex. Not paintings by some old count from Italy with one arm.

I scan the crowd for someone who could be Lulu, a thirty-year-old version of the girl in the painting. The gallery is jammed with people, all kinds of people. There are lots of dramatic hairstyles and costumey outfits. Almost everyone at a gallery opening wears the same self-congratulatory air. Even the babies look pretty damn pleased with themselves.

"I bet he lies about where he's having lunch," Jeffrey whispers to me. He points at Simon following the uninterested collector around the gallery.

"How did you know?"

"He can't help himself," Jeffrey says.

I'm still looking for Lulu when I see Connie and Andrew Kantor come into the gallery. Connie is hard to miss, in an enormous fur cap with earflaps. She has her big blue Birkin over her arm, and as she swings around to give her opinion of the Lulu painting to her husband, the bag comes close to scratching the canvas.

"Figurative painting," she says with a disparaging sniff, loud enough so Jeffrey and I can hear her. She has an unusually high voice, as though she's never getting enough air. "Our collection is all about ideas."

Andrew doesn't look up from his BlackBerry, but he must mumble something about leaving because her voice goes screechy in response.

"We're not leaving. We're going to the dinner."

More mumbles from Andrew.

"We never get invited to anything like an artists' dinner," Connie says. This is true. There are a lot of charity parties and big social events she can buy her way into. But the art world in the middle of a bubble affords some exclusivity. There's a hierarchy to the social life, just as there is in most worlds. And in this one, much to her dismay,

Connie is not A-list. She's lucky to be invited to one of Simon's dinners. And that's only because Simon was concerned about whether an unknown fifty-eight-year-old emerging painter would generate enough RSVPs to allow for critical mass. Simon's not exactly A-list himself.

"I'm not missing this opportunity," Connie hisses at her husband. "Even for an artist no one knows."

"Sorry," I say to Jeffrey, but he looks like he's enjoying himself now.

"Don't keep apologizing for things that have little to do with you," he says, still watching the Kantors.

"Sorry," I repeat, joking now.

When Dane O'Neill arrives, the whole mood shifts. Suddenly this is a happening. You can hear the buzz of his name spread through the gallery. Dane O'Neill. Dane O'Neill. His name is a brand. He's known for saying what shouldn't be said, doing what shouldn't be done, and commanding high prices for it. Dane O'Neill is expected to behave outrageously and make even more outrageous art. He never disappoints, even if his work does.

He wears a black T-shirt with a skull and crossbones painted neatly onto it. A T-shirt that intentionally makes you wonder. Did he paint it himself? Was it a gift from another artist? Is he licensing it to a fashion company to sell thousands of them, art world souvenirs? Where can I get one? As I said, it makes you wonder.

Like Simon, Dane understands the importance of a look. He knows he owes it to people to look a certain way, like an artist should, in their minds. Tonight he pairs the T-shirt with fairly predictable paint-splattered cargo pants and green boots. His hair is long and a bit wild. I've never met him before, but that doesn't stop me from falling a tiny bit in love with him as he makes an entrance, shouting out to Jeffrey.

"Finelli! You old prawn."

Jeffrey looks delighted to see him. I'm impressed. I didn't realize Jeffrey knew anyone in the New York gallery world, much less an international name like Dane O'Neill. Dane is an artist we all want to know. Dane is an artist the collector in the orange sneakers wishes he could own.

Dane hugs Jeffrey and kisses me, although he can't possibly know who I am. I have no problem with this familiarity. What does this say about me? That I'm shallow enough to covet attention from a famous artist? Of course.

"You're very pretty," he says to me. Even

though I'm one hundred percent certain he says something like this to every woman he meets, even seventy-year-old married ones, I'm flattered. Naturally.

Dane keeps one arm around the tiny Finelli, towering over him with a huge grin. It's hard for me not to suspect this jovial persona is an act. Almost every artist I know is inarticulate and introverted, like me. A visual person is not usually so verbally adept as Dane. But if it's an act, it's a good one. I'm almost convinced.

"How's it feel, old man? Selling out?"

"Hardly selling out. Not one sale as of yet," Jeffrey says. "I'm torn between desperately wanting them to love it and buy it and wanting to pull them off the wall in defiance of the brutal commerce of it all."

"That's what I meant by selling out. You've gone the commerce route, after all these years," Dane says. "It's become product, not process."

Dane's likable. And very good-looking, in a paunchy, uncombed, bloodshot-eyes, Irish-accent sort of way. I'm not the only one a tiny bit in love with him. I'm not the only one watching the two of them now.

"I know what you meant," Jeffrey says. "But all I've done is exhibit. I don't think any of them will sell."

"Are you mad?" Dane points at the Lulu painting. "This is a masterpiece."

Jeffrey shrugs, handing me his empty wineglass and shaking a cigarette out of the pack in his cardigan pocket. "They won't let me smoke in the gallery. I've been going out in the rain like a bad puppy."

"You're the man of the hour, light up," Dane says, wiggling his fingers at one of the babies. He opens his mouth wide and sticks his tongue out, making silly faces for the uninterested baby. He then gives me a rueful grin, acknowledging his lack of success at capturing the baby's attention. Is he flirting with me?

"I'm not one for conflict," Jeffrey says. He in turn eyes the baby like it might open its mouth and ask him for money.

Dane stops trying to engage the baby and steps closer to the Lulu painting. "My piece is intense."

It occurs to me to wonder at the possessive, but only for a second. I don't want to miss any of their conversation. It's the kind of talk I dreamed of overhearing when I took this job, two artists, dissecting their work. Just to be near creative people living out my dream, that's been almost enough for me. It's kept me here, in a job that's the antithesis of who I think I am, just to be near working artists.

Okay, I know I said I'd fallen a tiny bit in love with Jeffrey when I met him. Disregard that now. That was in a platonic, fan-to-artist sort of way. Dane O'Neill is much closer to my own age. Even if I'm not a big fan of his work.

"It's good to have a muse," Jeffrey says. He points the unlit cigarette in his hand toward Dane. "You should try it. Come back to painting."

"I should have a muse," Dane agrees. "I'm dry, mate. Dry as dust."

"I've got to have this thing," Jeffrey says, indicating the cigarette. "Back in a second."

He lights up on his way to the door, turning to blow the smoke away from the people still filing in.

Dane turns his attention to me. "You work here, do you?"

"Mia McMurray." I extend my hand, although we've already kissed.

"Irish?" He nods like he approves.

"My dad's family was from county Clare. He was born here. My mom was born here, but her parents were both Irish too."

"A fellow countrywoman," he says. "Lovely." Loovely.

Did I mention I have a weakness for a good accent? Dane O'Neill's brogue makes everything that comes out of his mouth sound sexy. Especially when he's looking at you the way he's looking at me now, all nodding approval.

Apparently there is a taxi. It is going too fast for the weather. Jeffrey Finelli had been in the middle of a street slick with rain, looking back at the gallery. There are skid marks. The cigarette is still lit, but he dies instantly.

When it happens, the rain is coming down so hard no one notices there is a dead man in the street. People arriving for the opening step right past his body. They don't even see him.

He's dead. Is that possible? Jeffrey Finelli is dead. At first there is a lag between the news making it inside the gallery and people moving outside to bear witness. For a few minutes they're all just standing around as nonchalantly as before, clutching their wineglasses in front of Jeffrey's paintings. And then the word gets out, and there is a herd movement toward the door.

When I hear what people are saying — there's been an accident, Finelli is dead — my brain refuses to process the information. I follow the crowd out of the gallery in an uncomprehending haze. He's dead? It doesn't register. And then I see the body.

We stand out there, in the rain, at least a hundred people who have nothing to do with each other or with Jeffrey, but bonded now, forever, as the people who had been at the opening, who will traffic in this anecdote, telling this story for years to come, embellishing it, torquing it this way and that, until the later versions bear little or no resemblance to what's actually happening here. We fall silent, waiting for the ambulance that has been summoned by someone with a cell phone and their wits about them.

I look down at my feet, not wanting to look at the body in the street. That's when I see a flash of silver. I bend down, without fully realizing what I'm doing. It's Jeffrey's lighter. The silver lighter that he kept in his cardigan pocket. I slip it into my pocket, clutching it for some kind of comfort.

The ambulance pulls onto the block. A figure is coming toward us. It appears to be a woman in a long gray coat with a hood. She's moving quickly when I first notice her, then her pace slows as she comes nearer, as if maybe she senses something and is attempting to postpone the inevitable realization of the truth. It's Lulu. I'm guessing. But I know it's her. And yes, as she gets closer I can see her face. The face from the painting, only more chiseled now, the beauty more fully realized.

She's very tall and impossibly thin. The long gray coat accentuates her length. She moves toward us, moving toward the inevitable painful truth; the uncle she hasn't seen in twenty years is dead.

There is a photographer videotaping the drama with the body and the ambulance and the crowd of culture vultures gathered in the driving rain. Someone yells to him to stop. It's raining so hard I can't really hear him, but what I think he says is, "Hey, man, this is art!"

Three:
Please Come to
Dinner in Honor of
Jeffrey Finelli

Later that night in March

Despite the fact that the guest of honor is no longer with us, we don't cancel dinner. It's like a piece of performance art; an invitation to dine with the artist, only he's not there because, sorry, he's, well, dead. I imagine Jeffrey popping in during the coconut flan. Miss me?

We convene at Simon's, three blocks from the gallery. Simon's flat occupies a full floor of a former warehouse building and is designed to highlight an ugly collection of fifties Swedish furniture and a few select pieces from Simon's inventory of art for sale. Simon is not passionate about either furniture or art, or collecting anything except personal luxury items, but it's important for his image, or so he thinks, to be perceived as living in the same manner as his customers, with the same lust for design, beauty, and a fine lifestyle.

Simon serves gin and tonics, although they make some people mean and others just stupid, and there is never quite enough food, but he's developed a reputation as a host. Maybe it's the accent.

"Come on in, everyone," Simon shouts as coats are shaken out and hung in the vestibule and umbrellas are stuffed into the holder or tossed on the now-slippery floor. There is a camaraderie to art collecting, a group dynamic that is fueled by parties such as these. It's a ready-made social life. The invitations that come in the mail, via e-mail, or over the phone make people feel like they belong to a world. It's comforting, I guess, to know one's presence is expected somewhere, to know there will be drinks and food and conversation with like-minded souls.

So they come. Even when the artist is dead. What do they care? In this case, none of them knew the artist. To me it seems unbearably callous, but everyone whose name was on Simon's invitation list files into his loft tonight.

"Jeffrey's niece went in the ambulance. With Dane O'Neill," Simon announces as his guests gather, kissing and asking questions. He wouldn't miss an opportunity to drop a name like Dane's. "They're coming here afterward."

Simon plays the part of the amiable but grieving dealer well. He holds the door open for his guests, spilling a little of his gin and tonic. He accepts condolences. He double-kisses cheeks and receives hearty handshakes. He looks appropriately grave while offering cocktails.

In fact, you might, if you were to show up at his home on this night or another, be taken in by his friendly British affability. You might note the smart suit — Brioni, right? — and the accent, and the smile that occasionally could truly charm, and think you could be Simon's friend. You might want to help him out, offering up your pressed hankie to sop the spilled drink, or proffer condolences of your own.

You might even become friends with Simon. Or so you might think. Oh, for a time, months, even a year or two if you didn't see too much of him. It would only be after he sells a piece of art you particularly want out from under you, or spreads a false rumor that causes a deal you've been working on for months to rupture, and tells blatant lies directly to your face without even so much as a flinch, then pockets that handkerchief, a gift from your grandmother, that you'd realize he could never be your friend.

That's if you're not a collector. If you're one of the few people Simon deems important enough or with enough potential to warrant the effort, you'd be positively swept off your feet by his charm. Charm is the one qualification absolutely required by an art dealer, although some are better actors than others.

Martin Better, despite his reputation for a sharp mind, has been on the other end of Simon's British charm for a while now, and he considers Simon a friend. For the past two years they've been hanging out together — enjoying regular dinners at Lever House or Mister Chow's and Saturday lunches at Pastis. They get together on Sundays to ride motorcycles at Martin's house in Greenwich. Martin's got bigger fish to catch than Simon's mediocre artists and more important dealers to befriend, but he enjoys Simon.

I understand it. Marty's an uptown guy. He's so far uptown he lives in Greenwich, Connecticut. Simon is downtown. Simon makes Marty feel cool and young. Simon understands how to do this. Marty likes being invited to Simon's flat, even though he hardly ever buys anything from him. He almost always shows up.

He comes through the door now in the dated-looking brown leather jacket he always wears when he travels downtown and gives Simon a buddy sort of hug, one arm smacking at his back.

"Sorry about Finelli," he says. Marty hardly takes a breath before adding, "I'll buy a painting."

Simon's carefully composed gravitas turns instantly to ill-concealed delight. "You will? Which one?"

"What was the cover of the invitation?"

"The Lulu painting. I sent you the jpeg. *Lulu Meets God and Doubts Him.*"

Martin lets out a dry laugh. "That's a mouthful. Terrible title. But I'll take it."

"You didn't see the show." Simon would be rubbing his hands together in manic glee if he weren't clutching that drink.

Martin Better shrugs. "The guy's dead? That's a limit to the supply. Should create some demand."

I can practically see the lightbulb going on over Simon's head. "Yes, yes, of course."

"Just put it on hold for me," Martin says. "I'll get over and see the show this week."

It is strange and awkward to attend a dinner for an artist who is suddenly dead. So we do what we tend to do in these situations:

drink. There are the gin and tonics and more of the clichéd chardonnay. There are also questions to which Simon does not have the answers. Is there more work? Did he have a will? Where will he be buried? Who was that girl in the big one?

I accept a glass of wine. Oh, why not? Under the circumstances, my self-imposed rule about not drinking during the week seems contrived. I hardly knew Jeffrey, I certainly can't claim an overwhelming loss, but I feel emotionally uncalibrated. A glass of wine, just one glass, should take the edge off, working its magic the way it does, genie in the bottle.

I'm hoping I'll get a chance to talk to Dane O'Neill again. I suspect I'm not the only one here with that hope. Collectors always seem to want to get to know the artists who make the pieces they covet. Especially artists who've already been anointed by the art world at large. Personally, I think it is a mistake to meet one's icons. Not that I've met many icons. Or any, really. Richard Prince smiled at me on the street one day, does that count?

Simon likes to invite three of the prettiest gallery girls to his parties. These are the women he thinks I'm talking to, when he wants to know "the poop." Alexis, Julia, and

Meredith; I call them the Weird Sisters. He thinks they are my friends. I guess they are. The three of them are almost always together. They converge on me now, offering air kisses and faux concern mixed with envy at my suddenly prime positioning in the middle of things.

"You're skinny," Meredith says, like she's accusing me. She means it as a compliment and a greeting, though also an accusation. She's a bit heavyset — the black sleeveless dress she's wearing doesn't help — and resentful of anyone whose metabolism is more forgiving than hers.

"Mia's tiny." Alexis Belkin is the alpha female of the troika. She's very tall and too thin for her black Prada dress, but remarkably striking, all angular cheeks and bony limbs. She intends for her comment — tiny — to seem on the surface like a compliment, but we all know what it really is, a tall-girl reminder of my diminutive stature. I'm five-four, taller than Meredith and about the same height as Julia, but Alexis likes to use the word *tiny* around me in a disparaging tone whenever she can.

"You're so right. What do you weigh, Mia, like ninety pounds?" Julia wants to know. I don't respond to this.

Alexis is usually the one with the most

accurate gossip, and she doesn't care about my weight. "Watch," she says. "Everything'll be marked up two hundred percent by tomorrow."

Alexis has worked for top dealer Pierre LaReine for four years and enjoys the rumors that she's spent a lot of time in his bed as much as the rumors that she's leaving any day to start a gallery of her own.

"Of course." Julia nods her head energetically. She's the pretty one, also in a black dress, a Prada knockoff. She had worked at LaReine for a year before moving on to a smaller gallery uptown where, as she explained it, there was less yelling. She tends to agree with everything Alexis says.

"And the work is terrible, isn't it?" Alexis says. "I can't stand this kind of thing. So easy."

Easy is a favorite word for Alexis. She uses it for any work that is visually pleasing, implying triteness.

"Oh, I know," Julia says. "Very easy."

"I heard the whole show's sold out already." Alexis has not heard this; she's fishing for information. She eyes me carefully now, to see if I'll take the bait.

"Martin Better just put the big one on hold, sight unseen," I tell them. "I don't know about any of the others."

"See what I mean?" Alexis says. She looks around, checking that the other two recognize how she's always right. Julia nods in approval.

"Isn't it sad? He waited his whole life for this show," Meredith whispers, veering away from sales talk. She comes from money, and therefore is not interested in it.

"Sight unseen?" Alexis looks at me. "What else is out there?"

The three of them face me in a black line, tallest, Alexis, to shortest, Meredith. Sometimes they scare me.

I don't respond to Alexis's question, so Julia fills the silence. "So sad," she states. "The art world killed him."

"Maybe it was a suicide." Meredith never, ever gets the stories straight.

Julia nods. "I know. Or maybe he was murdered."

She presents this thought almost in passing. The other two skip over it, moving on to other aspects of the story of the dead artist. Their conversation continues, but I don't move on with them. Jeffrey murdered? I consider the idea. Murder? Now there's a story.

But I dismiss it. Because, really, the story falls apart even before you start quibbling about how the taxi driver could have known

Jeffrey would step out for a smoke at that exact moment. The whole thing crumbles when you look to Simon as the murderer. Simon Pryce could persuade a lot of people to believe a lot of things — that he is really British, for one, that he is or isn't gay, that he has a long list of buyers for that piece you're deliberating on, or that he'd been "a close friend of Andy's" (that's Andy Warhol to you and me) — but it's hard enough to take him seriously as an art dealer, let alone a cold-blooded killer.

Meredith points to the door. "Look who's here," she says in a singsong voice.

Julia, Alexis, and I follow her gesture with our eyes. It's Zach Roberts. He's coming toward us, talking to Simon. In a tweed blazer and baggy wrinkled khakis, he could be a professor at a university rather than an art adviser. And in fact, if I remember correctly, he has a couple of degrees from Yale, proof, as he put it, that he couldn't figure out what he wanted to do when he grew up. He's very tall, with the kind of stooped grace of tall men who play sports like squash and golf, both of which he plays pretty well, or so I've heard. He leans over Simon to hear him.

"Nothing goes on in the art world without

him these days," Julia says, in an admiring tone.

All four of us fall silent, watching him. Zach catches sight of us and flashes a smile in our direction. Zach Roberts has one of the most charismatic smiles I've ever seen, a slow, sexy grin that could make even the stiffest old matron go light-headed. Our eyes meet, and his widen in recognition.

I met Zach five months ago at one of the fall auctions. He was sitting next to me, and he admired the doodles with which I'd covered my catalog. Our business, the art business, is comprised of a lot of male peacocks, men who dress to impress. In this world Zach's sloppy style makes him stand out. He wears faded jeans or baggy unironed khakis; soft oxford shirts untucked, the sleeves rolled up casually, or left unbuttoned.

That night he showed up at his seat at the auction room next to mine with his wavy hair still wet from a shower. We talked through the sale. If I read the body language correctly, he found me quite charming. When it was over, he invited me for a martini and a burger.

I said no. I was just coming off what I will refer to as the "situation" with Ricardo. Ricardo was a dealer from Milan who told me, in a very sexy Italian accent, that he adored me more than life itself. How was I to know that this was a euphemism for I wish to steal the first good artist Simon's found to show, and you, young lady, are going to help me figure out how?

Not to sound like the art world slut, but . . . before Ricardo there was Giles. And before that Manuel. Oh, and Jean-Pierre, but that was only one night. Compared to some of the gallerinas I'm practically a virgin.

(Can you be practically a virgin? Is that anything like technically a virgin?) What can I say? A classic case of looking for love in all the wrong places. I've not been as discerning as I should be. And I'm a sucker for a foreign accent. But I've learned my lesson. No more guys in the art world. Artists excluded, of course. One can always make exceptions for artists.

"I hear he's looking to hire a couple of people," Meredith says, sounding wistful. "He can't keep up with the demand on his time." She sounds like she wants a new job. This time she has her facts correct. Zach has very quickly become a star in the art advisory business. He has a reputation for being honest as well as smart, and that's not an easy reputation to come by in this world. If gallery receptionists are generally considered loathsome creatures, art advisers are thought of as worse. Lapdogs. Sleazy, obsequious, phony paid friends to the clients they're secretly ripping off while taking kickbacks from the dealers, isn't that what you've heard?

Marty Better pulls Alexis from our group to kiss her cheek. Meredith waggles her empty glass at us and heads off to the bar. Julia follows her.

Now Zach is talking to the Colancas. They're both in their late sixties, and very earnest, the kind of admirably serious art collectors who've been at it for years, studying, buying, donating. Serious, and seriously boring. They have him cornered.

"Save me," Zach mouths in my direction from behind Mrs. Colanca's back. He makes a comic eye-rolling sort of face, as if he's dying.

I make my way over to them. "I'm so sorry to interrupt, but Zach, would you mind? Simon wants me to give you something. He missed you at the opening."

"Of course," Mrs. Colanca says, patting Zach on the cheek. "He's very popular now. We knew him back when."

They let Zach move from the corner, and he kisses my cheek. He smells good, like soap and laundry detergent.

"Hey you." He has a deep voice, the kind of voice you almost feel inside your chest. His eyes are light blue, his skin and hair dark. He wears a light blue shirt that brings out the blue in his eyes.

"Hey. You."

"McMurray. I owe you one. Thank you." He smiles down at me.

How had I forgotten that smile? If I recall correctly — and that night is not easy to recall, after two martinis, or was it three — he made me laugh so hard I fell off my chair.

I did say no. At first. But I'm easily persuaded. And I have a weakness for tall men. So then I said yes. First we had a martini. Then we had another. We never got the burger.

Thank God I didn't sleep with him. I wanted to. We got close enough for me to know he wears boxers, not briefs or, worse, fancy designer underwear. But I held back, thinking there would be another time. And then he never called.

I suppose I did tell him not to. I did say, "Don't call me, I'm never going out with anyone who makes a living selling art." But I didn't expect him to listen. Aren't men supposed to know about our capitulation fantasies? Yes, some of us want to be won over by the force of will and charm. When we tell them we don't date anyone in our own field of business, we expect them to ignore us. We'd like to think the strength of their adoration for us will force them to call anyway.

I've only seen Zach a couple of times since then. He looked embarrassed. So did I, of course, but for me, embarrassment is pretty much a permanent state of being.

"How are you?" he asks now. He sounds like he really wants to know. Those words — how are you — could mean a lot of things. Like, what can you tell me about the Finelli market? Even when delivered with such sincerity. In fact, especially when delivered with such sincerity. Some of these guys are true thespians.

Zach is one of those men whose wholesome boyish looks make him seem incapable of guile. He always comes across as a nice guy, one of those guys about whom a certain type of person would say, "He has good energy." He looks genuinely concerned when he asks, "Did you know the artist?"

Did I know him? I was half in love with him. "Not well," I say. "Although I really liked him. He was very talented. You didn't see the show."

"Nah, I just came for the food."

This could mean he's hungry. It could also be translated to mean he came to assess a possible sudden demand for Finelli works. Or it could be a deadpan illusion to the insipid and cheap British food Simon insists on serving.

I check to see if he's joking. His half-smile makes it hard to tell. "The shepherd's pie?"

"I like shepherd's pie," he says. "Tell me about the show."

"What do you want to know? It's brilliant. Seven pieces. Two landscapes, two interiors, three portraits."

I tell him as much as I can about the paintings, starting with the interiors. I describe the colors and the way Jeffrey layered the paint. I explain the landscapes and the self-portrait. I take my time, being sure to include the details. I lead up to the masterpiece, the nine-by-twelve-foot *Lulu Meets God and Doubts Him.*

"He hadn't seen her in twenty years," I say, building to a dramatic finish. I like when a story, even a story about a show of paintings, has a good finish. "When she got to the gallery, he was dead."

"I love the way you talk about art," Zach says. "With so much passion."

"Why don't you say what you really want to ask me?"

"What is that?" he asks, grinning.

"You know, has anyone bought any yet? If so, which ones are sold? How much did they sell for? And to whom. Name names, please."

He laughs. "You're funny, McMurray."

Funny? I'm funny? Me? Oh, God, I'm glowing. Frankly, it annoys me, my reaction to his words. I'm not interested, remember? But I do like to think of myself as funny.

When I moved to New York, I expected to meet a lot of funny people, like in the movies. Unfortunately, I got immediately trapped in the art world, so I don't meet the funny New Yorkers. Mostly I meet people who take themselves dreadfully seriously, or ones who only think they are funny. Reference Simon and the aforementioned dealer humor. But Zach *is* really funny, with a dry observational wit that lets you know he's really paying attention.

"I did hear Martin Better bought the big painting," he says.

I take a big gulp of the wine in my glass before I answer him. Remember, I tell myself, this is what he wants. Even if he's not your typical art adviser, this is what they all want. Information. Don't confuse that with interest in you as a person.

"Where did you hear that?"

"It's these big ears of mine," he says, pointing at the side of his head.

"Your ears are perfectly normal," I say, looking at them. They are. Very nice ears, actually. Everything about him has a nice shape, I notice suddenly. Objectively. Nice shape and color. His nose is perfectly straight, his forehead a good height. His skin has a weathered sort of quality, as though he's been in the sun recently. His teeth are very white. His hair is a rich dark brown with the kind of highlights some women will spend a fortune to achieve. And those big eyes, an unusually pale shade of blue.

Simon calls us to eat. We move to the long table set with square white plates and green napkins. Down the center are flats of grass in which are nestled at least seventy votive candles, providing the only light. It's very stylish. Style is one thing Simon does pretty well. Even if he insists on playing Fischerspooner too loud, as he is now. Fischerspooner is not dinner music.

Connie and Andrew stop me in my move toward the table. She's still got the fur hat on. Isn't there some fashion rule about fur in March? There should be. She leans into me in a cloud of flowery perfume for kisses on either side of my face.

"I'm putting the big one on hold," Connie says, standing too close to me.

"It reminds me of Cindy Sherman," Andrew mumbles at her side, his face disappearing into his chin. He rarely speaks at all and almost never about art. Maybe this new verbosity is because he's feeling uncalibrated by the artist's death too.

"Cindy Sherman is a photographer." Connie waves her hand at her husband dismissively.

"Well, who's the painter I like who does all the women?"

She ignores him, eyeing me up and down blatantly as only a really competitive woman can do. Connie isn't thin or pretty or witty or kind or well-read. She's rich. It's come as a surprise to her that it's not enough.

"So? Are you going to tell me everything is sold?"

"I thought you said you wanted to buy Cindy Sherman," Andrew says to her. He defers all collecting decisions to his wife, with whom he's still infatuated. As the story goes, Connie and Andrew met at a dinner party. And depending on who tells the story, either she was seated next to him or she rearranged the place cards. Either she knew exactly who he was and his net worth to the penny, or she'd never heard of him.

It's been said that by the lobster appetizer she was touching his shoulder and by the main course — veal cutlets, I think — she told him he was the most fascinating man she'd ever laid eyes on. By the salad course her hand was in his crotch, and by dessert, a brownie sundae, he was in love.

They were married six months later. There was no prenup. She may not be thin or pretty or witty or kind or well-read, but you can't say she isn't smart.

"That painting belongs in THE collection," she says. She always refers to her collection as THE collection. As if there is no other. "It's absolutely brilliant."

And I wonder. Is it possible she could have suddenly changed her mind about figurative painting and seen the brilliance of Jeffrey's vision and the connection he felt between creativity and the spiritual? Um, no.

Simon always serves meager portions. Tonight's trays of shepherd's pie and mixed greens look alarmingly sparse. But by this point everyone is so drunk from the gin and tonics and the idea of the dead artist who was there at the opening and then poof, just gone, that we all just sit down and sip the wine that's been poured and wait for Lulu and Dane to show up.

We say obvious things. Life is too short. You have to live each day as though it could be your last. You have to make your life story a good one, you never know when it could end. And collectively we determine that this sudden tragedy will be a catalyst, to live how we're meant to live, to finally write that novel, take that trip to China, have a baby. For me, I vow to start painting again. In my head, I'm a Nike ad. Just do it.

Someone asks about Lulu and Dane, as though they're a couple.

"They met tonight," Simon clarifies, holding court with a wineglass held aloft. "He's her uncle's friend. She's his niece. And his muse."

I usually never talk much at these events. I'm used to being invisible. I like my role as an observer, rather than a participant, as the herd gathers, enjoying the bond that comes from pursuing the same goal, Art, with a capital A. And it can be hard to get a word in, or even to hear oneself above a steady drumbeat of name-dropping. But tonight I'm emboldened by the wine and the drama.

"She never even saw the show," I say, loudly, so everyone can hear me. "She doesn't know she was her uncle's muse."

They all look surprised. Simon looks the most shocked, but whether that's because he's never heard me speak up or because of the realization that Lulu might not have seen the portrait of herself, I can't know.

Zach finds me before he leaves. It occurs to me that he has very good manners. He's the sort who would never leave without saying good-bye and thank you. He thanks me, although I'm not the host of this evening, and then he asks, "Are you going to the Alex Beene opening next week?"

"I might," I say. I'm looking toward the door to see if Dane O'Neill has arrived yet.

Zach follows my line of sight. "Okay, then," he says. "Maybe I'll see you there."

Lulu and Dane never come to Simon's that night. The rest of us wait until it gets very, very late. There is coconut flan for dessert, and Simon gets belligerent. Jeffrey Finelli is dead. How is that possible? We're all drunk. Very drunk.

FOUR:
THE MUSEUM
COUNCIL INVITES YOU
TO A ROUNDTABLE
DISCUSSION ON THE
ROLE OF THE MUSE

The Mourning After . . .

At ten-twenty the next morning I'm drunk again. Three skim grande cappuccinos on an empty stomach will do that to a person. I'm high on caffeine and the anticipation of meeting Lulu Finelli in person. And on something else. It's the sort of adrenaline rush that comes from intimate contact with a now-dead person.

The day after Jeffrey Finelli's tragic demise, the gallery is officially closed for mourning. The mood in the empty gallery is somber, the space filled with dark gray light from the rain-heavy sky. Even the expression on the painted Lulu before my desk looks different, sad and sort of grim.

Simon seems to be feeling virtuous about this decision not to do business under the circumstances. Although he has the cell

85

phone glued to his ear, and I don't think he's just accepting condolences, if you know what I mean.

Simon needs time to come up with a plan. He needs time to figure out his timing. He can't cash out too quickly and risk squandering an opportunity. But he can't wait too long and risk losing the momentum either. So the gallery is closed.

Now, here's something you should know about my boss. As stylish as he is, he fancies himself an intellectual. He's vain about it. On the rare occasion that he receives an invitation to air his opinions in a public forum, he always accepts. Back in February, he was invited to join a panel of such experts for what is being billed as a "roundtable discussion on the role of the muse in contemporary art." He sent that response letter back so fast he got a paper cut. Much whining ensued, but the muse discussion has remained on the calendar all this time. It's today.

A roundtable discussion on the role of the muse? Sounds lethal. Today, Simon has a dead artist, a show of potentially hot paintings to sell, and a real-life muse on his hands, but he won't consider canceling his appearance. Are you kidding? This is confirmation that his view of himself is shared by the outside world. It's a chance for him to dazzle the public with his erudite thoughts. Even if the public is but a few desultory white-haired couples straggling into a conference room in search of cookies, Simon sees it as his duty and his privilege to dispense his infinite knowledge of art to such high-minded souls.

So I have to wait to meet Lulu. And Lulu has to wait to see the painting. According to Simon, she doesn't seem to mind.

"She's going to come after work," he announces, emerging from his office with a cup of tea as he usually does mid-morning. He's checking up on me.

I'm surprised to hear she's going to her job, after the devastating events of the previous night. I know I personally would have grabbed the opportunity for at least a week of mental health days if I had a dead uncle, even one I hadn't seen in twenty years.

"I can't believe she wouldn't come straight here," I say.

The young Lulu in the painting hovers over his shoulder. He leans over my desk dunking his tea bag and doesn't return my gaze.

"She didn't know her uncle," he says with an indifferent shrug. He's focused on the bobbing sack of Earl Grey. "She didn't even realize he existed until he rang her up out of the clear blue."

"Isn't there a funeral? Does she have to go to Italy?"

Simon looks pained. Too many questions. He doesn't like me to be the one seeking information. That's his job. "The contessa is making the arrangements."

I try to remember what Jeffrey had told me about the contessa. I think she was married three times, twice to the same man, the count of something or other. Each time she married for love, but her true love was the third husband, a genius inventor who choked on a chicken bone and left her a nice amount of money when he died. That's when she met Jeffrey.

"Is she really a contessa? I thought they weren't married. Would he still be allowed to use the title, then?"

Simon finds these sorts of details, if they don't pertain directly to him and some way that he might benefit, tedious. He sighs deeply, with dramatic heft, to indicate clearly just how tedious I am.

"He's to be buried in Florence. Her family plot dates back to the Medicis," he says. These are the kinds of details he does like. Privilege comforts him, even if it doesn't pertain directly to him.

"Is Lulu his beneficiary? What does she inherit? Is there more work?"

This is too much talk for Simon. He's very buttoned up today, quite taken with the idea that he's done the right thing by closing the gallery. His posture indicates his pleasure, his chest puffed, spine straight.

"The contessa and Miss Finelli will arrange the details." He turns toward his office with the cup of tea, all proper British, rolling his *r*'s around in his mouth. "There's to be a memorial service at the end of the month. Now, where's my briefcase?"

"Isn't it funny?" I ask, as he's moving away from me. "You're going to talk about muses, and this real-life muse doesn't even know she's a muse."

I don't expect him to respond, but he halts and speaks from the door at the far end of the gallery.

"That's right," he says. He resents my implications. "She doesn't know what she's missing."

He disappears into his office. I lose myself for a spell in the painting before me, curious about the girl who inspired it. I wish I'd asked Jeffrey more about her. Were they close before he moved away? Was there some sort of a rift in the family, or did they just drift apart, as families do? Why her?

"Come along, then," Simon says when he returns with his index cards and his brolly, ready to set off in the rain.

"You want me to come?" I never attend events outside the gallery during the day. I'd been looking forward to some quiet time to myself with him gone and the gallery closed. I'm still feeling uncalibrated.

"Of course," Simon says, adopting a more emphatic version of the tone he tends to use with me, a combination of familiarity and disdain. "The gallery is closed."

He opens the umbrella, an inverted bucket-shaped contraption designed for old ladies leaving the beauty parlor and needing maximum protection. He looks at me expectantly.

"That's bad luck," I tell him.

The panel discussion takes place in a large conference room at the museum. Seven people show up. A real crowd. There are tea sandwiches and Milano cookies and the requisite tall green bottles of San Pellegrino water.

The other members of the panel seated at a half-round table include two artists I've never heard of. There are also two curators from the museum staff and a woman with long red hair who claims to be a muse. She has a foreign accent of indeterminate origin and keeps pronouncing it "mooze." This alone would have made it hard to take her seriously, but she also keeps making self-important statements like, "A mooze is more of an artist than the artist, but the artist must never know," and "Moozes must always be inspiring, never boring."

Simon's theory on muses — and I'm not surprised to learn he has such a theory — is that a muse should never try to figure out what it is about her that inspires the artist. According to Simon, it is not up to the muse to analyze the process or comment on it.

"In fact," he says, "I was just having this discussion with several of my artists. Myself, Carlos Peres, and Maria Ueffelman were meeting at . . ."

Now, I'm sure I'm the only person in the room who finds that grammatical blunder grating. It gets under my skin, the way he tries to sound so eloquent and then starts a sentence with *Myself.*

Could this be any more boring? I want to get back to the gallery and meet the real muse, not listen to Simon, whom I'm fairly certain has had little contact with any muses.

"It's a burden, being a mooze," the red-haired woman complains. "A mooze can't just be a face on a painting. A mooze has to inspire, to draw out the work. Then a mooze has to sell product. Nowadays moozes have to have clothing lines. It's about branding. And money."

An interesting point, but I start to slip on my raincoat, certain no one is even still awake, let alone alert enough to ask a question. Let's go, folks! A stout gentleman in a three-piece suit rouses himself and proceeds with a long-winded diatribe on whether a muse is actually an artist in her own right. Only he gets confused by the red-haired woman's interjections about the role of the mooze, and then he starts pronouncing it "mooze" himself, and she thinks he's making fun of her and gets angry.

It's the kind of thing that usually affords me a little private laugh, but I can't even enjoy it today. I want to be released. Come on, people.

Finally, it's over. Simon looks like he wants to linger, basking in the glow of this public exertion of his intellect, but I remind him that Lulu will be waiting for us downtown.

■ ■ ■ ■

She is. Waiting for us, that is. We pull up to the gallery in a taxi, and there she is. She isn't conventionally pretty. Well, yes, of course she's pretty. She's beautiful. If by beautiful you mean that fragile blond kind of beauty that make artists want to capture it on canvas. If you mean the kind of stunning and unusual looks that usually belong to supermodels who are paid huge day rates. Yes, she's beautiful, if you mean the kind of gorgeous that usually makes other women very uncomfortable. Her face is almost heart-shaped, with sharp, high cheekbones and the wide-set round eyes that I recognize from the painting. Jeffrey's eyes.

As we shake hands, my eyes meet hers. I see in them the very quality Jeffrey captured so brilliantly in the painting, a sort of distance in a cloud of doubt. I've seen a lot of gorgeous women in my time in the art world. Some days it seems like half the female population of downtown New York is made up of tall beauties with ridiculously high cheekbones and coltlike legs. But I've never seen anyone this beautiful, in such an interesting way.

"Hello," she says simply. Her energy is calm. She wears a long fitted gray coat with double rows of buttons hooked up to her neck, and her hair is as straight and fine and light as it looks in the painting, when she was nine. She doesn't just look gorgeous, she looks cool. Chic.

Simon goes positively giddy at the sight of her. I imagine this is the way most men, even ones with wavering sexuality like Simon, must get in her presence. What a strange thought, to be able to make grown men feel silly, just by being. Simon gets all flustered, goes to kiss her cheek as she extends her hand to shake. They almost collide, and he tries to turn his movement into a sort of bow. Then he fumbles with the keys to the door and keeps lowering his head in her direction.

"I've just given a lecture," Simon tells her as he tries to get the door open. "On the very subject of muses. You would have found it insightful."

It was a panel discussion for an audience of seven, and he's making it sound like it was him at a podium before a crowd of hundreds. I can see by the way her eyebrows knit together that she doesn't realize why a discussion on muses would even be relevant to her. But she puts her hand on his arm, a light and flirtatious gesture that seems very natural.

Simon runs his hands through his hair, restoring it to its perfect shape, although the wind and the rain have hardly had an effect on it. He finally swings open the door to the gallery and holds it open for Lulu. Just as I'm about to follow her, Simon lets go, sliding in behind her as the door catches me hard on the shoulder.

Lulu's eyes go straight to the wall that separates the entrance from the actual gallery space. There on the chalky white of the plaster Jeffrey Finelli's name is stenciled in black sans serif letters. She reaches out and rubs her hand on her uncle's name.

"Did he tell you anything about the show?" Simon asks. He has his roll of Smarties in his hand, and he holds it out to her as is his habit.

She shakes her head, still feeling the letters as if they're braille.

"He said we come from a long line of failed artists," she says.

Simon takes her by the elbow. "He just liked the way that sounded. He was hardly a failed artist."

She catches my eye. She has an air of wanting to make us feel at ease. I wonder if that's how she always is with new people, if it has something to do with being so beautiful. Or maybe it's just that she understands the strangeness of the situation in which we find ourselves, how life can bring together such a seemingly random selection of human beings into a forced intimacy. Like this, the three of us clustered awkwardly around a set of letters on the wall.

I try to imagine what she is about to experience. To be unexpectedly confronted by a painted image of myself, one large enough to cover an entire wall, executed by an uncle I hadn't seen in twenty years who is suddenly, dead? It's hard to conceive, although she's the first person I've met, I realize suddenly, who, like me, has lost all of her family.

Jeffrey told me Lulu was an only child who lost both her parents. Like Lulu, I was an only child too. I guess I still am. Then my dad died when I was eleven, and my mom six, no, six and a half years ago. It hits me as our eyes meet; she understands. She knows what it's like to be completely alone in this world, as I do.

Simon leads her around the wall and into the gallery. Lulu looks at the whole space once quickly, taking in all the works. Her eyes go back to the large painting where they stop. "That's me?"

I'll give Simon credit. He is patient. He allows her plenty of time to absorb what she's seeing, just as he would with a client viewing a new artist for the first time. He doesn't say anything until she does.

I let my eyes rest on the large painting as hers do. The colors are so intense, all those bright oranges and pinks and many shades of yellow, that I lose myself in them. I love the way Jeffrey uses, or used, paler whites and yellows to create the illusion of natural light, the kind of natural light I imagine you might see in Florence. God, he was a good painter.

The three of us stand there, riveted by the girl on the wall. Even Simon appears to be moved by seeing the work with Lulu at his side.

"I don't understand," Lulu says, after a long while. Her voice is thick, as though she might cry. "Me as a little girl with a paintbrush? What does that mean? I assume it has some kind of meaning."

Simon has an answer. He responds quickly, as though he's rehearsed it. "You represent pure creativity. All children have it, a relationship with their own inspiration. And thus, with God."

I'm impressed. Simon really sounds like

he understood what Jeffrey was talking about. "He talked about the doubt, as it pertains to faith, and to art," he says. "Self-doubt."

Lulu steps forward to inspect the other paintings, the landscapes, more closely. She moves with grace, as though she once studied dance. Simon follows her, maintaining the same respectful distance but keeping her company. I stay where I am.

"Jeffrey believed the creative endeavor is the only way to connect with the spiritual," Simon continues. "To feel God, who was the original Creator."

She looks perplexed. "What does that have to do with me?"

"You're the next in that line of failed artists," he says.

"I'm not an artist," she says softly, looking down at her feet. "I'm a bean counter, the furthest thing from an artist."

"Your uncle felt it's in all of us, to be an artist. To create," Simon says.

"I work on Wall Street," Lulu says.

It's a shock to hear her say she works on Wall Street. She just doesn't look anything like anyone's idea of a woman with that sort of job. Wall Street. It sounds so manly, so serious. Wall Street is the real world, a place where everyone makes money, even the secretaries. Somehow I can tell Lulu is not a secretary.

We all go quiet then, staring up at the enormous canvas on the wall, searching it, as though we're looking for clues.

"How about a spot of tea?" Simon suggests after a bit. It occurs to me a few seconds later that he wants me to produce the tea, but by then Lulu has spoken, and the idea of tea goes away.

"Where did he get this stuff about being a count?"

"Maybe he bought the title," Simon suggests. "Americans are always doing that." He loves to point out what Americans always do, the expatriate commenting on the natives.

Simon had turned his phone off during the muse discussion. He turns it back on now and checks his messages.

"Seventeen new messages?" he exclaims. He moves toward his office with the phone at his ear, a look of wonder on his face. There seems to be a new confidence to his manner and a strut in his step that wasn't there before last night.

"Sorry, will you excuse me for a brief moment? Stay, spend time with the painting of you," he says to Lulu. "Get used to the idea of yourself as the unsuspecting muse."

She smiles at him, lifting one hand in the tiniest wave. It's a charming gesture, one that implies intimacy. Simon looks enchanted as he returns the wave and backs into his office.

The unsuspecting muse. Wish I'd come up with that one.

"There's a contessa," I tell Lulu once he's gone. "I think that's where it came from. He never referred to himself as a count."

She fixes her eyes on mine now in a way that reminds me of Jeffrey, full of curiosity. "Yes, she called me this morning. I couldn't understand half of what she said."

"She's making the arrangements."

"I think that's what she said. I'm not to come there for three weeks. That's when she wants the service."

It's like an optical illusion, the young version of the face on the wall, looming large above the same face in front of me, only twenty years older. Her face is more chiseled, less rounded, more grown-up beautiful, but otherwise looks very similar. Scientifically and mathematically pretty.

"What did you talk about with my uncle?" Lulu asks.

What did we talk about? I can't remember anything specific. Madagascar. The shepherd's pie. "He was very excited to see you."

"Then why did he wait until the day before the opening to call me?" Lulu wears a thick silver band on her thumb, and she plays with it. It's not a very Wall Street accessory, I think. Although, what do I know about Wall Street?

"I'm sure it was a surprise," I say. "To hear from him after all those years."

"A surprise? I thought it was some kind of identity theft."

Lulu stays at the gallery into the evening. She stares at the painting of her for stretches, then drifts around to the other pieces before going back to it. Sometimes she gets very close, inspecting the brushstrokes. Other times she stands way back.

I sit at my desk, trying to work. As I stare at the large canvas before me, I feel overcome with what I can only describe as resentment. I want to be there, on the wall, in the form of my own painting, not behind the desk dealing with the business of selling what's on the wall. *Resentment,* that word lacks momentum. And what I experience then, in the presence of both the painted and the real Lulu, is more like inspiration tinged with guilt at how easily I've allowed myself not to paint, simply because I'm not good enough. Momentum, that's what I feel.

It's getting dark when Lulu says, "It's very moving, this painting. Isn't it?"

"As though it's imbued with some kind of power," I add. And it does seem that way to me, as though this painting has taken hold of me.

"Is this contemporary art, though? This kind of painting? I'd expect more cutting edge, plain black canvases and boxes of hair. What's all that about ready-made things, like urinals? This is so different."

"Every artist is different. Each has their own style," I say. "And there's a conceptual component to your uncle's work. In the way he relates it back to the creative process."

"I wish I'd asked more, when I spoke to him," she says. She steps back to take a wider look of the portrait of her.

It's getting late, past the time when I would have gone home. Simon has not emerged from his office. I'd like to suggest that Lulu and I go somewhere, for a coffee, or a bite to eat. But I think it might sound odd, so soon after we've met. She sees me look toward the door.

"I'm so sorry," she says. "Is it late?"

"Not at all," I say, although we usually close at six, if we're open.

"Do you have plans?" she asks. "I'd love to hear more about my uncle. Want to get something to eat?"

I peer around the door to Simon's office. He's leaning way back in his chair, his John Lobb handmade shoes on the desk, one arm reaching up and around his head to cradle the phone to his ear. He's animated, with the ebullience that usually only emerges when he's drinking. It occurs to me to wonder, almost in passing, whether I was wrong in dismissing my murder suspicions. This is all working out a little too well for him.

When he notices me, he asks the person on the other end of the phone if they would mind holding for just a brief second. "I don't want to lose you," he says into the phone, adding a snort of a laugh. God, he's annoying.

"Lulu and I are going to leave," I tell him. Once again I dismiss my suspicions. Simon Pryce can be mean, he can be petty and spiteful and silly, and certainly, he can be greedy, but he's not a murderer.

He must have forgotten Lulu was still there. At the mention of her name he jumps up and quickly extricates himself from his call.

"You can't imagine the demand," he says to me, practically dancing at my side.

"I guess I can't."

"You'll be impressed," he says. As if he could impress me. Oh, Simon.

"I've used this leverage to presell some of the Carlos Peres works from our next show," he continues.

He pauses, waiting for me to applaud. I don't, so he keeps talking. Now he adopts a conspiratorial tone, as though we're in the habit of exchanging confidences. "I know there must be more Finelli work. Although the Italian woman is being mysterious," he says. "I'm devastated, of course, to lose an artist like Jeffrey."

He hardly looks devastated, all rosy-cheeked and happy and light on his feet.

"I'm leaving with Lulu," I tell him.

"Right." He nods, as though this makes sense, the ambitious assistant moving in to befriend the niece/muse. He's got it wrong, of course. Not that I'm not curious about Lulu, and not that I would mind befriending her, either, but it's not the way he would envision such a friendship, with an agenda.

He follows me out of the office into the gallery, where Lulu looks forlorn, staring up at her portrait.

Simon kisses her on both cheeks to say good-bye, less awkward now. "Let me take you to lunch tomorrow. We've so much to talk about."

"I'd like that very much," she says, putting her hand on his arm. "But I don't go to lunch. I work on Wall Street."

"We're staying closed again tomorrow," he says. "Out of deference to the artist. Why don't you come back and see the show again? It's always a different experience the second time."

"Well," she says. "Maybe if it's a late lunch."

Lulu and I step out onto the spot in the street where Jeffrey died at almost the exact same time only the night before. We pause in front of the gallery, on the rain-slicked sidewalk where tonight it's very quiet. Now the gray and white and charcoal expanse of sky is moody and expressive, filled with oddly defused light, like a bad painting of a city sky.

Five:
Dinner with the Unsuspecting Muse

March

Lulu and I start walking east, toward Ninth Avenue. Her stride is impossibly long, and I struggle to keep up, although she keeps slowing down to let me catch her. We chat easily as we walk. At first, we talk about how we're both addicted to caffeine of the Starbucks variety, even though we hate the way they can't just call the sizes small, medium, and large.

Then we move on to exchanging background history, where we grew up, where we went to college, where we live now, that kind of thing. I spent my childhood on Long Island, Lulu moved around a lot, New Jersey, Colorado, Connecticut, Baltimore, even a year and a half in Paris. I tell her I feel grateful on a daily basis for my studio sublet in the West Village, where I live now. I expect Lulu to say she lives downtown too, but no, she lives on East Thirty-eighth Street. Not the kind of neighborhood that inspires tremendous gratitude.

We're almost to Sixth Avenue when Lulu surprises me.

"Would you like to come to my place?"

Once the words are out, she looks almost as startled as I feel. People our age never entertain in our homes. The small spaces into which we cram ourselves are not conducive to dinner parties.

"We can order Chinese," she says. "And I'd love a glass of wine."

We hail a cab. Simply by asking, she leads me to believe her apartment will be large, or very design-y and stylish, or some kind of space worthy of an invitation. So I'm surprised when our taxi pulls up to a nondescript brick building.

The apartment inside is even more of a surprise, a tidy white box of a studio. It's almost empty, with only a white daybed covered in white pillows along one wall and a small round table with three chairs around it on the other. There's a fluffy white rug in the center of the floor and a television.

It's very neat, almost sterile. There is no art on the walls. There are no family pictures, no trinkets lying on the tabletops, no belongings, really, to speak of.

"Did you just move in?" I ask as she throws her gray coat on one of the three chairs and puts mine on top of it.

"Is that how it looks?" She looks around, as though seeing her space with new eyes, and lets out a small laugh. "I guess I'm just not into stuff."

She has an iPod in a speaker set, and she turns it on now. Again, I'm surprised. It's not the Strokes or the Gorillas or music you'd expect someone who wears low-slung jeans this well would listen to. Instead, what pours from the speakers is the kind of music they play in yoga class. What is this, Enya?

Lulu takes a bottle of white wine from the small refrigerator, where there are three matching bottles of an Italian pinot grigio. Tonight, I decide, is not a night for my rules about mid-week drinking. One glass.

There are no photographs at all in the whole apartment. I'm usually too reserved to reveal my curiosity about other people. So I surprise myself when I come right out and ask her, "You don't have any family photos?"

She takes a corkscrew from one of the kitchen drawers and opens the wine before she answers me.

"My mother destroyed them all," she says, pouring wine into two glasses.

See, this is why I'm better off keeping my mouth shut. Now I'm embarrassed. "I'm sorry," I say, accepting the glass of wine. "I shouldn't have said anything."

"No, no," she says. Her earlier reserve has disappeared. "It's okay. I have a weird family. Had."

I sip the wine, enjoying the way it immediately offers its fuzzy comfort. My reserve seems to have disappeared as well. I feel extremely comfortable with Lulu, not at all like I normally feel meeting new people. It almost feels as though we've known each other before. "Don't we all?"

"My dad died when I was nine," she says.

"I was eleven when mine died," I say.

Another look of understanding passes between us, like earlier in the day when we met for the first time. "I'm sorry," she says.

"I'm sorry too."

"I think my father hated his brother," she says, sliding her feet gracefully underneath her on the sofa. "That's why I didn't know my uncle. My parents never talked about him. I mean, once or twice I remember my father referring to the genius artist in a mean tone. Enough that I understood that an artist was a lame thing to be, according to my father. But that was it."

"Jeffrey didn't come to his funeral?"

"They never spoke. I don't even know if he knew his own brother had died," she says. "I'm not sure my mother ever contacted him. I think my father felt pretty strongly about never wanting anything to do with him. I never found out why. One time I asked my mom why we had no relatives, and she said we were lucky. I asked her about the uncle I could only sort of remember, and she said she imagined he might have died. That was exactly how she said it. 'I imagine he might have died.' "

"It must have been a shock to hear from him on the phone," I say.

"I told you," she says with that small laugh. "I thought it was some kind of identity theft. The name Jeffrey Finelli meant nothing to me."

"And seeing the painting of you, that must have been even more of a shock."

"That was strange. But oddly comforting. And this is going to sound bizarre, but it's almost like that painting was speaking to me."

"That doesn't sound bizarre at all," I say.

"My mother teetered elegantly on the brink of insanity. For years," she says. "Then she just sort of unraveled. She said she suffered from a disease called perfectionism. In the end I think that's what killed her."

Her words hit me with a slap. Perfectionism. That sounds like my diagnosis. It seems like a relatively benign ailment. But my prognosis is not good.

"My mom found religion," I say. It's liberating, talking about my family. "She died four years ago. But we'd grown so far apart by then."

Lulu is looking at me with that same half-smile she wears in her portrait. "I've never met anyone whose story is so much like mine. I think my mom had always wanted to be an artist. She never told me that, and she never did it. But somehow I thought that's what she would have wanted for herself."

She unfolds herself from the sofa, opens a drawer, and pulls out a binder full of take-out menus organized in plastic flaps. The names of the restaurants are stuck to labeled tabs and alphabetized.

"I know, I'm anal." She laughs, acknowledging my look. "Pick something."

She fills our half-empty glasses with more wine. So much for my one-drink resolution. "After my father died," she continues, "my mom, she went slowly insane. One day I came home from school, and she'd started a fire in the living room. She burned all the pictures. Every last one. That's why there's nothing here."

"Lulu, I'm so sorry."

"We had a complicated relationship. I guess most people do, with their mothers. With their families. That's why it meant so much to me when my uncle said he was giving me the painting."

At first I don't quite realize what she's saying. "What does that mean," I ask, "giving you the painting?"

"I don't know," she says. "We had the strangest conversation. He called me the day before the opening. I had theater tickets. So I said I was too busy to come."

She looks down at her wineglass. "Isn't that crazy? He was my uncle. I hadn't seen him in twenty years. He said, 'Busy? You sound just like your mother.' And then he said, 'You have to come. There's something you have to see.' "

I remember then what Jeffrey told me that night in the gallery, he had to promise her the painting to get her to come. "He never gave us your name or address. We would have sent you an invitation."

"Well, that explains why I never got it," Lulu says. "So he asks me, 'Didn't you get the invitation? The picture that is on the cover of the invitation is for you. It's my gift to you.' The painting of me. Today was the first I heard of it."

Is that what he meant when he said he was giving her the painting? His masterpiece? *Lulu Meets God and Doubts Him?*

"I don't even want it," she continues. "I mean, what would I do with it? Even if I could live with a huge portrait of myself, it wouldn't fit in here."

I don't offer an opinion about what Simon might have to say about this. Why would Jeffrey give away a painting that wasn't his? Simon owns those paintings, remember? Simon is planning on selling the Lulu painting for as much money as he can get.

"Chinese okay?" Lulu shows me the menu for Shun Lee.

"My favorite."

"Mine too," she says with a grin.

We like a lot of the same things, Grand Marnier prawns, moo shu pork, dumplings, and we order enough food to feed thirty people. Lulu pours more wine. I ask about her job. I'm fascinated by people who have regular moneymaking jobs and aren't afflicted with creative aspirations. "Wall Street. It sounds so serious."

"It's just a job," Lulu says with a shrug of her bony shoulders. "Sometimes I wonder why I ever thought it was a good idea."

"We all have to make a living," I offer up, me at my most trite. "I feel the same way about my job."

"I felt this pressure," she says. "You know, to be the breadwinner. I'm a family of one. I had to take care of myself. It was out of fear that I went that direction."

"I could say the same," I tell her. "Except being a gallery girl doesn't pay much."

"I know nothing about art," she says. "I was a business major. Although I did study painting in college. But I know absolutely nothing about contemporary art. I have no idea if my uncle's show would be considered any good. Is it?"

"It is now," I say.

Over dinner, after we've loaded up our plates, she brings up Dane O'Neill. "My uncle told me about him on the phone," she says. "I guess I was supposed to know who he was. And be impressed."

"He's the darling of the art world," I tell her, through a mouthful of moo shu pork.

"He made quite certain I knew that when he came to the hospital with me," she says. "What an ego."

"I just met him at the opening," I say, wondering if I should tell her I fell a tiny bit in love with him. "The standard favorite

Dane O'Neill story has him stripped down to nothing but purple striped socks at the first party in his honor. He makes it memorable by dancing naked on the dining table —"

At this she laughs, interrupting me. "Can you imagine? What a lot of bobbing around."

"It becomes a signature," I say. "You know you're at a good party if Dane O'Neill has gotten naked."

"And let me guess," she says, spearing one of the dumplings with a fork. "The show sells out."

"I think I like him," I tell her. I blurt it out. I'm not in the habit of discussing my poor choices of romantic candidates with my friends, not even my closest friends from college like Azalea or Joey. Usually the perfectionist in me dismisses the choices before I get a chance to have a conversation about them. And even that doesn't stop me from ending up in their beds. Although come to think of it, even the perfectionist in me thought Ricardo was the real thing.

"Dane O'Neill? No. You seem so grounded, so grown up," she says. "He seems like such a baby."

"He's at least ten years older than I am."

"I'm not talking about age," she says,

pouring more wine for both of us.

"I haven't been very lucky in love," I say. "Maybe an older artist would be a good change."

"I don't know," she says. "I haven't been lucky either. I tend to play it safe, going out with very boring, safe guys I can't possibly fall in love with. As though that will keep me from getting hurt."

She eats a lot, for someone so thin. I, of course, keep up. I'm not one to turn down Grand Marnier prawns under any circumstances.

"You play backgammon?" she asks, when we've eaten as much as we can.

"I do. I love it," I say, gushing a bit. "My dad taught me when I was little. We used to play a lot. Then when I was in college I worked evenings at the school studio space. All I had to do was sit there and check people in. The janitor and I would play backgammon almost every night. I got really good at it."

While I've given her more detail than I'm sure anyone would want on my backgammon history, she's pulled out the board and started setting it up. "Not for money," she says. "Not the first game, anyway."

She places the pieces quickly, like someone

who has done this many times. I'm more slow. It's been a while since I've played. The last time was with a French secondary market dealer named Jean-Paul. I beat him. Then he told me he loved me. I believed him.

We each roll one die to get the game started. She rolls a six to my one, and in a flash two of her pieces are neatly blocking the point just outside her home base.

I roll a three and a four and slowly count out the weak moves available to me. We continue chatting, the words just flowing out of us. We've got good chemistry, it seems, the two of us, and remarkable parallels in our lives. If it weren't for the fact that she's stunningly beautiful and I'm, well, not, we're very similar.

We've been rolling the dice and talking, and before I realize what's happened she's got six of my men off the board and blocked up her entire home base. Obviously, Lulu's playing the game on an entirely different level.

"Sorry," she says. "I should have told you up front. This is how I put myself through business school."

It's after one in the morning when we finally say good-bye. By this point, I feel I've made a new friend, even if she beat me soundly at a game I seem to recall bragging about earlier in the evening. It's a good thing we weren't playing for money.

I'm at the door in my coat when Lulu asks, "Do you think Simon knows Jeffrey gave me the painting of me?"

"I don't think so." In fact, I know he doesn't, but now doesn't seem the time to tell her that Simon actually owns the paintings. She'll learn soon enough that Simon is gleeful about the death of the artist that will pull him out of debt and onto the roster of dealers that are rewarded for their ability to pick winners.

"How will he take it?"

"Not well," I tell her. This is an understatement. It's too late at night to get into why Simon won't be at all thrilled to learn about Lulu's claim on his painting. "He's very excited about selling the piece."

"The art world is totally foreign to me," she says. "Will you be my guide?"

She smiles at me, that wry doubting half-smile, almost an exact duplicate of her face in the painting. I nod, yes, I will be her guide, although something tells me she doesn't need much guidance. In fact, I have a feeling she will be more of a guide to me.

"I really want to learn," she says. "Can we go to some galleries and museums together?"

I explain that I work on Saturdays, but I usually see new shows at other galleries' openings. "It's the beginning of the month, so there should be a few this weekend if you want to go."

"Thank you," she says.

My apartment looks different to me when I get home, a shift in perspective that feels sudden and jarring. I remember feeling so lucky when I found this place, an illegal sublet on the fifth floor of a walk-up building. An artist's garret, I think I actually called it, when I came to New York full of all that earnest and misplaced ambition. Just like so many eager artists before me.

Not for me is hipster Brooklyn. For one thing, I'm not hip. Not hip at all. Hip scares me. And my rent-controlled sublet is cheaper than anything I could have found in Williamsburg when I moved. I was one of the lucky ones, somehow, miraculously able to find a home on the overcrowded island of Manhattan. Lucky, that's how I've thought of myself, at least in terms of real estate.

Lucky until now, that is. I had thought my teeny-tiny studio apartment was cozy and charming. Now I see it's closed in on itself, with piles of junk and stacks of books cluttering the few surfaces. Before tonight, I thought of it as authentically prewar, with details that were original to the 1930s. Now I see it's just dirty, no matter how regularly I get the cleaning bug, the tiles grimy with years of ground-in dirt. I thought I would paint brilliantly here, but, well, that hasn't happened.

The mess, this is part of the problem. As an artist — and it's hard for me to even use that term to describe myself, it sounds so vain — I crave order. I'm in love with symmetry and neatness and precise placements of objects. The clutter in my apartment is symbolic, if there can be such a thing as symbolic clutter.

When I first moved in, I hung my own work on the walls to hide the holes and the places where the paint was chipped. What hubris. Back then, I confused scale with emotion, and my canvases were as big as I could afford. A huge portrait of my favorite professor. An even bigger one of a class model named Mark. Good only for hiding the peeling pink paint that was never my color choice. Now the hooks where those works used to hang are forlorn reminders of my ambition. Ambition. My dirty little secret.

I kneel at the foot of my bed. There, behind shopping bags of clothes I'll never wear but haven't been able to give away, a carton of hangers, and my huge green suitcase, is the box that contains what's left of my painting aspirations. This is where I keep my sketch pads, some brushes, tubes of paints, and a few small stretched canvases, empty and waiting.

There's one canvas on an easel in the corner of the room, but it's been a few months since I've worked on it. A few months? Who am I kidding? It's been at least a year. A couple of coats are draped over the easel, hiding the evidence. Every time I've tried to work on it, I get so frustrated, trying to capture what is brilliant in my mind's eye, but horribly not brilliant at all once it's on the canvas. Some days I'll get very strict with myself. I'll tell myself I have three months to finish, say, six canvases. Enough to show a dealer. Maybe even Simon. Other days, I give up entirely. It's just too depressing not to be brilliant.

I used to love to mix colors, spending hours playing with small bowls of acrylics, dripping white into red, adding dollops of ecru and cerulean blue. My teachers at school and in the workshops I took when I first moved to New York would compliment me. They'd call me a true colorist, and I reveled in the praise, even as I suspected that's what they called all the students who couldn't draw.

I've held on tight to my identity as a painter. I'm an artist in New York. I know it's supposed to be difficult. That's okay, I've been more than willing for it to be difficult. I'm willing to study, to pay my dues. I'm even willing to be poor — artists are supposed to be poor. I'm willing to work for little money in a second-rate gallery, just to make ends meet and be in the art world. I chose a gallery because the job fed my hope that one day I might go from receptionist behind the desk to artist with work on the wall. But somehow five years have passed, and the likelihood of such a transition seems now . . . um, impossible.

From my prostrated position before my bed, I slide the box toward me. I open it and breathe in the familiar turpentiney smell of the clean brushes. A deep breath. Okay, here goes.

I throw the coats off the easel to reveal the painting I'd been working on the last time I quit. A self-portrait. Talk about hubris! But it's too late to start something new now, so I position the easel before the mirror in the way that I had when I first conceived this piece. I take a plastic plate from my little kitchenette to use as a palette and squeeze brown, gold, and ecru onto it. I pick up the smallest brush and set to work on the hair.

There's a certain alchemy that has to happen for a painting to be successful. It all has to come together. It's after four in the morning when I decide I'm not an alchemist. And I have a feeling I'm not a figurative painter either.

Six:
A Private Viewing
of New Paintings
by Jeffrey Finelli
at the Simon Pryce
Gallery

Just because we're closed doesn't mean we're closed, if you know what I mean. Word seems to have gotten out about Martin Better's interest in the dead artist. By late morning, the two landscapes have been sold to two different collectors. *Where Is God When We Need Him* went to the Keeping-It-Real yoga guy in the orange sneakers who had shown so little interest the night of the opening. *Yearning for Family* went to an Ohio collector who had received only a jpeg of the work before the show. They both paid nearly double the initial price Simon had considered charging: $85,000. There is a museum discussing *Studio at Dusk* if they can't have one of the figurative works.

Three people have holds on *Mona's Bedroom.* Simon is working the phones with the collectors interested in Jeffrey's self-portrait and *Finding and Losing Faith*. And there is lots and lots of interest in *Lulu Meets God and Doubts Him.* Suddenly there are plenty of people claiming to have witnessed the power of this particular painting. Even people who haven't actually witnessed the painting itself. All this interest leads Simon to decide not to sell the painting right away.

This morning Simon is holed up in his office with the telephone, high on the sweet narcotic of having a supply to meet a demand. A masterpiece! What is that worth? Certainly more than a thousand words. He's taking orders, placing multiple holds on all the available works. This is a new experience for him. Rep of a hot artist.

Oh, sure, he's sold out a show every now and then. I mean, it *is* a bubble, even if Simon has not exactly had his finger on the pulse of the art market. But now, here he is, with some very hot paintings to sell. Paintings that he owns.

We're closed, yes. But there are private viewings today. The very word *private* acts as a velvet rope for certain collectors, and Simon has done his best to entice them to take advantage of the opportunity. Martin Better's coming down to see the piece he has on hold. And, big news, a celebrity is coming in. It's a young actor, one who prefers to remain nameless. I would prefer he remain nameless, as he seems overexposed as it is. Simon, the world's greatest name-dropper, has never had a celebrity client. Needless to say, he is very excited at the prospect.

"Go ahead, you can say it," he crows when I interrupt his telephone negotiations to tell him the actor's assistant says he'll arrive sometime between three and seven. "I'm a starfucker."

"I'd rather not."

"You can say it, Mia. Go on." This is Simon at his most jovial, when he actually seems to like me. "Starfucker!"

Martin Better appears at noon exactly, on time. He bangs on the glass to get my attention. The door is locked, and I open it for him.

"Thanks, babe," he says. He's chewing cinnamon gum. "You look great. Love you in black."

"Would you like a Pellegrino?" I ask as he strides into the main gallery, art lust in his eyes. There is something magnetic about Martin Better, despite the paunch under the suit and the patch of skull shining through the thinning hair. It might be those coconuts.

"Just tell me what you think of the piece I got on hold. Which one is it?"

He's stopped in front of the Lulu painting. He's easily turned on, like a horny teenager, and a look of rapture comes over his face as he stares at the piece. What earlier in the week was just a painting is now *the* Jeffrey Finelli. The definitive Finelli.

"The one that stopped you in your tracks," I say, and he turns to grin at me.

"Gotcha," he says.

Simon, although he's not a very polished salesman, has a sixth sense for activity in the gallery. He emerges now with a strut in his step, elaborately clapping his cell phone shut. He offers Martin a Smartie.

"I don't know," Martin says to Simon. He shakes his head to decline the candy, pointing at his mouth to indicate the gum already occupying that spot. "You really think this works in my collection?"

"It's a masterpiece," Simon says. He shrugs as though it doesn't really matter whether Martin agrees with him or not. "There's so much demand, I can't get off the phone."

As if on cue, Simon's cell phone tootles in his hand. He looks down at the number but doesn't answer.

Martin says to me, "I told the wife I'd take a break from art a bit. She says I'm an addict. But you're not addicted to something if you can quit when you want to, right?"

"Frankly, I'm not even sure I want to sell it," Simon says, clearly impatient with any talk of quitting art.

"Tell you what," Martin says. "Send it up to Greenwich for me. I got to see it in context."

This is a presumptuous request for a show that's just opened, but Simon's got a whale — yes, a buyer like Marty is a whale — on the line, and he'll do anything he can to hold on to it. "Monday, just for the day," Simon says, back to sounding cheery. And why shouldn't he sound cheery? Martin Better wants to do business with him. Everyone wants to do business with him.

After Martin Better leaves, Simon heads off too. It's time for his lunch. He lies, and tells me he's meeting a client. I'm used to this, but today his lie annoys me more than it should. Of course, that could have something to do with my agitated state of mind, since I've already downed three cappuccinos in the size that Starbucks persists in terming Venti.

There's no need for Simon to lie about

where he goes. I couldn't care less where he goes. I only care not to be lied to. All I know is, he's not there when Pierre LaReine comes into the gallery for the first time. Simon is going to be completely rattled that he's missing this visit from the biggest contemporary art dealer in New York. Somehow this will be my fault.

Pierre LaReine is with Dane O'Neill. Their presence in the gallery can mean only one thing — LaReine wants in on the action. The buzz on the Finelli goods must be better than we thought. Pierre LaReine doesn't usually get interested in an artist until the work gets expensive enough. Pierre LaReine's definition of a great artist? One whose market is in the millions.

"I'm telling you, this bloke's for real," Dane is saying as they come through the door.

Dane looks like he hasn't slept since Jeffrey's fateful opening. His eyes are rimmed in red, and he has several days' growth on his face. He's wearing the same clothes he was wearing two nights ago, the hand-painted T-shirt, the cargo pants now spattered with more colors. I'm reminded of something I heard about him. He supposedly did time, jail time — in the slammer! — in Ireland and was in the army, or was it the Irish secret police? His muscles are thick, like he's used to physical labor, and there's a roughness to him, like someone who definitely could've spent time in the big house.

Pierre LaReine, by contrast, the dapper Frenchman, looks like he just stepped out of the shower after a ten-hour sleep. He's perfectly groomed in a charcoal gray suit that slouches just so, comb marks in his silver hair. On his wrist, a large Franck Muller watch; on his feet, highly polished Berluti shoes. I recognize the names from the way Simon covets these personal style items. Simon covets everything about LaReine, especially his lifestyle. LaReine's lifestyle is famous.

So is his business acumen. I've seen LaReine walk by on nice days, hair glinting in the sunlight, on his way, perhaps, to meet a client for a lunch at which he will not even mention the eight-million-dollar price tag on a piece of art that sold at auction for three million only a season or two ago. And somehow, or so I hear, by the time the espressos are placed before them, the sale will be complete.

Or LaReine might be meeting an artist represented by another gallery, only for a casual meal, not to discuss business at all.

But by the end of their lunch, the artist might be invited to a dinner with collectors at Pierre's country farm. There might be the offer of a lift on Pierre's helicopter, and in a month or three, the artist has new representation.

They pause at my desk, and I stand up to greet them. Dane kisses my cheek. It's a distracted kiss, but a kiss nonetheless. I am now on kissing-hello terms with Dane O'Neill, the world-renowned artist. I will admit that this thrills me.

Dane introduces me to Pierre LaReine, who gives me a halfhearted handshake. He's already moving on, into the gallery, to see the Finellis.

"It's nice work," LaReine says. He has only the slightest French accent, with a subtle *z* sound replacing the *th*. "What's he asking for the big one?" *Ze big one.*

"I don't care, I'm buying it." Dane sinks to his knees just in front of the painting of Lulu. He looks at it closely, inspecting brushstrokes. "He was after me to get back to painting. I haven't stopped since that night."

"What's the price?" LaReine says again. This time the words are directed at me. *Ze price.*

"I'm not sure." I wish I had an answer. I

sound insipid. But Simon told me he isn't going to put any prices on the works until the gallery reopens. That $75,000 number, the price he dismissed the night of the opening, is no longer relevant. And if I say it out loud, someone could hold me to it. "Four of them are sold."

Dane keeps talking from his kneeling position in front of the Lulu painting. "He was always after me to paint. Paint, paint. That's the real thing. And I'd say, No one wants to buy a Dane O'Neill painting."

Pierre isn't listening to him. "Is there other work?"

"There must be," Dane says, standing now. As he turns, our eyes meet. Do I just imagine it, or does something pass between us? Oh God. I think something just passed between me and Dane O'Neill.

After a pause, Dane continues. "Finelli was very prolific. He would tell me he could paint ten or twelve big canvases a year, sometimes more."

"Who controls it?" LaReine wants to know. He throws it out there, for either one of us, it seems.

As though to answer the question, Lulu Finelli's presence suddenly fills the gallery.

Both of the men turn and stare at her as though she's a ghost. And she *is* like an apparition, just suddenly there, the girl from the painting. My new friend, the real Lulu, is so thin you could almost see through her.

She hugs me hello and moves into the main gallery. She gives Dane a small wave, almost regal, but then she smiles, and it is all warmth and light. I thought she was shy. Now I see there is nothing timid about her.

Dane swallows, and his face goes pale as though he really is looking at a ghost. He stares at the actual Lulu.

Pierre LaReine is staring too, but he suddenly snaps to attention. He comes forward with his hand outstretched to introduce himself. He is notoriously comfortable with lovely women, having been linked in the past to some famous beauties, models and socialites, trophy women. Although he's rarely alone, he's uncharacteristically single at the moment, unless you believe the rumors about Alexis and him.

He takes Lulu's hand and bows over it. He doesn't touch his lips to her skin, but just bends quickly over her hand in that European aristocratic way, just as Jeffrey Finelli had done to me when I met him for the first time.

"I know who you are," Lulu says to him. "You're the king of the art world."

It's clear he likes the sound of that. "I'm in love with the show," he says. "Especially this piece." It's sexy, the way he says it in that accent, *zis piece,* intimating that he's in love with the subject as well as the piece.

"I am too," she says, like she's talking about him now. This is interesting. A new side to Lulu. We all watch as she slowly unhooks the long row of buttons on the gray coat.

"That painting is crazy," Dane says, pointing at it. He seems to want to interrupt them. Perhaps I did imagine that thing, whatever it was, that passed between us when our eyes met. Or it was a very fleeting thing. Because Dane can't take his eyes off Lulu.

"Listen," Pierre says. "Are you by any chance free for dinner?"

"I'm not sure," Lulu says, sounding coy. Does she know he's a legendary ladies' man? As Alexis likes to point out, he doesn't hire anyone who isn't pretty. And often the women he hires end up being more than employees, if I understand Alexis correctly. Does Lulu know he's called off a wedding once or twice? Does she know he's been responsible for more than one broken marriage?

Pierre LaReine takes Lulu's hand in a

practiced move, pressing his lips to the top of it. "Give me your number."

He punches it into his cell phone. "I'll phone you. Dane, I like the show. Let's find out more."

He moves past my desk. "Nice vernissage," he says, on his way out.

Lulu then turns her gaze to Dane, taking in the disheveled hair, the manic eyes. "The painting isn't crazy. Maybe you're the crazy one."

This makes him laugh, a loud, short burst of laughter. "I am, I am. The painting is making me so. It's a crazy painting."

She appraises him calmly, her quiet steadiness in contrast to his frenetic energy as he paces back and forth before her.

"My uncle gave me that painting," she says. "That crazy painting."

He doesn't respond right away. Then he says, "It was always assumed I would buy it. He never thought anyone would want it."

"It was probably also always assumed he would stay alive."

She turns to me. There is no more doubt in her eyes. It's been replaced by something else, a kind of steeliness. "Last night I wasn't sure I could live with it. But I can't stop thinking about it."

"You see," Dane says. "There's something

crazy about this painting."

Simon opens the door then, returning from his supposed lunch with a client. What client, I'd like to know. He looks thrilled to see Dane O'Neill in his space. This means he raises his eyebrows several times in succession. Then he shakes Dane's hand too enthusiastically. Come on, Simon. Try to be cool.

Dane and Simon have met many times before, danced around each other in the way unique to artists and dealers who don't represent them. It's a cha-cha, forward and back, never an outright suggestion, never a firm rejection, just a dance, tinged with possibility.

"How d'you like the gallery?" Simon asks him, fishing for the compliment. No, he can't play it cool.

"I like the light," Dane says. "And the way you come in around that wall."

I listen, waiting for the pebble drop of the architect's name from Simon's lips. But Simon plays it modest, a new affectation somehow worse than his old ones. I see that Lulu is watching them too, assessing the two of them with a half-smile.

"Music to my ears," Simon says.

"Did you know Finelli told his niece she

could have the painting of her?" Dane swings an arm in Lulu's direction at the word *niece,* but she doesn't say anything. She stands very still, just watching.

Simon's face goes slack. It's not a good look. "What d'you mean?"

Dane laughs. He looks almost unhinged. "Did Finelli tell you I promised him I'd buy it?"

Simon shakes his head. No. No, this is not how he would have envisioned this playing out. Although, I can see him thinking, maybe if Dane O'Neill would consider switching galleries . . . But that's impossible. No one leaves a gallery like Pierre LaReine for one like Simon Pryce.

"What are you saying? These paintings were not his to give away. Or to promise for sale." Simon looks panicky at the news that these two, the brand-name artist and the muse, are both laying claim to his newfound cash cow. Lulu and Dane exchange glances, suddenly allied.

"You should buy the self-portrait, Dane," Simon says, trying to recover his charm. "That's the one for you."

Dane shakes his head. The smaller works are not nearly as strong as *Lulu Meets God.* There really is something powerful in the large canvas, maybe even something crazy, as Dane put it. We all eye the other works now, comparing them.

There's a pause. We hear the door to the gallery open. Swoosh. There is a click, click, click, of high heels slapping against the poured concrete floor.

"We're closed," Simon calls out, flashing me an exasperated look, although he was the last one through the open door.

"It's me. Connie Kantor."

Simon makes a face, but he greets her cordially, perhaps relieved at the reprieve. He's cordial but cold and dismissive, making it clear he has no interest in Connie's potential as a client. This is typical of Simon's shortsightedness as a businessman, but I can hardly blame him. I wouldn't want to do business with Connie Kantor either. Especially as she has a reputation for being slow to pay. And she always wants a discount.

I catch Lulu's eye here, and she raises one eyebrow at me in reaction to the vision of the fur-clad woman who's just clattered into our midst. Connie has another Birkin bag on her arm, this one a deep ugly red, and high-heeled shoes that almost, but don't quite, match. Underneath the sable she's got on a too-tight suit that is all wrong. As usual, she's a sight, making you wonder,

Doesn't she own a full-length mirror?

"Dane O'Neill!" Connie cries out, practically swooning into the artist's arms. "You're coming to my house. For the museum party."

Dane doesn't look like he knows what she's talking about. "In your honor?" Connie adds.

"Yeah, that's right," he says, still sounding doubtful.

Connie's never been able to get on Pierre LaReine's list of buyers for Dane O'Neill's work. But there was a grossly overpriced piece being shopped around for a while by a Swiss secondary-market dealer of questionable ethics, according to Alexis, who tends to know these things. Connie was finally offered a Dane O'Neill once all the other collectors the Swiss approached had balked at the price. Naturally, she's having a party to celebrate.

She turns to Simon. "You're coming too. I saw your name on the list."

"Yes, wouldn't miss it," he says. I'm probably the only one who catches the slightest rolling of his eyes. Who is he to be snobby about a client like Connie? He should be delighted to sell her any works of art she wants. But there's something about Connie that just rubs people the wrong way.

Even dealers like Simon who should want to help her spend her money on art but are too shortsighted to see that she could be a whale.

Connie is not stupid. She knows there's something repellent about her. When it comes to having a party, she understands the wisdom of securing a hot guest of honor to make for a desirable invitation. She's done so by promising the piece to the museum in addition to a large sum of money to underwrite an upcoming retrospective of Dane's work.

"You," she says, pointing at Lulu with a rude jab of a manicured finger. "You come too."

"Wait till you see my installation," she says to Dane. "You're going to die."

At least she realizes her last sentence is insensitive. "Sorry," she adds. "Poor choice of words. Of course you're not literally going to die. At least, not at my house."

She's the only one who laughs. She juts one hand awkwardly toward Lulu. "I feel like I already know you, from the painting."

Lulu takes her hand and shakes it. "I'm Lulu Finelli."

"I know," Connie says. Another forced laugh. "I know *all* about you."

There are implications in her delivery, as

though the things she knows are top secret. But she lets it go. She waves a hand at her face to fan herself. "I'm so thirsty."

The diamond on her finger shoots rays of light across the white wall. "So thirsty."

She wants to be offered a Pellegrino. The offering of a water, this confers status on a collector, at least in Connie's mind. That Pellegrino means something. It means that she is considered a backroom player, not simply one of the masses who peruse the paintings and suffer attitude from the receptionist — who, me? — when they ask for a price list.

But Simon doesn't take her up on the hint and suggest a drink. So I don't either. There is an implicit message in the simple glass of water. I can't take it upon myself to confer Pellegrino status on a collector who doesn't deserve it. That's just not the way it works.

There's silence. When no one talks, the gallery is deadly quiet, as though all the air has been sucked out of it. It always reminds me of church, when I used to wait for my mom, times when there was no mass but she'd stop in to light a candle or two in Dad's memory. Or because I had a test that day. Or because it was supposed to rain. My mother clung tightly to her Catholicism. As I got older, I failed to see the point of it

141

all. When she died, I gave it up for good.

We all look up at the Lulu painting, waiting for someone to make a move. Connie, realizing a Pellegrino is not forthcoming, flutters both hands at her face as she steps in front of the rest of us to get closer to the painting. "I'm so glad I put this on hold."

"I did say you had to talk to Simon," I remind her. It's not that I'm trying to help Simon out. I've decided that Lulu should have the painting. And as her guide, I'm going to do what I can to help her get it. It's the doing-what-I-can part that might get tricky. Because, really, what the hell can I do? It's very simple. Simon's going to sell it for as much money as he can. End of story.

Connie encroaches on Simon's personal space. "Simon?"

He responds by retreating into his sales mode, like a turtle into its shell. "There is, uh, a certain universal spiritual longing that this work evokes. It, uh —"

"I told her I was taking it." Connie points a manicured finger in my direction.

Simon purses his lips and nods as though this makes sense, proof of my insatiable drive to take over his business. "Mia isn't in a position to take holds on these pieces."

Okay, is that necessary? When it suits him, he'd be more than thrilled for me to keep track of who's holding what.

"I did tell you to talk to Simon," I repeat, smarting a bit at my lack of authority.

"Here's the trouble," he says. "We're closed."

Connie gets even closer to him, backing him almost into the painting. "It's because I'm a woman, isn't it? This is a man's game, trophy hunting. And I'm disrupting the rules of the game."

It seems this really is what she believes. She's convinced herself she's on a feminist mission.

Simon wouldn't know anything about a feminist mission. "There's so much confusion right now," he says. "I might be able to sell you this one."

He points at *Finding and Losing Faith.* But Connie shakes her head. "I want *Lulu and God.* That's what I put on hold."

"Possibly *Portrait of the Artist as a Confused Young Man,*" Simon says, ignoring her words. "Although someone has a hold on it. And there are second, third, and fourth holds too."

I wonder if that's true. Before Connie can get even more agitated, Simon goes on to say, "These are remarkable paintings by a

143

gifted soul whose life ended far too early. Let's wait until the gallery reopens to discuss business."

It's hard to argue when there's a dead person involved. Somehow this works. Connie clacks her way to the two-toned Maybach and driver waiting in front of the gallery, determination sewn into her features.

"You know," Dane says to Lulu as she buttons up her coat, "I've got a sense Jeffrey might have been speaking metaphorically when he said he was giving you this painting. The painting of it, and your seeing it, that's the gift. The message of the painting, that's what he was giving you."

As though she's looking right through him, "Then why didn't he say, I'm giving you the message?"

He shrugs. "I think what he wanted was for you to know the artist inside you. He wanted for you to paint. And that's the power of this piece. Inspiration."

I'm listening, trying to remember now if Jeffrey had sounded like he was speaking metaphorically that night of the opening. I have no clue, not having had much experience with people speaking metaphorically.

■ ■ ■ ■

Simon and Lulu head off for their planned lunch date. Dane watches them leave, then turns back to the Lulu painting. It's just the two of us now, very quiet in the gallery. Too quiet.

To break the silence, I tell him, "I'm a big fan of your work."

This is a lie. I don't really care for his large-scale installations, although they are sensational, in the sense of causing a sensation.

He turns, as though surprised that I'm still there. "Thank you," he says. He moves toward my desk and peers down at me, assessing. "Has anyone ever painted you?"

Instantly, I'm flattered. "My portrait, you mean?" Is it possible *I* could be a muse?

"I mean you," he says, putting both hands on the counter before me. "Painted your body?"

So I'm not a muse. I didn't think so. "My body?"

He leans over my desk. "Paints are very sensual, you know. The way they feel on your skin, it's something special."

Okay, who am I kidding? I'm way too conservative to be comfortable with someone like Dane O'Neill. Painting my body? I don't think so. And he gets naked all the time, remember? All that bobbing around? I sense this is part of the persona, that underneath this wild-man exterior beats the heart of an orderly symmetry-craving artist. But still, no body painting for me. I just want to fall in love.

"We should try it," he says. And I understand. He's offering to do me a favor.

I shake my head, laughing. "I'm not that girl."

I know, I've cultivated and nurtured the fantasy of falling in love with an artist. And here's a famous one, a handsome one, one who could teach me things in the studio and the bedroom, how's that for a fantasy? But I don't need any favors, thank you.

"Good-bye, lovely Mia," he says, in that Irish way of his. *Loovly.*

After lunch Lulu comes back to see me. "I brought you a present," she says, handing me a small package, beautifully wrapped in turquoise and orange tissue paper tied with raffia.

Gifts embarrass me, but I'm touched. "Thank you. This is amazing, thank you."

She shakes her head to dismiss my gratitude. "Open it."

"What did Simon say?" I ask. "Is he going to let you take the painting of you?"

"Of course not," she says. "I'm going to have to work it."

And that's when I see it, underneath the distracting beauty, the thing that must make it possible for her to work on Wall Street. Determination. "Open your present," she says.

"It's too pretty," I protest, but I pull open the ribbon anyway. Inside the delicate layers of tissue paper is an orange leather journal with a small gold pencil attached to the binding.

"I thought you might have some interesting stories to tell," she says, and winks on her way out.

By six o'clock the actor still hasn't arrived. His assistant has called at least seven times, first to tell me he's running late, then he's on his way, then he's almost there, he's five minutes away. It's after six when he finally arrives — the assistant calls, He's pulling up! Okay, okay, alert the media.

He has two friends in tow. They all look to be about my age, but I'm quite sure the actor is at least thirty-five. He must be doing something right, drinking wheatgrass juice maybe, or doing those colonics. He's very tanned, his teeth impossibly white against his bronze skin.

There's no art lust in those eyes. He's not going to get aroused by the Lulu painting or by any other work. This is someone who is turned on by what collecting art can do for his image, by the way that an interest in the conceptual can wash away the taint of an upbringing in a poor neighborhood where college was not an option. But he puts on a dramatic show of being knocked over by the paintings, grabbing his heart and staggering around the gallery, making sure both Simon and I are watching along with the friends-for-hire. "I'm blown away. Fucking blown away." What a phony.

Simon's gone glassy-eyed with delight. A celebrity, right here in his humble art emporium. He watches the performance with glee, like he's ready to applaud.

"Whaddya think, fellas?" the actor asks his friends. He's already told them what they're supposed to say, with his performance.

"Cool," one of them says. "I like 'em."

"This is the one I want," he says to all of us, pointing at *Lulu*. "I like size."

The two friends snicker at that, of course. I don't hold it against them. We all do what we have to, to survive.

The actor doesn't ask the price. He moves toward the door; just before he comes around the wall, he turns and makes a gun-shooting motion with both hands toward Simon. "You'll hold it for me, right?"

No, no, I want to say to Simon. If you're to use this painting to your advantage, you don't offer it up to an actor. The smart thing to do would be to get someone like Martin Better to buy the piece. Or Robert Bain. Or give it to Lulu. Just think of the publicity you could get out of that kind of gift. But Simon is not very smart. And he said it himself, he's a starfucker. So he allows the actor to put the Lulu painting on hold. Wait, didn't Connie already put it on hold? Doesn't Dane O'Neill have a hold on it too? And isn't Simon sending it up to Martin Better's house in Greenwich? Yes, yes, and yes. All in a day's work here at the Simon Pryce Gallery.

SEVEN:
CHELSEA GALLERY TOUR AND LUNCH AT BOTTINO

Friday

Seven seconds. That's the average amount of time a viewer will spend looking at a painting before moving on, according to a study done at the Museum of Modern Art. In the case of the Finelli, people linger. Ten, even twelve seconds at least, to my calculations, before they look away.

On Friday we're more crowded than even the busiest Saturday. That's not to say there are crowds at the recalcitrant door. But there is a steady flow, more than a trickle, of people coming in to stand in front of the Finelli masterpiece and stare at it. For at least seven seconds.

It's almost lunch time when Simon comes out of his office. He makes his way through the people in the gallery, his arms pumping. He has a folder in one hand and the cell phone in the other, held open, and on his face is a look of pure venom. With that look on his face, he almost looks capable of killing. Maybe my original suspicions were accurate. I consider resuscitating my murder theory.

"When were you going to tell me Pierre LaReine was here?"

I didn't mean to forget. Yesterday just got away from me. But, oops, I guess I should have mentioned it. "Sorry."

"This is unacceptable," he says. He can't get too loud, as there are people in the gallery, but he leans way over my counter and hisses at me, spraying saliva too close for comfort. Tea-scented breath, nice.

"First you try to sell the painting out from under me. Then you're meeting with Pierre LaReine behind my back?"

I try to explain that it's not like that. I really did just forget in all the excitement. I mean, Dane O'Neill wanted to cover my body in paint, should I tell him that part?

Simon won't listen. "Ambition is an insidious thing," he says. "Don't be a victim of the ego's need for stroking."

"Um, okay." I lean back in my chair to avoid the saliva shower.

Now, in all my years at the gallery I've never told Simon what to do. I have good survival instincts, I suppose, and I could tell early on that offering my opinion too frequently would not work for our relationship. And yet today, for some strange reason, the words just seem to flow out of me. "I think you should let Lulu have the painting."

He couldn't look more shocked if I suddenly pulled a Dane O'Neill and shed all my clothes. He straightens himself fully upright with a pompous air. "Whose name is on that door? Because that's who's going to decide what happens to that painting."

"I just thought —"

"You thought what? You thought you'd neglect to tell me LaReine is honing in? You didn't think that would be relevant? I've a good mind to dismiss you for this."

Now there's a thought. Dismissal. Like at the end of the school day. If it weren't for the fact that I have exactly seven dollars in my savings account, I might like the idea. Dismissal, yes. In fact, the old reason this job made sense — as my entrée into the gallery world — is starting to feel a little stale. Five years in, I don't have much in the way of finished work to even show Simon, let alone any other dealer. And the art world is not exactly awaiting my big emergence, if you know what I mean.

Simon glares at me once more, but then he turns on his heel. He's not going to dismiss me. Of course not. What's that term for what we are, codependent? Yes, I think that's it. We're codependent. Dysfunctionally needy of each other. I actually do want Simon to like me. Maybe it has something to do with losing my father at such a young age. Or maybe I still want to hold on to the fantasy that one day I'm going to come in here with two or three canvases in a shopping bag and stun him to tears with my accomplishment. Ha!

When I started working for Simon, I think I viewed all art dealers as godlike figures. Well, they have the power to anoint. You, you're an artist. You, you're not. I wanted to believe Simon was the Messiah. I saw him as the keeper of the key to the kingdom, the person who could make my life begin, who could say to me, You, you're special.

Over his shoulder the Messiah says, "I sold the self-portrait. Three hundred thousand. To Mark Banashek. Send an invoice."

At twelve forty-five two policemen appear at the door. New York Police Department cops, in their blue uniforms. So this is it, I think. They're coming to arrest Simon. I was right to be suspicious! My mouth goes dry as they pull at the door. I don't have to volunteer any information, I tell myself. I just have to answer their questions. Simon Pryce can't possibly have murdered anyone, I can say. He's a silly man, I'll say, a small man in every way, but not capable.

I watch them open the door — hips, good — and come toward me. I'm frozen. Murder, now this *is* a good story. I wonder how Simon will fare in the big house. The slammer. How will he look in an orange jumpsuit? Will he have to be someone's bitch?

I can't muster even a smile. They don't seem to be expecting one, however. Maybe they know about us gallerinas. They walk right past me, meandering into the middle of the gallery. Then they do something surprising. They look at the paintings. They linger for a few minutes — just about exactly seven seconds per painting, it appears to me. When they've seen all of them, they head for the door.

All this time I'm holding myself rigid in place, waiting for Simon to be dragged out in handcuffs.

"Your wife's really into this stuff, huh?" one cop says to the other. He's shaking his head.

"It's not my thing," the shorter one says, in a thick Brooklyn accent. "But the one of the girl's not bad."

And they're gone. No handcuffs, no drawn guns, no Miranda rights. Just a couple of guys, New York's finest, looking at art on their lunch break. So much for my short-lived murder theory.

Mrs. Rachletminoff's galleries and museums tour group arrives right on schedule at one ten, on their sixth stop before lunch at Bottino. Mrs. Rachletminoff, a stocky woman in a tweed suit and navy blue pumps who admits to a "bit of work around the eyes," holds open the door and waves her ladies in.

Her group comes in from the suburbs, and they dress up for their day in the city. They shuffle in on the tail end of their tour, gossiping a little as they wait for their guide to explain what they're looking at. They're all surprised to learn the artist just died.

"He was one of the greats," Mrs. Rachletminoff says, sounding like someone who has studied Jeffrey's work at length, although I know she's seeing it for the first time herself. Her eyes fill with tears.

"That's terrible," one of the ladies says. "Eerie," another one adds, their eyes passing quickly over the paintings on the walls.

Mrs. Rachletminoff lets them talk for a bit

and then gathers them around her with little swimming motions of her hands, taking a spot to the left of *Lulu Meets God and Doubts Him.*

"They're very real," I hear one of the ladies say. Her friend, sunglasses perched on her head as she holds small reading glasses to her eyes, peruses the label. "It's called *Lulu Meets God and Doubts Him.* What the hey does that mean?"

"I hate that title," another woman states emphatically.

The one with the two pairs of glasses nods. "At least he didn't make everything untitled. I hate when they do that."

The woman who said they were "real" is dressed in pink from head to toe, including pink shoes. She wears pink lipstick to match. "I like titles. Tells us what we're looking at."

"But what are we looking at? Where's God in this painting?" Sunglasses wants to know.

"You don't actually *see* God," the pink lady explains patiently. "Just like in life."

Sunglasses is getting vexed. "I don't get what the title has to do with the painting."

"You're not supposed to get it," the emphatic one announces to the whole group. "It's conceptual."

Mrs. Rachletminoff gestures gracefully at

the painting, doing Vanna White demonstrating the wares. Like many in her cottage industry, she possesses an antiquated degree in art history and some, but not much, concrete knowledge of the contemporary world.

"*Lulu Meets God and Doubts Him*. Oil on canvas. A portrait. This is one of the most stunning works of contemporary painting I've seen in years. We see this young girl, holding her own work of art, as they so often did in classical portraiture. She's probably his daughter."

No one ever seems to be listening when these groups come in, so I never bother correcting. Does it matter if they think she's his niece or his daughter? But her comment makes me wonder what Lulu's father looked like. Lulu herself resembles her uncle in several ways, particularly in those eyes.

"What does he mean, about doubting God?" Sunglasses asks.

"It's a metaphor," Mrs. R says, dismissive.

"What do you call that, the way he uses so much paint, in layers?" asks another of the women.

I don't hear the answer. One of the women says loudly that she's hungry, and another informs Mrs. Rachletminoff that they will be late for Bottino if they don't go now.

"Are we having wine today?" the woman with the two pairs of glasses asks the others. The general consensus seems to be that they most certainly are. "That's what I like about art class on Fridays," she says to a round of nods.

"What's this guy's name again?" someone calls out.

"Jeffrey Finelli," Mrs. Rachletminoff says as they begin to file out of the gallery. "A tremendous talent, isn't he? Aren't they breathtaking? Can you feel the emotion?"

But the ladies have moved to the door. Lunch beckons.

"I don't think they're so great," Emphatic comments as she passes my desk. Everyone's a critic.

Mrs. Rachletminoff holds the door open for her ladies as they step back out onto the street. She's closed it behind her when the pink lady reappears. The woman pulls at the door but can't get it open and gives me a pointed look I know well by now. It's a look that says, as clearly as words, Get off your butt and open this damn door before I pull my arm out of its socket, isn't that your job?

I open the damn door before she pulls her arm out of her socket and let the pink lady back in to the gallery. I assume she's forgotten her pink purse or wants to use the bathroom before the walk down the block, but she surprises me and asks for a price list. I explain that there isn't one.

"That's strange." The pink lady eyes me as though she thinks I'm the one who could have committed murder. "How much is the big one?"

"I don't know," I say. I'm being truthful, not evasive. "I'd have to check with Simon. But I think it's sold."

"Sold?" She shakes her head, like she doesn't want to believe it. Pink lipstick is flaking off her lips. "If it's sold, you should know how much it was."

I shrug. "I'm sorry."

"I want one. A small one. When will you get some more?"

I explain that we probably wouldn't get any more paintings, as the artist is dead.

"They must be very valuable then," she says, before marching out of the gallery in a huff. She has no trouble with the door on the way out.

As it happens, like the ladies from the suburbs who've spent their morning in the galleries, I'm also having a Bottino lunch today. Mine is a mozzarella and tomato sandwich from their takeout shop next door to the restaurant that I'm washing down with my fourth cappuccino of the day. I get to eat half of it before Simon makes me put it away. The gallery is too busy for me to eat lunch. I wrap up the other half to take home, although I suspect he's going to ask me for it later.

Connie Kantor must sense that the Finelli situation does not bode well for her — was it the Pellegrino showdown? — for she's hired an art adviser to act as intermediary. Not just any art adviser either. I've just stashed my sandwich in my bottom drawer when she comes into the gallery with Zach.

My first thought is, What's he doing with her? Actually, that's my second thought. My first thought is, He looks good in that camel overcoat with that blue shirt underneath. My second thought is, Not Connie Kantor. And then my third thought is, Who do I think I am to have an opinion about his clientele? And why do I care?

"I want you to do something," Connie's saying to him as she passes my desk without looking at me. Connie doesn't say hello to receptionists. She's been around long enough to know experienced collectors don't bother with rude gallery girls. She points toward *Lulu Meets God and Doubts Him.*

"That's it."

Zach stops and leans over my counter with a slightly sheepish smile, as though he knew what my second thought was: Not her. "McMurray," he says.

I can't help returning the smile. Our eyes meet for a second. Suddenly I feel like all the breath's been knocked out of me. What's going on here? I look away as Connie calls out from her proprietary spot in front of the painting. "Tell Simon we're here."

He leans closer to me to whisper, "She says she's got the piece on hold."

"You'll have to talk to Simon," I say, willing my heart to stop racing. Is it him or all that caffeine in my system? Must be the caffeine. A fourth cappuccino is never a good idea.

Zach has a small digital camera in his pocket, and he pulls it out now, directing it at me. "Smile," he says.

I hold up my hand to block the lens. "Get that thing out of here."

When I put my hand down, he snaps a shot. "Sorry," he says, pressing the shutter again, and then again before he slips it back into his pocket.

He looks like he's going to say something else. I know how this works. These guys, the guys who make a living selling art, they

161

know to play their cards close to the vest in the trading game of information currency that makes up most of their communications. Reveal a little, one card, maybe, to get a little, a card or two in return. Zach looks like he's going to play a card. And then he seems to change his mind.

The moment is gone as Simon comes through the back door, adjusting his lemon yellow tie.

Simon likes Zach. Well, I don't know that he likes him, although most people seem to like Zach. Simon doesn't really like anybody. But when he senses someone can do something for him, he likes that.

"Can I offer you anything," he says. "Water? Pellegrino?"

"I'd *love* a Pellegrino," Connie says, a note of triumph in her shrill voice.

"Two Pellegrinos," Simon orders from me as he takes them into his office.

When I open the fridge to pull out the water, I see — and smell — Jeffrey's cheese. It immediately conjures an image of the elfin artist with the one arm handing over his precious gift so graciously. I wonder what he would have to say about all this, collectors stomping into the gallery with lust in their hearts, yearning for a work by the unknown dead count.

I pour two glasses of the sparkling water and close the fridge. Poor old Jeffrey. All this hoopla, maybe it's making him laugh, wherever he is. Up there somewhere. Meeting God, I suppose.

I bring the Pellegrino into the office, where Connie sits opposite a large color photograph by one of Simon's young Germans. Rudolph Spaetzel. Not exactly a household name.

I try not to notice the victorious gleam in Connie's eye as I hand her the coveted glass of Pellegrino water.

When they emerge twenty minutes later, Connie owns the Spaetzel.

"Tell me about Lulu Finelli," she says to me. She's still holding her precious Pellegrino. "I hear you're trying to be her friend."

"I'm sure she doesn't need to try," Zach says, coming gallantly to my rescue.

"I Googled her," Connie says. "There wasn't much. She's involved in some charity for kids in Harlem."

Zach seems to have found a warm joking tone that works with Connie. "Why in God's name are you Googling her?"

"I want to be her friend," Connie says, as though it's perfectly normal to Google new

163

acquaintances. "Although she's got some nerve. Claiming her uncle gave her this painting. When he's conveniently dead."

She puts the Pellegrino glass on my counter. It's still full. "Zach, let's go."

She heads for the door, heels clacking. He pauses, looking at me.

"I owe you a burger," he says.

"I'm a vegetarian." This is my attempt at sassy, though I'm not sure I even know what sassy is, let alone how to pull it off.

"Really?"

Sassy is hard to get right. "Just kidding."

Around five thirty that evening Lulu comes back to see the painting she, and I, have come to think of as hers. She also wants to talk to Simon, and I had told her the end of the day would be the best time to try to reason with him.

She hugs me and goes straight to the portrait. "Why do I love this painting so much?"

"It's you," I say.

"Isn't that totally narcissistic?"

"I understand it," I tell her, because I think I do. "He made this for you. There's a message here, from someone who obviously had very strong feelings for you."

"I wish I could understand the message," she says. "What's all this business about meeting God? I don't think I believe in God."

When Simon comes through the back door to meet Lulu, he looks tired. His newfound ebullience is wearing on him. There are faint lines showing around his eyes, and his hair is a little less buoyant, the knot in the yellow tie sagging.

Lulu is forthright. "You said if there was anything I needed, I should come to you."

He goes all proper and self-righteous, doing his English gentleman thing. "Right. Right."

"This contessa person in Florence says I'm to inherit whatever is in the studio."

"So I understand," he says. He pulls himself up as tall as he can, but she is still quite a bit taller, and he has to look up at her.

"She won't tell me what's there. But I'm not sure I care. This is the one I want." She points at the vibrant pink-and-orange canvas on the wall. "This is the one he gave me."

Simon lets out a sigh. "You know I bought these paintings from your uncle. He had conflicted feelings about selling them. The contessa wouldn't let him show them without first selling them. She was the one who insisted he take the money up front, which is not how we normally work."

"Why did he want to show in New York?" she asks. A good question. "Why not in Florence, or somewhere in Europe? And why with you?"

"Well, I offered," Simon says. "I discovered him. And I suspect the reason for New York has something to do with you. And something to do with it being his hometown. He was coming home."

Lulu plays with the ring on her thumb. "This painting means a lot to me. It's the only thing I've got from my family."

Simon does a very good job of looking sympathetic. "I understand. It's the only one I have left now too. I sold the self-portrait and *Faith* today."

Wow. That was fast. Simon's made a lot of money on Finelli already. Maybe even enough to pay off the debt he racked up opening this big gallery.

Lulu nods. "The contessa won't tell me what's there. I can't get anything out of her over the phone. But I could see having you show, and sell, whatever else might be in my uncle's studio. With an appropriate split, of course. We could work something out," she says. "In exchange for this one painting. I'm sure you didn't pay very much for it, no

166

matter what you think it might be worth now that he's dead."

I'm impressed. She seems to have figured out exactly how to play this. He listens, a rare occurrence for Simon.

"Right," he says again. "The early work was different, if I recall. He said he painted a lot of scenes, contemporary versions of religious panels, full of people. I only saw two. I don't know if they're still in the studio or if he sold them on his own. This work is much, much stronger."

They go back and forth a bit, but Simon agrees. It's just too tempting, the thought that there might be objects of desire for him to sell piled high in a studio in Florence. He will not sell this one last painting until after the memorial service. Ironically, the service is scheduled for the same week at the end of the month that the show is coming down.

Eight:
Alex Beene:
Works in Bronze
Barbara Hartman
Gallery Opening
Reception
6:00–8:00 p.m.

March

Lulu and I leave the gallery together. Simon's already gone on to a dinner at the Guggenheim — busy, busy! — and I'm the only one here, so I lock the door behind us. Over the years there have been other employees. Bookkeepers and salespeople and assistants, summer interns every now and then; when we first opened the big new gallery, there were four on staff. But they would all move on, usually pretty quickly, forced out by meager pay and Simon's mercurial personality, or lured by better opportunities. Since Jose left to work down the block at the Cassidy/Landman Gallery, it's been just me and Simon.

"What's going on?" Lulu asks, pointing down the street where a few people are gathered.

I look. "Barbara Hartman's gallery. She's got an opening tonight."

"All those people for an opening?"

"You should see what it's like when La-Reine has one."

"Can we go?" Lulu asks, already moving down the street in the direction of the opening, one of many at galleries big and small in Chelsea tonight.

"Sure." I catch up to her. "He's a sculptor. Large works in bronze."

We make our way through the people gathered at the front of Barbara Hartman's gallery. Inside, she's installed four pieces, all female figures with oddly formed limbs and elongated faces. There is something sad about the works, but proud at the same time. I like them.

Lulu does too. "These are amazing," she says. "I can't believe this is bronze. It looks like it would be supple and bend, but it's so solid."

We stand in front of one of the women, the one with the saddest-looking face.

"I like her. She's creepy," Lulu says.

From behind us, a deep voice adds, "He said he thinks of his women as monsters you fall in love with, haunting and creepy. They're all portraits."

Lulu turns, startled. Zach is behind us, still wearing the color combination I'd noticed earlier in the day, Mediterranean blue shirt that matches his eyes and camel overcoat. "Hey you," he says to me.

"Lulu Finelli, Zach Roberts," I say. "Zach, this is Lulu."

"I recognize you from the painting," he says. I wait for him to act silly or bumbling or start talking too much in reaction to Lulu's looks, but he just smiles affably at her and then turns to me.

"McMurray," he says. "How about my new client, Connie Kantor? How badly does she want that painting?"

"You're the one who has to play lapdog to these people," I say. "I don't know how you do it." Sassy, that's not. But I wouldn't want him to get the wrong idea, like I might be interested in him.

"Ouch," he says. He smiles. Either he's flirting with me, or he wants something. "You hear that, Lulu? Lapdog. That's not nice."

Lulu grins at him. "What Mia meant to say is, she's very impressed with your success."

He bows deeply, kidding around. "Thank you. We all have to make a living."

"Yes, but, Lulu," I add, going for a similarly teasing tone, "what Mr. Roberts here is leaving out is, we all don't have to make a living being a weasel."

"Weasel," he repeats with a laugh. "Is it lapdog or weasel? You're mixing your animals. Helping my clients buy works of art is being a weasel?"

I meet his gaze. "Helping your clients buy works of art is not being a weasel. Lying by omission, or acting on insider information, or slithering your way into deals, that makes someone a weasel."

"If I recall, McMurray, last I checked, which was today, you too make a living this way. On the sale of art."

Touché. He's got me there. I move away from them toward the large sculpture in the corner. It's an impressive accomplishment, this solid piece of bronze cast to seem so fluid. There's movement in the sculpture, although it probably weighs at least five hundred pounds.

I'm still admiring it when Lulu and Zach join me. "Lulu wants to see more," he says. "Kranach has a young painter. From Arizona. She grew up on a reservation, dirt-poor. Her father's an Indian chief or something, but there's no money at all. Her work has a lot of Native American stuff, really interesting."

"Come on, Mia," she says. "I think I've been bitten by the art bug."

The three of us head down the street together to Kranach. Native American images, powerful colors, some text. Strong stuff, yes, but I can't help feeling that I wouldn't mind being born poor on a reservation, if I knew I was going to be a painter with a show in a Chelsea gallery as a result.

"You really feel the artist's hand in these brushstrokes, don't you?" Zach asks me as we stand in front of one of the paintings, side by side. Lulu's moved on to another piece.

"All those powerful reds," I add. "She's got a good feel for color."

"There's something primitive, though," he says. "It gets you in the gut. Kind of like Basquiat."

The gallery is crowded, but we're alone in the middle of a space between people. As I do sometimes, I lose myself in looking at the work before us, caught up in the mood of the painting. Zach is one of the only people I've met with as much enthusiasm for the art as I have. The other guys — come on, there weren't that many — were much more interested in the art of the deal than the art itself.

"What do you think?" he asks me, quietly. He sounds like he really wants to know. There's that sincerity thing again.

"I feel like I'm on a reservation," I say. "How does she do that? Like she's transported you somehow, to another place."

"I'm not sure I really want to go to that place," Zach adds. "But I agree. It transports you."

From there we go on to two more openings, one a show of photographs of convicts, the other an installation involving a lot of grass and flowers. Zach knows so much about art history, and he teaches both of us as we walk through the shows. There's something really sexy, I suddenly realize, lightbulb-over-the-head fashion, about someone this smart. Zach seems to keep an enormous amount of information in his brain.

It's nice, the way he subtly takes charge, pointing out the strengths in each of the works, referencing artists who paved the way. Lulu and I both listen intently.

"Any of you have it in you to do another show?" Lulu asks when we've headed out of the flower-scented gallery. "I could just keep on going."

"Anyone hungry?" Zach looks at both of us in turn.

"Actually, I'm starved," Lulu says.

"Me too," I add.

"I live on Eighteenth," Zach says. "Let's go to my place. I'll make something."

I remember then, from the martini night, he said he was an amateur chef. A foodie, I think, is what he called it.

Zach's apartment is gorgeous, all warm woods and soft lighting. There's a large living room with a kitchen that opens into it and a dining table along one side. One whole wall is lined with books; the others are hung with photographs.

There's a fireplace. "A fireplace!" Lulu and I exclaim, in unison. I'm immediately drawn to the photographs and move closer to inspect them. I recognize Diane Arbus, Robert Frank, Lee Friedlander, but not all of them.

"I'll light a fire," Zach says, taking a box of long matches from the box of firewood stacked alongside the mantle. A backgammon table sits in one corner, by the tall windows, mid-game, from the looks of it. The two sofas look deep and really mushy, like you could sink into them and never want to get up.

"Nice," I say. "Are you sure you're not gay?"

"You're not the first person to wonder," he says, laughing. "It comes with the art territory. But if I am, I'm still latent. I haven't come out of the closet."

"Then you're what they call a metro-sexual," I add. I don't recognize myself in this person I'm being. I think I'd better give up on the sassy routine, if that's what this is. It's definitely not working. "Did you do this apartment yourself?"

"With a lot of help from my mom."

"Mia, he plays backgammon," Lulu says, pointing to the table. "We'll have to challenge him."

Zach opens a bottle of red wine, one he says is his favorite, and pours it into three glasses. He moves with lanky grace around his apartment, comfortable in his skin. He's very likable, and I like him. But I'm determined, now. I'm not falling even the tiniest bit in love with anyone in the art world ever again. Not an artist, not a dealer, not a collector, not even a curator. I should find a nice scientist, or an architect, maybe even a teacher.

"To Jeffrey Finelli," Zach says, raising a glass. Zach strikes me as one of those people who appreciate when life should be celebrated. He's probably the kind of guy who would throw you a surprise party for your birthday, or send you flowers because it's Friday.

"To Jeffrey," Lulu and I add, glasses raised.

"Who's the photographer?" Lulu asks. "I mean, they're not all the same, right?"

"Those two are Diane Arbus, not vintage prints," Zach says, pointing at two of my favorite Arbus photographs.

"That's Robert Frank."

"Who took these?" Lulu asks, pointing to three misty photographs of old ruins, castles. They're beautiful prints, but I don't recognize the style.

"I did," Zach says, pulling a frying pan from a drawer in the kitchen area.

"Wow," she says.

I look at the pictures again. Evocative. Moody. Not my taste, but very interesting.

Zach sets to work, wielding a big knife. While he chops garlic into tiny particles and sets spaghetti to boil and whisks a salad dressing, Lulu and I lay silverware and napkins on the table.

As he cooks, the most amazing smells waft around the apartment, and Lulu and I bring Zach up to date on the Finelli show. "All sold," I tell him. "Except the big one. The one Jeffrey told Lulu he was giving her."

"Well," Lulu says. "Now I'm not sure. Dane said he was just giving me a message. Not the actual painting."

"He said, I'm giving you *the* painting? Not *a* painting?" Zach clarifies.

"I'm giving you a painting. It's the cover of the invitation for the show."

"And I heard him say it too," I add. "He told me he had to give her a painting in order to get her to come."

"So was it *a* painting or *the* painting?" Zach asks, pausing at his work at the stove to sip his wine.

I try to play back Jeffrey's words. The smell of roasting garlic is intoxicating, and I realize I'm ravenous. "I can't remember now."

"It doesn't matter," Lulu says. "I know which painting he meant. I just don't know if he meant he wanted me to have a message from it or the actual painting. And even that doesn't matter, because now I want it. I want that painting of me."

"Then you'll have to make Simon Pryce agree to sell it to you," he says.

"She went even better," I add. "She offered to trade. Whatever is in the studio, he can have to sell, if he gives her that piece."

Zach nods. I realize this is exactly the kind of information he wants, but I'm enjoying the warmth of the fire and the cooking smells and the soft light too much to care if what I'm saying might help him strategize to get Connie Kantor the painting.

We fill our plates. Spaghetti perfectly al dente with pesto sauce, thin chicken cutlets in a lemon gravy, a crisp green salad with unbelievably good vinaigrette dressing. Zach is a really good cook. I suspect he's probably good at most things he does.

After accolades for the food, the conversation takes a circuitous route, touching on religion, art, the perfect chocolate pretzel. Zach is not afraid to poke fun at himself or his clients, and he's got great stories. He knows everything that goes on in the art world, and in the stories he's always the straight man, the sane one in a world of crazy people. He acts out certain parts for us, doing spot-on imitations of some of the accents. Lulu and I can't help ourselves; he keeps us laughing.

"Come on, McMurray," Zach says when we've put the dinner plates in the sink. "Some gammon. Lulu, you take the winner."

"No, that's okay, you guys play," she says. "I should get home."

"Not before dessert, you don't," Zach says.

"No, really, I have to be at work early tomorrow," Lulu says. "Although I've decided I hate my job."

As Zach moves toward the kitchen to get dessert, Lulu pulls me to the backgammon table and whispers, "Sorry. I'm such a third wheel."

"Don't be ridiculous," I say. "I'm probably the third wheel, if anyone is."

Oh, God, the thought occurs to me then; I'm the third wheel. And I don't even know it.

"Are you crazy? You two have this incredible chemistry. I should go," she says.

"Don't you dare," I tell her. "There's no chemistry. None at all. This is strictly business. He wants information, that's all. You're the one he wants to get to know."

Zach's put a pie in the oven to warm. "Strawberry rhubarb. It will just take a few minutes," he says

Lulu and I both spin around to face him, incredulous. "You just happen to have a pie," she says. "You didn't know we were coming here tonight."

I add, "Who keeps a pie in their refrigerator?"

He shrugs. "You make it sound like a loaded gun."

The pie is amazing, sweet and tart, and

warmed up in the oven with fresh cream poured over it. We devour the first pieces, and then we each have seconds. I'm going to weigh three hundred pounds by the time this story goes anywhere.

After dinner Zach and I play one game of backgammon. He plays like someone who knows what he's doing. Give me a break, I think. Another thing he just happens to be good at.

I suspect he lets me win. Not necessary, I want to tell him. Lulu begs off playing the winner, and the two of us leave together.

"That was really fun," she says, in a taxi on our way home. "He seems completely crazy about you."

"You're what's crazy," I tell her. "I'm not interested."

"Why not? He's adorable. Good-looking, smart, funny. The three big ones. That's a catch."

"If he's such a catch, you take him."

"What's wrong with you? He's obviously interested. You had a smile on your face the entire night. Why would you turn down such a great guy?"

I don't want to have to tell her the whole story, about how they all come on so strong. And then, so quickly, once they've gotten what they want, gone. I don't want to have to tell her about Ricardo, from Milan, who told me he loved me. Then I'd have to add in about Giles, and Jean-Paul, and the others. I'd have to do the accents, as I did for my friends, turning the shameful parts into anecdotes, as though that takes the sting out.

"Let's just say I've got my reputation to uphold," I tell her. "No more art guys. I am absolutely, definitively, totally uninterested in Zach Roberts."

Lulu shakes her head. "Methinks thou dost protest too much."

That night, on the wave of warmth and hope from pie, wine, and friendship, I try again to work on the self-portrait. I position the easel in my symbolically cluttered apartment just so, squirting the expensive oil paints into small containers for mixing, trying to get the angle of my head right. There's something in my eyes when I look at them in the mirror, what is that? Not doubt. More like insecurity. I want to convey an expression of what it's like to be twenty-eight, knowing you're a grown-up but wondering what you're supposed to be when you grow up. I want to capture what it looks like when you start to realize you have to let go of your dreams. I want the pain of my own artistic yearning to appear there, on the canvas.

As I paint, I lose myself in the joy of the work. Later, I'm overcome by an old familiar feeling of faint hope, that maybe I'm capturing something there on the canvas, some essence of what's in my mind's eye. Is this what Jeffrey meant, about meeting God? God, is that you?

In the cold light of morning, of course, there's another old familiar feeling. Dread. What I imagined as a kind of questioning look is more like a primitive muddle of ugly brown paint, in the vague shape of an eyeball.

Nine:
Please Come for March Book Club at the Home of Mrs. Martin Better

Monday

On Monday Simon hands me the keys to his beloved Jaguar. "Go up and give Martin Better some sex," he says.

By sex he doesn't mean actually undress and have intercourse, although if that's what the client wants, who am I to turn him down? Wink wink. "Sex," as used here in the course of normal business, simply means I should make Mr. Better feel, well, better about his choice. It means I should sex up the piece he's about to buy. It means fueling his art lust with eye contact, flirting, giggling, and a promise of something. That's all.

Martin Better is a receptive audience. There's something about the way he looks at me — the same way he looks at a work of art before he says, "Fuck it, I'll take it" — that tells me he'd be willing to negotiate any sort of deal I might have in mind.

He likes young artists. Especially young female ones. What kind of deal could I suggest? A monthly stipend for a studio, a first look at the works, introductions to the museum boards and gallery owners willing to do favors for a man who can write a check for twenty-five million dollars without blinking an eye.

This is how I entertain myself on the very pleasant drive to Greenwich, developing and elaborating on this fantasy as I maneuver Simon's luxury car along the Merritt Parkway. I've held on tight to the belief, for the past few years, that time is the issue. I don't have time to paint because I spend all of it working at the gallery. Yet working at the gallery was supposed to be the job that led me to showing my work. After that, acclaim, sales, museum shows, maybe the cover of *Artforum.*

Time, money, encouragement, I'm lacking all three. Oh, and talent. Talent is kind of an important one, don't you think?

Before I know it I'm playing chicken on the backcountry lanes of Greenwich with the gardening trucks towing leaf blowers and lawn mowers. On each side of the narrow streets are acres and acres of perfectly landscaped properties that need endless care. It's spring cleanup season in

Greenwich.

As I drive, my cell phone chirps rudely, interrupting my reverie. My ring tone for this week is the theme from *Mission Impossible*. Martin Better's three assistants are coordinating his arrival at his home along with mine and that of the truck bearing "the goods." This involves many calls to determine exact locations and ETAs.

Mr. Better is flying into White Plains Airport in a Sikorsky helicopter. The assistants warn me, in several phone calls, that I will be arriving at the estate before he does and should plan to wait, as Mr. Better, whose time is worth millions of dollars, can't possibly be expected to wait for me. This is how they refer to his home, "the estate," and to the helicopter, the "Sikorsky." And to Martin, "Mr. Better."

I knew I'd be waiting. This is why I've brought the notebook Lulu gave me. I figure I'll jot down some of my thoughts about art and life. At least it will give me something to do. I do have some good stories — isn't that what Lulu said? I love stories. Who doesn't? Let's face it, even when it comes to art, we like it better when there's a good story attached.

When I pull through the wrought-iron gates of the enormous stone manor that is the Better residence, I see that recording my scintillating thoughts is not going to be on my agenda, at least not this afternoon. There are a minimum of twenty Lexus SUVs in different colors parked haphazardly up and down the long driveway. There are a few Mercedes wagons and the occasional Porsche Cayenne, but the Lexus seems to be the vehicle of choice here. What's going on? The assistants have mentioned nothing about a Lexus convention.

There are also trucks and lawn mowers and machines that chop wood and at least seventeen gardeners wielding blowers that direct leaves and debris all over the property and at me. I park at the gate and walk up the long gravel driveway, dodging flying twigs.

The house is a builder's spec fantasy of an English manor, so big it's hard to tell where the front door is. The whole thing is made of stone, massive blocks of granite weathered intentionally to look old, although the house was finished, rather famously, as it was then the most expensive home in Greenwich, less than two years ago. The place makes a McMansion sound small, a little cheeseburger of a residence, while this, this is a castle. The cobblestoned driveway circles the house, but the first way

I walk leads to the garage, so I have to go all the way back around to the other side before I find the front door.

I ring the doorbell and explain to the housekeeper who answers the door that I've come from the Simon Pryce Gallery. She looks at me askance. Perhaps she can tell that I have no business advising anyone on buying art. Or maybe she can't hear me over the whine of the equipment the team of gardeners is using on the Better property.

"I'm meeting Mr. Better," I tell her again, shouting so she can hear me. "He's not here yet."

"Mr. Better no here," she says, smoothing down her gray-and-white uniform.

"I know," I say. "I'm meeting him here."

"Mr. Better no here," she repeats, suspicion lacing her words.

"I'll wait for him," I say, offering a friendly smile. I don't want her to think I'm a typical gallery girl. "His office called."

"Office?" That must be the magic word. She steps aside.

I'm left in the enormous center hall. It's so big Martin could land his helicopter right here if his Greenwich neighbors weren't ornery about things like that. There are two painters, and by painters I mean men in overalls patching the walls, not artists, working to repair the plaster. The art that usually hangs on these walls has been moved out. The only piece in the space is a sculpture of a metal grid that forms a sort of bench, with what looks like dried blood layered over the top of it and dripping around the edges.

It's a piece I've seen before. I should know the name of the artist and where Martin Better bought it and how much he paid for it and what the last one sold for at auction. But these are the sorts of details that don't seem to get any traction inside my brain. I just remember the color of the paint used for the blood and the way it's caked into the metal.

One of the painters has placed the can of paint he is using on top of the sculpture. I wonder if I should say something. I probably should. But before I have a chance, Martin Better comes through one of the arched doorways into the center hall. He must have arrived at the back of the house.

Martin is about to greet me when he spots the offending tin of decorator white. "Not on the art," he cries out, lifting the can by the handle and jerking it off the sculpture.

He gives me a hand signal then, to indicate that he'll be right back, and rushes off through another arched doorway leading to what must be at least thirty-five thousand square feet of ill-conceived home.

"My fucking ass, that's a piece of art," one of the painters says to the other.

"Dude, you call it art, it *is* art," the other one says. I wonder if he realizes he's referencing my hero Marcel Duchamp.

Their exchange makes me want to laugh, but these two don't look like they're trying to be funny, so I keep quiet. I wait there for a few minutes, hoping Martin Better comes back soon. But when someone does come, it's not Martin. It's his wife, Lorette, dangerously thin, with a carefully blown-out bob of blond hair. She charges into the hall with a furious pumping of bony arms.

"What the hell is going on in here?" She eyes me, assessing my viability as a rival, possessive of her husband's attentions in the manner of second wives who know how easily they can be replaced.

"I'm Mia," I say, extending my hand to shake hers, although we've met at least three or four times before, on the rare occasions that she's accompanied her husband to one of Simon's gin tonic parties.

"I've brought the Finelli painting, for Mr. Better."

She takes my hand with a limp grasp, long nails scraping at my palm, and lets go quickly. She's not happy to meet me, and she makes that clear. Okay, got it.

"I'm hosting my book club," she says, her crisp tone indicating that she suspects I'm crashing her exclusive gathering to sell her husband sex in the form of an expensive work of art. Yes, she knows about the sex. And she hates art. Lorette Better is vociferously disdainful of contemporary art. Hey, better he be interested in art than his secretary, I want to say to her. And then I remember, Lorette *was* his secretary.

She gestures that I'm to follow her. I do, as she moves quickly down the hall, leading me into the oversize living room in which the Lexus drivers are gathered. On the coffee table are a few of the books, opened, so I can't see the title, and several half-consumed glasses of white wine, stained with pink lipstick. There are at least twenty-five women, most of them blond, and almost all of them skinny. They wear a lot of camel and pink cashmere, dressed up for their Monday book club. Some of them look to have had their faces changed and lifted. Most seem to have had their hair done for the occasion.

The walls are covered in art. There are paintings and photographs and drawings hung salon-style on every surface, one on top of the other. There's so much art, some by big names, some unknowns, that it's hard to know where to look.

"Ladies," Lorette Better says loudly, looking to make sure I can see she is the queen bee in this town where cash is king. "This is . . . what's your name again?"

"Mia," I say, wishing it came out a little more forcefully. I find these sorts of women terrifying. "Mia McMurray."

"Mia, from a gallery in Chelsea. She's come up to sell Martin a piece of art." Her tone indicates that no one understands better than she about the sex part. They all eyeball me suspiciously, understanding it themselves, gathering around Lorette protectively.

Lorette Better raises her voice so they can all hear her. "I thought it would be fun, before we start talking about our book, to see what she's brought. Who wants another glass of chardie?"

The art handlers have appeared at the curved entranceway, along with Martin Better and the nine-by-twelve-foot canvas of Lulu. They have on their white gloves, and they place the painting gently against a wall on which a set of four drawings is clustered. It almost looks small here, on the double-height wall. Lulu eyes the group of Greenwich ladies with her wry smile.

"Let's hear what everyone thinks," Lorette says, waving the book club members toward the piece. "I know nothing about modern art." She adds this last line boastfully.

"It's kind of creepy," one says.

"It's so big," another one adds.

"Her eyes are funny."

"Figurative painting is so old-school," offers one who must have taken an art class or two. I wonder if she knows Mrs. Rachletminoff.

I don't tell them what I'm supposed to tell them; there are museums interested, the critics are gushing, there are ten people who will buy this very rare painting by a dead artist in ten seconds flat if her husband passes on it. Dead artist, get it? Talk about rarity. That's what I should say. But I stay quiet. I let them talk, waiting for Martin to make it stop.

"It's just too big," one of the women says. Her eyes are so green, I'm guessing she's wearing contact lenses color-coordinated to her cashmere twin set. "Where would you put it?"

"He doesn't care if he's got any place to put it, he just keeps on buying the stuff," Lorette says. A bitter note has seeped into her voice. The sun shifts just then, and a ray of light catches her harshly. The lines around her eyes seem deeper, and I can see that she is a frightened woman. I feel a pang of sympathy for her, aging, while her husband indulges himself in a passion for an art world where old gets old really fast, and new and young is what everyone wants.

Poor old Lorette Better clearly feels no such sympathy pang for me. "Don't waste your time," she says. "He's not buying that painting."

Yup. That's the idea. With him out of the picture, so to speak, Lulu stands a better chance of getting it.

"Sorry to disturb your lunch, ladies," Martin says, coming into the living room with his arms up to greet all of us at once, like a politician.

"It's book club," Lorette says, making it obvious that he's interrupting.

"Marty," one of the women coos. "We're talking about the painting."

"I like it," another woman offers now.

"It's really big," one says, but now she makes it sound like a compliment.

Martin looks at the piece carefully, licking his lips. I should speak up. This is where the sex part would come in. First, as foreplay, the painting should be unattainable. A rare and special object with much demand. I should explain that there's a list. I should drop the celebrity's name. I should tell Martin about the museums and the critics and the collectors from all over the world who want the painting. I should make the situation seem impossible. But that's just the tease, the allure of the unavailable.

Then, I should allow him to imagine attaining it. I should talk about how well it works on this wall, right here, how it would add to his collection. I should play up the notion of Simon as the caring dealer looking out for such a discerning collector, offering the placement of the finest of rare and precious pieces in such a collection. I should remind him that the artist is dead. There will be no more of these paintings.

I should reference other art collectors — recognizable names, important names — who've made similar choices, putting him into a rarefied category of person that will be flattering to him. I should indicate how smart and clever and, by the way, handsome he is for even considering it.

I don't say anything. I allow the book club ladies to take the sex appeal right out of the Lulu painting.

"We love it," one of them says, ignoring

the look on Lorette Better's face.

"I'll think about it," Martin says, walking me through the kitchen to the side door.

"I think Simon wants to know today," I tell him, noticing that he puts his hand on my back to guide me. "The painting has to go back to the gallery now."

"Maybe I could take you to dinner," he suggests when we've stepped outside, away from the uniformed housekeepers arranging lettuce leaves in the tiled country kitchen. "We could talk about it over a bottle of Opus One."

And there it is, the tease of the only slightly unattainable on his part. What is he suggesting? Only what I wish to read into it.

The smell of freshly mowed lawn is sweet. I breathe deeply. It's not a scent I get to enjoy often. Trees, sunshine, fresh air. I feel inspired to paint out here in the open. I know, what a cliché!

"Simon wants me to come back with an answer," I say, uncomfortably aware of how Martin's looking at me, like he could seduce me, if I were willing.

He seems to have turned up the magnetism in the way he's focusing on me. He's stocky, yes, but there's an underlying strength that is kind of sexy in an older-man way. I can see something appealing about the extra weight he carries as a result of foods like Kobe beef and scrambled eggs with caviar, all washed down with big crystal goblets of expensive wines like the afore-mentioned Opus One. Dinner with him would be fun.

He leans against one of the stone pillars, folding his arms. He fixes an assessing gaze at me, offering a challenge. "You think about opening your own gallery?"

"No." I shake my head. "That's not part of the plan for me."

He's still looking at me intently, as if he's trying to figure me out. Good luck, I want to tell him. I could use some help in that area. "An auction house," he suggests.

"An auction house? Not a chance."

He smirks. It's charming, from this rich and powerful man. He's charismatic. I wonder if his charisma existed before he was rich, if it's what helped him get there. Or is it something he acquired along the way, the same way he acquired many other things? "So what do you want?"

Okay, I might as well confess. I do briefly, very briefly, consider sharing a version of the fantasy I'd concocted on my way there. But I realize how silly it would sound. Besides, I wouldn't have any paintings good enough to show him. Old art-school stuff.

That awful unfinished self-portrait now gracing my bedside? Please! "I don't know," I say, vowing to bring more focus and intensity to my painting.

He knows I'm lying. "Listen," he says, chewing on a piece of red gum. "I'm thinking of going cold turkey. No more art."

Now this is interesting. "Why?"

"My wife complains a lot," he says. "And I'm kind of bored. The first few times you buy something, it's a thrill. When you acquire something rare, something that other guys are chasing and you get it, that's fun. But on your hundredth piece, or four hundredth piece, it's not such a big deal."

"I can imagine," I say, although of course I can't possibly imagine what it would be like to spend millions of dollars on a hundred pieces of art.

"I tried to be quiet about it," he continues. "But that's impossible. Too many people know what I'm buying, no matter how discreet I am. The whale that spouts gets harpooned."

"What're you going to do, sell it all?"

He kicks at a clump of dirt on the stone step that the gardeners with their blowers must have missed. "That's the problem," he says, laughing. "Do you have any idea what happens when you want to sell a piece of art? The minute you go back to one of these dealers with something you've bought from them, you're the bad guy. Then it's not such a masterpiece as it was when you bought it. Then it's not worth half of what it was worth when the dealer made you feel so special by allowing you access to it."

He delivers this without bitterness, and I'm not sure how to react.

"So you won't be getting rid of your collection?"

"Nah, I won't sell, I just won't buy anything for six months. No art. I'm going cold turkey."

I notice one of the housekeepers watching us through the window.

"You think you can do it?" There's doubt in my voice. I've seen how passionate he is about art, horny for it. If he doesn't buy the Finelli, he'll buy something else.

"I don't know," he says, with another dry laugh. "I need Art Collectors Anonymous. I'd like to know what it feels like, not to feel like the sucker, with all these guys feeding my addiction, like it's crack."

"But you're so passionate about art."

"Art is money," he says. "Anyone who says it isn't, doesn't get it. It's a market, like any other."

"What about just making art, enjoying the

creative process, instead of buying it?"

He smiles in a contented sort of way. "I probably won't be able to do it," he says. "Not buy anything. Anyway, keep the Finelli on hold for me, will you?"

On my way back to the city, I get a call from Lulu. She's whispering into her cell phone so I can hardly hear her. "I'm at Byron Tollman's studio," she says. "This is so cool."

Byron Tollman is one of Pierre LaReine's less well known artists. He's considered an artists' artist.

"You're not at work?"

"I had lunch with Pierre LaReine. Then he offered to bring me on this studio visit. It's amazing. You should see how many people work here."

"I was in Greenwich with your painting. I think Martin's going to pass on it."

"Why doesn't he want it?" she asks, sounding slightly offended.

"It's good that he doesn't want it. Clears the field for you."

"Mia, I can't believe there's this entire world of art I never paid any attention to. I feel like I'm suddenly looking at the world in a totally different way now."

"Just be careful with Pierre LaReine," I say. "I'm sure he can be very seductive."

"The whole thing is seductive," she says. "The man, the lifestyle, the art.

We make plans to meet for drinks and backgammon before she goes out with La-Reine for a late dinner, and I click my phone shut.

My next call is from Zach. "McMurray," he says. "Where are you?"

"I had to go to Greenwich to give Martin Better some sex."

There's a pause. Then his laugh. I will confess that I find it somewhat irresistible, that laugh. "The Finelli?"

"Of course the Finelli."

"Connie's getting nervous," he says. "I have another client who wants it."

"Well, Zach, we all want what we can't have," I say. I imagine I'm delivering a pithy line.

Ten:
Hello/Goodbye,
A Group Show:
Cassidy/Landman
Palladium and
Drone, New Works
by Jason Avery
All Done,
Nina Rosenbaum Gallery,
Amatyias Johnson,
mixed media,
Pierre LaReine Gallery

March

On Thursday night I'm at Lulu's apartment playing backgammon when I get an e-mail from Zach with an attachment. I've checked my BlackBerry during a bathroom break, and there it is, his name in my in-box, with an icon of a paper clip next to it. For a second or two I'm afraid to open it.

Get over your drama, I say to myself. I'm very stern. This is business, nothing more.

Standard operating procedure for an art adviser in Zach Roberts's position. He has to work the receptionist — me — as he angles a position for his client.

There are no words in the actual e-mail, and nothing in the subject box. There's just an attachment I have to open.

"Anything good?" Lulu asks when she comes out of the bathroom.

"Zach. But it's an attachment. I'll open it when I get home."

"Open it now," she says.

"Aren't you bossy?" I say, joking around with her.

"Use my laptop," she says.

"We're in the middle of a game," I remind her. "And after giving you four wins, I think it's finally my turn. I'll do it later."

I did think I was going to win this time. But Lulu rolls double sixes twice in a row, and she beats me. Again.

At home I click and wait for the jpeg to assemble itself on my computer. The image is so large I can't immediately tell what it is. Just a bunch of pixels. But I hit minimize and keep minimizing until I see that it's a photograph. It's a picture of, what? A cheeseburger?

Yes, a close-up of a juicy, dripping burger, cheese melting down the sides. It's an elaborately seductive picture, so fresh and sizzling I can almost smell the grease. I wonder if Zach took the shot himself. Underneath are the words TOMORROW NIGHT?

Do I want to have dinner with him? If only there were a simple answer to that question. I like Zach. I enjoy his company. But is he the man of my dreams? Of course not. Absolutely not. The man of my dreams is not an art adviser. Yes, I realize how obnoxious that sounds.

Needless to say, I agonize over my response to his e-mail, typing and retyping at least two hundred versions of yes, no, and maybe before settling on simply "yes."

Zach's response comes only a few minutes later, in the form of a questionnaire.

WHERE WOULD YOU LIKE TO GO? CHECK THE BOX NEXT TO YOUR CHOICE:

1. The Classic. Twenty-one. The original twenty-one-dollar burger.
2. The Politically Incorrect. DB Bistro. Fancy French burger. Foie gras and Kobe beef.
3. The local. My favorite bar. Down and dirty. With an ice cold beer.

My response, after another angst-filled round of editing: "Is this a test?"

His comes quickly: "Not a test. Options."

"Number 3," I type back.

"Great choice," he writes.

So it was a test.

Zach is picking me up at seven at my apartment, and we plan to stop in at a couple of openings before the vaunted burger. I've left the gallery at six, raced home for a shower, and by six forty-five I've tried on and discarded every option in my meager wardrobe and settled on jeans and a black turtleneck. That's when Azalea stops by on her way uptown. "You're going on a date dressed like that?

Azalea herself is wearing a red tulle skirt, a turquoise floral print top, and a hat, an ensemble that she somehow pulls off. Azalea is one of the most talented unheralded artists I've met, although her day job is professional stylist. She takes fashion decisions seriously. "I can't allow it."

"It's not a date," I tell her. "Just two work colleagues going to some openings and then out for a burger."

"You're going to openings too?" She looks horrified. "How many times have I told you, you can't squander your sartorial opportunities. Now, take those things off."

My preference for plain clothes in somber colors is an issue for my friend. The last time I saw her, I was wearing a gray sweater and skirt, and she asked if I was going to a funeral. Now, she flips through the choices in my closet. "Ugh, the wire hangers," she says. "Black, gray, brown. What are you, a sparrow?"

This is a typical exchange with the colorful Azalea, so I let her do her thing. She pulls out a black vintage cocktail dress I usually wear when I have to go to events with Simon. It's much too dressy for a Friday-night burger.

"This, I like," she says. "Let's see it on."

"Too dressed up," I say, although I've pulled off the jeans. "I don't want to look like I'm trying too hard."

"This is just business, right?"

I slip the dress on. "That's why I don't want to look like I'm trying too hard."

"If it was just business, you would have gone straight from the gallery. Why did you bother coming home to change?

"I wanted to take a shower." I'm starting to sound defensive. I zip the dress up and turn to face her.

"Beautiful," she says. "Very Audrey Hepburn if we do a pearl choker with it. And let's put your hair up."

I don't have a pearl choker. But I do let her put my hair up. When the buzzer goes off, indicating that Zach is downstairs, it's too late to change back into the jeans. So I'm overdressed, and that's something I never want to be.

"Wow," Zach says when I get downstairs. I immediately feel ridiculous. He's much more appropriately dressed in old Levi's and a navy sweater, his coat open.

"You look incredible," he says, seeming awed.

"Don't sound so surprised," I say, breathless. How is it possible that my rational mind and my physical self can disagree about him so vehemently?

"I like it," he says. "Very grown-up."

"Appearances can be deceiving," I say as we move down the street.

"You don't feel like a grown-up?"

"I don't even feel like a sophisticated teenager. I think I'm still a kid." Oh, God, what am I saying? I sound like an idiot. There's something about him that feels so comfortable, like I can say anything to him. But at the same time my nerves are all jangled, and I feel like I might throw up.

Zach laughs. He's acting like I'm the most charming person he's ever met. I immediately assume this means he wants something.

"Do you still want to go see some shows? Or should we go straight for the burger?"

"I don't care," I say, although I wouldn't mind a break from the art world. I'm all art, all the time, it seems. And it only makes me all too aware of the insignificance of what little contribution I might offer to the world in the form of my painting.

"How about one show?" he says. "I had a look at a new painter today. I think you might like his work. He does portraits."

"Okay, then. One show."

There's a green Vespa parked in front of my apartment building. Zach points to it and says, "Want a ride?"

"That's yours?" I say, with a laugh. I didn't picture Zach on such a European set of wheels.

"Born to be wild," he says, poking fun at himself. "I can't afford a car. But you're wearing a dress, so let's take a taxi."

He hails a taxi, and we slide in together. "The artist we're going to see was in jail. A drug dealer. Says he was wrongly convicted. When he got out, he gave himself what he called a community service duty. He went around to the parks in Zurich where the junkies hang out, and he found six women who were addicts. He painted these incredible portraits of them, had them sit for him for weeks, sometimes longer, and he wrote down what they told him about their lives. He's done a book, with the portraits and the stories."

The show, in a small gallery at the edge of Chelsea, is really good. The women in the paintings are simply hinted at, in thick swirls of paint that somehow evoke the pain and confusion of a heroin addict's life. I'm mesmerized. These are the kinds of paintings I dream of being able to do myself. If only.

"They're good, aren't they?" Zach says.

"I like them a lot." That's an understatement. Or maybe an overstatement. I don't actually like these paintings — I feel thoroughly depressed by them. I can't imagine being able to paint like this. Ever since *Lulu Meets God and Doubts Him* was hung on the wall opposite my desk, I've started to question what it is that made me think I could ever be an artist.

I don't want to tell Zach all this. I mean, really, what would I say? You think I'm a gallery girl, but what I really want to do is — cue dramatic drumroll — paint.

"They're not like Finelli's," he says, gazing up at the painting thoughtfully. "Very different style, but they both capture the human figure really well."

Okay, enough. How about that burger?

We're seated in a booth at the back of a dark bar with a forgettable name with ice-cold beers in hand when he says, "Simon's never going to sell that painting to Connie."

"Nope, not if he can help it," I say.

"Do you think Finelli really told Lulu she could have it?"

I pause. "I guess we only know what she tells us. But he did say to me that night that he had to promise her a painting to get her to come to the opening."

"A painting," he says. "What does that mean? Why would he give her one that he'd already sold? He might have meant another painting, one in the studio."

As he talks, his eyes linger on my face in a friendly way.

"Dane O'Neill says he might have been speaking metaphorically. Like, I'm making you a gift of this painting but, you know, not actually meaning she should take it home and hang it on her wall."

"That makes more sense," he says. "Simon probably prefers that explanation too."

We order cheeseburgers with grilled onions and french fries and another round of beers from a guy with a long stringy beard.

"I was hoping Simon could turn out to have murdered him," I say, the beer on an empty stomach going straight to my head. "It's a more dramatic story that way."

"Simon? He'd be afraid to ruin his manicure."

We laugh. "I know," I say. "It could muss his do."

"What's up with that hair?" Zach asks.

I take a long sip of my second beer, realizing how much I'm enjoying myself. "But it would make for a good story, wouldn't it? If he killed him."

He nods, grinning. "Even better if Pierre LaReine did it. You watch, if there's money in Finellis, it won't be Simon Pryce making it. It'll be LaReine."

"Lulu's out with him again tonight," I tell him. "She says she's, and I quote, 'Finding it impossible to resist his strenuous seductive powers.'"

He laughs. "The wolf. In sheep's clothing. He wants to get his hands on what's in that studio."

"But she's beautiful, and smart, and really nice," I say. "And supposedly he loves beautiful women. You think the studio's the only thing he's interested in?"

"Come on," he says.

"Maybe Lulu can work it to her advantage."

"Connie's become obsessed with her," he says. "She keeps asking me if she's coming to her party. She wanted to know what size shoe she wears. How the hell would I know the answer to that?"

The cheeseburgers are fat and juicy, piled with grilled onions and cheddar cheese and accompanied by bowls of crisp french fries. "Aren't you glad you changed your mind?" he says, through a big bite.

This is the most delicious cheeseburger I've ever tasted. I chew for a few seconds before I can answer without spraying him with crumbs. "About what?"

"About the burger," he says, dunking a fry in ketchup. "Seeing as how you swore you'd never go out with anyone who works in the art business."

"I told you that?"

He points the fry in my direction. "You said I should never call you."

"I did?" I don't remember much about that night of the three martinis, but I do recall telling him not to call me. "I think that was an attempt at flirting."

His eyes fix on mine across the table.

"Obviously I'm not very good at it," I add.

He reaches over with his napkin to wipe my cheek. "I get the sense you manage quite well."

I almost choke on a french fry, so quick am I to scoff at his words. "Nothing could be further from the truth." I sip my beer quickly, shaking my head.

He smiles slow and sexy. It's the kind where the eyes get involved. "Is that why you were so unfriendly the first time I came into the gallery?"

"You never came into the gallery," I say, after another bite of my cheeseburger. "We met at auction."

"Nope," he says. "I came into the gallery before that. I asked you for the price list, and you rolled your eyes at me."

"Then it couldn't have been me," I assure him. "I'm single-handedly working to dispel the myth of the nasty gallery girl."

He laughs. God, that's a nice sound.

"At the auction you asked me for a pen, and I gave you the only one I had," I remind him.

"Come on," he says, tossing his napkin at me. "I never would have gone to an auction without a pen."

I throw the napkin back at him. "It's impossible, what you're suggesting. I would have remembered you."

It's true. The perfectionist in me doesn't like this version of the story at all. And the story of how a couple first meets is very important. Wait. We are not going to become a couple, so why would the story of how we met be at all important?

"You said you couldn't trust anyone who makes money selling art," he says. "And I said I don't make much money."

This makes me laugh. "What did I say to that?"

"You laughed, just like you did now," he says.

"You see, I was right to be wary," I point out. "You were lying to me the whole time. You probably had three pens in your pocket."

"At least three," he agrees.

We linger at the table until after midnight. There's just something about a guy who can make you laugh. Even though I remind myself sternly that this is a business friendship, nothing more, I can't help thinking I'll never go out with anyone without a sense of humor ever again.

It's a warm night. One of those magical New York evenings when spring makes a quick shy appearance in winter before disappearing for a few more weeks.

As we walk, we talk about ourselves. He tells me about his passion for photography and asks how I came to be working at the gallery. Instead of avoiding the answer, I tell him the truth. "I'm, um, well, I'm an artist. Um. A painter."

Now, I know there are plenty of people who can speak those words comfortably but my little admission comes out all stammering and embarrassed, as though I've just revealed a deeply personal secret. I guess I have.

Zach simply nods and asks me what I like to paint. "I'd love to see your work," he says. Music to my ears. The problem is, there is no work.

He walks me home through SoHo, where groups of people are gathered outside the restaurants and everyone seems to be laughing. We cross Houston Street, and he holds my hand as we run to beat the changing light on the far side. At the door to my building we face each other. I've already told myself he can't come up. He doesn't ask to. He kisses my cheek and says, "Good night, McMurray."

That's it. But it seems right. Although entirely against my will I seem to be falling a tiny bit in love with Zach Roberts. That I appear to have no say in this matter baffles me.

Eleven:
Museum Reception in Honor of Dane O'Neill at the Home of Constance and Andrew Kantor

Late March

Simon and I are the first ones to arrive at the Kantors' Park Avenue apartment. "Bloody hell," Simon says. "You've got to manage our time better. We're early."

He's in a sour mood. He still hasn't sold *Lulu Meets God,* and he's nervous that excitement about it might be waning. It's time to move on to the next big thing. There's no need to point out that he created this situation by waiting to sell willingly and greedily. He's just moody, so I don't bother reminding him he was the one who said we should head uptown before six. I hand my coat and umbrella to a man in a tuxedo and head for the bar.

Sometimes Simon will bring a date to one of these networking events that pass for social functions in our line of work. There are always girls from the auction houses or galleries, Condé Nast editors, or pretty public relations managers who are distracted enough by the accent and the hair and the fact that he owns a gallery that they convince themselves his callous indifference is attraction and agree to hang on his arm at a party.

Sometimes there are even young men, although these he doesn't call dates. And he doesn't allow them to hang on his arm.

But usually Simon prefers that I accompany him. He insists it's part of the job, which is true, I guess. He doesn't like to waste time on a date when he could be chatting up a potential customer at a party. He also insists that *I* chat up potential customers, which I do, to the best of my ability. The fact that my ability in this area is nonexistent tells you what you need to know about Simon's business savvy. Yet he's always sidling up to me at parties, imploring me to "mingle, mingle."

Simon is unkind too, with the petty meanness of a boy who stomps on bugs just because he can. It probably has something to do with having been sent off to boarding school at age seven. He knows I despise this part of my job: the phony friendliness; the trawling for information; the pretentious artspeak; ugh, the networking. (I even hate that word.) I'm convinced Simon makes me go just to see me squirm.

At first I was so self-conscious I could hardly say hello. My mouth would always go dry, making my voice crack in odd ways. And I'd end up talking to someone like the caterer's cousin or the security guard protecting the big collector rather than anyone helpful to Simon's business. Simon would get annoyed and make faces expressing his disappointment in me.

Now I'm a lot less squirmy than I used to be. For one thing, I do love to look at art. And the art gives me something to talk about, if I have to talk. There's an instant bond I can find with anyone who also loves art, even if they're from another country and can hardly speak English.

Also I'm insatiably curious about the acquisitive gene of the collector. I'm curious about a lot of things. But collectors? They're freakishly fascinating. I love to see how new collectors ease in through the gentle stuff: editioned works that are not so hard to score or live with, like photographs or prints, works on paper. Some stay there, in the mellow marijuana high of a photography collection. Others move on to harder stuff, paintings, large sculptures, works they can't even live with. I like seeing how people live with their collections. Even when the people are Connie and Andrew Kantor.

At the bar, I decide between a martini, white wine, or a Diet Coke. The martini wins. I'm handed an enormous triangular glass like a mod fish bowl with three olives in it. It's the biggest glass I've ever seen; I almost need two hands to hold it. What is Connie trying to do to people? Simon opts for a gin and tonic, and the two of us split up. I take the opportunity to wander.

When I began receiving invitations to collectors' homes, I was surprised how comfortable most of them seem with strangers peering into every corner of their private spaces. At first it felt funny, standing in someone's bathroom with their pill jars and their ointments and their toothbrushes exposed, looking at the Damien Hirst medicine cabinet they've hung so cleverly next to the actual medicine cabinet. Or breathing an older couple's bedroom smell, their reading glasses on the night table, slippers tucked under the chair, admiring the Matthew Barney above the headboard. Now I've gotten used to the intimacy of it. And I really enjoy it. But you've got to admit, it's kind of weird.

The Kantors are into the hard stuff. Shock value. Like the Dane O'Neill in the foyer that practically hits you over the head when you walk in. It's a piece that features, among other things, a taxidermied rat, an ax, and a rusty garbage can. I wouldn't say it's one of Dane's strongest works, but it has a certain, I don't know, existential charisma.

Lots of the pieces in the Kantors' collection are the kinds of things some people would call, well, pornography: a huge photograph of a bum, a little red and pimply; a bad painting of a woman clutching her pendulous breasts; a series of pictures of a couple fucking, both of them looking bored. None of these pieces are by any recognizably named artists. No wonder the Kantors wanted to throw a party for Dane O'Neill.

There's French furniture of all periods. In every room there is one jarring piece. Okay, we get it: shock value! In the living room it's a remarkably hideous red chair in the shape of two kissing lips. In the dining room an artist has been hired to paint the sideboard with monkey faces.

The table in the dining room is set, although the Kantors are not planning on serving dinner. No, the table's been set to highlight an ancillary collection of monkey stuff. Everything on the table continues the monkey theme: the plates, the knives and forks, the glassware — climbing monkeys on the stems, the definition of cute — and the napkins. Even the art on the walls of this room sticks to the curatorial missive, with a series of paintings of monkeys engaged in what appears to be, yes, more fucking.

I move on from the monkey orgy quickly. Next stop on the tour: the library. Here I come across two white-haired biddies in stodgy cocktail suits. "I only came to see what they've done with the place," one of them is saying to the other. "They paid so much for it."

"After those two board turndowns, they were desperate for any co-op that would have them."

"Lucinda would be turning over in her grave," her friend says with a swig of her scotch. They don't seem to notice me.

"It's the emperor's new clothes," the second lady says with a self-satisfied wave of dismissal.

I head back to the entrance hall, on the lookout for Zach. I'm surprised at how much I'm looking forward to seeing him. Surprised and, if I'm honest, a little annoyed at myself. I have no intention of falling for

Zach Roberts. My plan is to ignore him. Let him come to me. Sassy, remember?

I linger in front of the Dane O'Neill, in the perfect position to listen to — okay, eavesdrop on — our hostess. It's not that I deliberately try to overhear other people's conversations. I just happen to have unusually perky ears that jut out from the sides of my head. They pick up a lot.

"When you go into a gallery," Connie is saying, speaking with grand authority to someone, a new collector from the sound of it, "talk about anything but art for the first ten minutes. Never show too much interest. You've got to establish a rapport, break the ice, you know?"

I turn slightly to get a look at the woman Connie is lecturing. All I can see from behind is that she has long hair that looks ironed.

"But don't take no for an answer either," Connie continues. "If you want to be a top collector, you have to be a bit of a bulldog."

The woman's head bobs enthusiastically. Bulldog, got it.

"Feel free to name-drop. Everyone does it. Particularly about the other artists in your collection. It's helpful to claim one or two of them as personal friends."

The other woman says something I can't

hear. Her voice is much lower than Connie's shrill shriek, so it doesn't carry, but I think she is clarifying that she has no claim to any artists as personal friends.

"Shaking a hand at an opening certainly makes them a personal friend," Connie says, getting too close to the other woman. "And whatever you do, don't admit you haven't heard of an artist. Lie if you have to."

She pauses to sip from one of the gargantuan martini glasses. Connie's drink is a strange hue — what is that, blood orange, passion fruit? The color is something in the burnt sienna family. It clashes wonderfully with her turquoise flower-print dress. You know how there are some clothes so ugly you wonder how they ever get made, let alone sold? Connie's wardrobe seems to be made up exclusively of very, very expensive versions of these clothes. Hers have labels on them, but even great designers make mistakes.

"When you run into other collectors, never tell them what you're buying," Connie continues. Her glance bounces off me, and she turns indicating that she has no intention of interrupting herself to say hello to me. "Like with this Finelli painting. I'm obsessed with it. But I'm careful. There are so many copycats all wanting trophies. The art world is made up of lemmings."

The ironed-hair listener forces what sounds like a laugh.

"Don't bother being modest," Connie goes on. "No one else is. And don't think you have to admit you don't own something by an artist who's hot — just say you sold one or you're working on one."

Connie bobbles for a second on her spindly Jimmy Choo heels. "Oopsy," she says, catching herself. Is she drunk, or is it just the shoes?

"I don't need guidance," she goes on. "I know what I like. But it's not a bad idea to hire a consultant. They can give you access, do the dirty work, even though they'll want credit for every idea and they'll bilk you for as much as they can get in the process. And don't think they're not getting kickbacks on the other side too."

The woman's nods slow a bit, as though she's confused, and she mumbles what sounds like bewilderment.

"I'll give you a guy," Connie the know-it-all says. "He's young and pretty full of himself. But I think he's honest, which is more than I can say for most of them. He'll be here tonight, I'll introduce you."

They move on before Connie says anything more about Zach. I revert my attention to the painted skulls at the base of the Dane O'Neill. Skulls. What is this endless fascination with skulls? I'm inspired now. I want to do my own version of a skull painting. I'm contemplating my next body of work when I hear loud whispers indicating the entrance of an intriguing couple.

Someone says, "Who is that with LaReine?"

"I've seen her before," someone else says. "Very attractive girl."

Lulu and Pierre LaReine are standing together in the center of the foyer. He's whispering into her ear.

In the past week Lulu's taken three days off from work and had three dinners with LaReine, one of which was at the country home of a well-known Rothko collector. This one they arrived at in a helicopter in which LaReine presented her with a gold bracelet. She's visited four different artist's studios and spent a day at the closed Whitney Museum in the company of a curator for a private tour. Then she slept with LaReine.

Lulu sees me and waves. LaReine gets pulled into another conversation, and she comes over to hug me.

"Is this the piece?" She points to the wall

with Dane O'Neill's piece. The rat tail hangs to about eye level for her, as she's so tall. "My God," she says, laughing.

"It's supposed to make you think," I say.

"It makes me think all right. Makes me think the artist is crazy," she says. "And the person who bought it is even crazier."

"We like to think our artists are crazy."

"This one is crazy, all right."

"Is he? Or does it just help if we think that?" I ask.

"This artist really *is* crazy," she says, emphatically.

The artist in question appears between us suddenly. Dane's laughing at something someone in the other room has said and he pops his head in between Lulu and me. "What artist?"

"The artist who made this piece," she says, pointing at the installation behind him. It's a flirtatious gesture, taking any sting out of her words.

"Yours truly," he says, almost but not quite sheepish.

"You're well hung," she says. Now that's sassy.

"And you're very clever." Dane points one finger at her. "I've never done well with clever girls."

"I've never met a clever man," she says in

a straight deadpan. "Only ones who think they are."

"My dealer is the cleverest man I know," he says, giving Lulu a pointed look. "And the most seductive. He can talk anyone into anything. Anyone."

She returns his gaze steadily. "And your point is?"

"My point is," he says, "be careful of clever people. Stupid people are much more comfortable."

"You're stupid, are you?"

"You have to be pretty stupid to make stuff like this," he says, waving toward his own piece on the wall.

"Your dealer tells me you've completely stopped making this kind of stuff," Lulu says. "You won't even finish the work for your show. He says all you're doing is painting."

There's a pause. I feel suddenly that this is a private moment and I shouldn't be standing there, but I'd have to interrupt to move, wouldn't I? Or could I just slip off? Frankly, I'm riveted. Any sense I might have had about Dane O'Neill as a possible love interest for me has dissipated so entirely I can hardly recall feeling it.

"Ever since I saw the finished painting of you," Dane says softly, "it took hold of me."

Lulu nods. I nod too. I can't help myself.

"Would you let me paint you?" he asks. Clearly he doesn't mean painting her body, I think, recalling his words to me that day in the gallery. Did he really ask me that? It seems so cheesy now.

Lulu shakes her head. "One painting of me out there in the world is enough."

Someone, probably the museum's director of development, gets everyone quiet then so Connie can make a speech. Connie giggles, covering her mouth with her notecards as though she's shy. Andrew watches, silent as usual, his tiny troll eyes darting suspiciously from face to face as his wife ducks and acts embarrassed, daring anyone not to find her charming.

"Welcome, everyone," Connie says, with another giggle. "I hope you're enjoying the food catered by Daniel Boulud. Make sure you try the potato with caviar. Beluga is practically illegal these days."

As she speaks, Pierre LaReine moves toward Lulu and drapes one arm around her waist. Dane stands at the other side of her, staring straight ahead.

"Everything in this apartment is something," Connie states portentously. "Furniture, art, collectibles. Please take the opportunity to view the entire collection."

As she speaks, the people who were in the other rooms of the apartment move in to the foyer, summoned in urgent demanding whispers by the museum staff, eager to get their proposed gift and underwriting acknowledged in public. They know how much harder it is for a donor to renege on a pledge once it's been spoken out loud.

"We're honored to have added Dane O'Neill's name to the collection with this piece you see behind me," Connie is saying as I find myself surrounded by the gallery girls, Alexis, Julia, and Meredith. All three wear variations of their usual black dresses, although Julia's has an unfortunate bow at the hip, and Meredith sports a long-sleeved knee-length number and a necklace with a wooden cross so she looks like a nun. They all kiss me hello, not bothering to be too quiet about it.

Connie flashes them a look, but she drones on, congratulating herself on her wealth and taste. "A collection of this caliber needs a Dane O'Neill."

Dane seems more interested in watching LaReine and Lulu than in what Connie is saying about his work. Connie goes on to pat herself on the back for her extreme generosity.

"I've given this work to the museum," she

announces, making no mention of her husband, Andrew, who, even here, can't be parted with his BlackBerry. Like Dane, Andrew doesn't seem to be listening to Connie. "Along with the necessary underwriting for a planned Dane O'Neill mid-career retrospective."

When it's over, finally, there's weak applause and we're released to continue drinking and talking. I'm still holding the enormous martini glass, although I've only had a few sips. Dane stops to say hello to me. "Simon here?" he asks. The art girls are all suitably impressed, and cluster around waiting to be introduced.

Dane knows his audience. He shakes all their hands, repeating their names with his Irish spin, rolling the *r* in Meredith, dragging out the *e* in Alexis. They're all delighted. Even Alexis, which is apparent even though, or perhaps because of, her expression, which reads: Get out of my sight, you dirty lowlife. She works for his dealer, but either they've never met or, worse, Dane doesn't remember her.

Just as he's finished with the greetings, Connie is there, pulling him toward a photographer. "I want *New York Magazine* to run it."

"Is it true she has an artist's clause in her

prenup?" Meredith whispers, with a head bob toward Connie and Dane. "Something that says if she can get an artist to sleep with her, she can go ahead?"

"I know. Dane O'Neill probably would do it, he's such a sellout," Julia says, not bothering to whisper. "Can you believe this is the same guy who once handed a collector back a check and threw his own work in the garbage?"

"That was Malcolm Morley," Alexis says, with disgust. She expects people to have their facts straight.

"Dane O'Neill did it too," Julia replies snippily. "In homage."

"Anyway, there is no prenup," Alexis says, trumping her. She turns to me, hands on her hips. "I hear my boss is interested in Finelli."

"You're so right. Robert Bain and Martin Better too," Julia adds. She assumes her usual position, hovering just behind Alexis.

"That's all it takes," Alexis says. "This is the last bastion of legal insider trading."

"Connie Kantor wants it too. But only because they all want it," Meredith says, always pointing out the obvious.

I acknowledge that there's been a lot of demand, especially for the Lulu painting.

"I know. It's all these young people with

too much money," Julia says, clearly parroting something she's heard someone else say. Young people? She's all of twenty-six.

Meredith and Alexis both nod in agreement. This is all the encouragement Julia needs. "After they buy the big apartment and the beach house and the plane, the next thing is the art collection. They want it instant. That's why there's this bubble. But what's going to happen when they move on to wine?"

Julia pauses, her head darting around to see if we're all listening. "The bubble will burst," she says, with drama.

"Not anytime soon," Alexis says, bursting Julia's own bubble of excitement at holding the floor for that long. This is a tough audience. "Who's buying the *Lulu Meets God* painting?" she asks me. She still has her hands on her hips, and now she juts out one foot, aggressively daring me not to tell her.

I drop the celebrity's name.

"I thought Martin Better bought it," Meredith says.

"He put it on hold. They all did. Or think they did. Connie too." I say this in a low voice so no one can eavesdrop. I know how easily that can occur in these crowds. "But

Lulu says it's hers. Her uncle gave it to her."

Meredith, a former aspiring actress, clamps her hand over her mouth in disproportionate shock.

Julia says, "What?"

"She has no claim to it," Alexis points out. "Doesn't Simon own the paintings anyway?"

"She looks like a real bitch," Meredith exclaims, looking over at Lulu, where she stands in the corner of the entrance hall with Pierre LaReine on one side and Dane O'Neill on the other. Lulu is all poise, standing very still between them as the two men move and gesticulate around her. She wears a pale gray silk dress that shows off her shoulders, and she listens as they both seem to be talking at once. She manages to look cool and detached while still interested.

"She's not a bitch," Alexis says. She should know, being a world-class bitch herself. "She's overwhelmed."

"Well, it's pretty bitchy to think you can walk off with a painting, just because it's of you," Julia says.

At this point Alexis is bored. "She's not going to walk off with it. Simon's trying to sell it to Marty Better. And I'm doing everything I can to talk him out of buying it. What does he need that crap for?" She heads into the crowd, looking for prey in the form of a collector. She's not one to waste time at a party like this.

"There's Zach," Julia says, pointing toward the door as Alexis moves away from us. My heart lurches at the sound of his name. Zach.

Meredith giggles. "They're like such the art power couple. Alexis and Zach."

What's she talking about? This can't be right. Meredith never gets the facts right.

"I know," Julia adds. "I know" is one of her catchphrases, along with "You're so right." "They've gotten hot and heavy really fast. She says she could marry him."

Is this true? Zach and Alexis? Not possible. Absolutely not possible.

Meredith adds, "She says she'd have the wedding in the main gallery at LaReine."

Oh, come on. Isn't this the ultimate irony? I'm rejecting the very idea of Zach, and he's not even available.

"They're talking about doing business together, looking for things they can buy," Julia says.

I can feel the bile rising in my throat. That's something I would do, vomit all over Connie Kantor's floor. I rush to the hall where I'd seen a bathroom as Julia says something like, "What's with her?"

I lock the door to the Kantors' guest bathroom behind me. I splash cold water on my face. I want it to be impossible that Zach would be interested in Alexis, but there's a certain logic there. Art world power couple, huh? Zach and Alexis, it has a ring to it. I take a deep breath. Just as I was allowing myself to get interested in him. I had tried to be so strict with myself. No one in the art world, remember? I didn't listen, did I?

After more deep breathing and cold water and stern words to myself, I unlock the bathroom door. As I come out, I see that Connie's got Lulu cornered in the hallway.

"Isn't it great, this apartment? Do you like it?" Connie is standing too close to Lulu. "I knew we'd have the same taste."

Lulu sees me. "Is that the bathroom? That's what I was looking for."

Connie takes her hand. "You didn't go in the powder room yet? Wait till you see the mother-of-pearl inlays. It took a year to install."

She pulls Lulu past me, into the bathroom.

"Mia, wait," Lulu calls out. "I'll go with you."

"You can't leave," Connie says. "I have to show you my collection of perfume bottles."

"Mia and I have to go," Lulu says firmly, as an adult to a whiny child.

"You'd better make sure Simon sells me that painting," Connie yells after me. "I'm buying it, mark my words."

In the elevator Lulu says, "Who uses that expression? Mark my words?"

"Mark my words," I say. "He'll never sell her that painting."

"Was it just me, or was that awful?" she asks. "So pretentious. And all those people acting like they knew me, expecting me to be a nine-year-old painter. It's like they were disappointed —" Suddenly she stops, peering intently at my face. "What's wrong?

I shake my head, as though it's nothing. But then the words come tumbling out of me. I tell her about Zach. "And the whole time I've been talking myself out of him. But it wasn't working."

"How do you know it's true?" Lulu says as we take our coats from the coatrack in the lobby of the Kantors' building.

"Meredith and Julia are her best friends," I point out. "They would know. They would make it their business to know."

"They only know what she tells them."

"It doesn't matter," I say, trying to sound convincing. "The last thing I need is another fling. And I told you, he's not the one. I don't even remember meeting him the first time he says we met."

We walk out of the building together. "I'll take you out for dinner," Lulu says. "But not up here. Let's go downtown."

"What about your date, Mr. LaReine?"

She shrugs. "I think I'm losing interest."

"You said you were hooked," I remind her. "On the man, on the art, the strenuous seduction. You said he was irresistible."

She grabs my arm to make me stop. "He's small. And uncircumcised," she says. "Need I say more?"

I burst out laughing. "Resistible?"

"Not a good combination," Lulu adds, laughing herself. Suddenly the two of us are out of control, falling against each other we're laughing so hard.

It's cathartic, our laughter, and I feel much better as we head downtown in a taxi. It's a relief, I convince myself, to write off Zach Roberts. I never liked the story anyway. Who meets the love of their life and doesn't remember him?

Our taxi driver cuts over on a side street

toward Fifth Avenue to head downtown. We pass the five authoritative blocks of the Metropolitan Museum with its enormous galleries filled with art from ancient times to now, and all seems right again in the world, the way it does sometimes in the company of a good friend.

Twelve:
Please Meet
Pierre LaReine at
Teterboro
Wheels Up: 8:00 p.m.

At the end of March

Wheels up at eight o'clock. That's the message I get, delivered in a lingo only the privileged few speak. That I am now one of these people is pretty funny to me. This is the dialect of private flight. It means, I learn, that we depart — the wheels on the plane go up — when the owner of the plane wishes to depart.

There are only a very few art dealers in the world who can dictate what time the wheels go up on their own plane. Pierre La-Reine is one of these. Most dealers, if they're lucky enough to fly privately, do so at the behest of their well-heeled clients. But they are told when the wheels go up. They're certainly not doing the telling. Simon has never been on a private plane, although he tries to act like he knows all about NetJet shares.

Somehow, in the strange way everything

239

seems to have been turned around since Jeffrey and Lulu Finelli came into my life, it's come about that I'm invited to join Lulu to fly to Italy for Finelli's memorial service on LaReine's G-5. I'm still not sure how this happened, but there are some things in life you don't examine too closely.

My travel arrangements makes Simon crazy of course. Irate. This means he drags the word *right* into five syllables. "R-i-i-i-i-ght."

When I point out that he's been encouraging my friendship with Lulu, seeing in it potential for an angle from which he might benefit, he pouts. He wants to be flying on Pierre LaReine's plane. He wants to *be* Pierre LaReine.

"People will talk," he says, as though the flight is a betrayal, further proof of my uncontrollable ambition. He seems to think I've plotted this myself, hoping to get closer to LaReine. And what? Ask him for a job?

"What people?" As if anyone is tracking my career.

"The art world is fueled by gossip," he states, as though he's come up with the world's greatest insight.

"Reeallly?" I plump the word up with an injection of sarcasm.

"It's all in the image one projects," he says

in all seriousness, lacking a sarcasm radar. "One's image is critical to the selling of images."

Is this another sound bite he's picked up somewhere, or did he make this one up himself?

"It's something Pierre LaReine has certainly figured out," Simon mutters grumpily. "A G-5. Bloody hell."

The right thing to do when invited to fly on someone's private plane is to show up at least fifteen minutes before wheels-up time and be waiting on the plane when the owner arrives. What you should not do is get lost on the way to Teterboro Airport and arrive more than half an hour late. The fact that no one who has not flown on a private plane would have any clue where to find Teterboro Airport in New Jersey is no excuse. Teterboro is part of the lingo, and knowing how to get there is part of the deal.

The other thing you should not do, if you happen to get invited to fly on someone's private plane, is show up with an enormous battered green suitcase that looks like it should be strapped to the top of the Beverly Hillbillies' jalopy. This makes the owner of the plane — Pierre LaReine in this case, waiting out on the steps for us — glare at you as though wondering what you're doing there.

Lulu's bag is as big as mine, but not as ugly. Hers is black and serious. Both our bags get quickly loaded into the cargo space of the plane at the back as we make our way up the steps toward our host.

I notice that LaReine discreetly eyes Lulu up and down, in that way some men have, like she's a purchase he's considering. "I'm happy to see you," he says, in an intimate voice.

Lulu wields power here, that much is obvious. There is the power bestowed on her by the others, because of her connection to the paintings and her uncle, the artist. There's the power she knows she holds over LaReine and his interest in a potential estate that would be hers to control. And there is another power I'm seeing unfold within her. Call it the power of the muse. I don't think she's unaware of it.

Dane O'Neill is on the plane, and he grins at Lulu as we step into the luxurious cocoon. "I just won twenty pounds," he says, in a teasing voice.

Lulu gazes at him steadily before responding. "You wiped the chocolate off your mouth and sold the napkin as a piece of art?"

He looks pleasantly surprised, as though he wasn't sure she was capable of joking back at him. "There's an idea," he says. "I may use it in my next show. Apparently I'm experiencing a dry spell when it comes to the kind of work that will sell for lots of money. It has my dealer very worried."

"Then you'll owe me the twenty pounds," she says, attempting to slide past him.

"Don't you want to know how I won?" he says, stepping aside to let her pass him.

"Not particularly."

"I want to tell you," he says.

"Of course you do," she says. Sassy.

"I bet that you would be at least twenty minutes late," he says. "And I always win my bets."

The plane is sleek and tailored, stylish, like its owner, all pale woods and tan chenille seat cushions. There are sky blue cashmere throws everywhere and Molton Brown products in the bathroom. I had heard it said once that LaReine kept three Picasso drawings on the plane, but they are nowhere in evidence for tonight's flight. There is also no red, not one speck of red, because, as legend has it, Pierre LaReine has a total aversion to red. No red in any of the galleries, not in the décor or the flowers, or on any of the employees. Red is allowed only in the art.

Besides Pierre and Dane, there are two other travelers on the plane, along with a very friendly flight attendant named Joy. One is a client of Pierre's named Robert Bain, flying to Florence because Pierre has arranged for him to see a piece in which he's expressed an interest, although that part is hush-hush, according to Alexis. Pierre LaReine introduces us.

"I'm a big fan of your uncle's work," Robert Bain says to Lulu, shaking her hand energetically. Apparently he bought Warhols when they couldn't give them away, Koons when he had just stopped working on Wall Street. He owns de Koonings and Pollocks and Johns, and he knows who else does too. "The portrait of you is a masterpiece."

"Robert's trying to buy it," LaReine tells her. "Among other things. Simon Pryce is playing coy."

"Isn't that what dealers are supposed to do?" she replies, playing coy herself. She's flirting. She does it well, I note. Subtle. She doesn't smile too often, so when she does, it's like a gift. All three men seem to hang on her words. This is pretty heady company. But Lulu is perfectly able to handle the attentions of not only the world-renowned art dealer but also the global artist and the high-profile billionaire.

The other passenger is a severe and unfriendly curator named Sybil Worthington whom I've heard referred to as Dane O'Neill's sometime girlfriend. She is oddly dressed, in an avant-garde white garment with fraying sleeves. A dress? A tunic? Hard to tell.

She is working on a retrospective of Dane's work and appears to be in love with him, gazing intently at his face as though she's imagining herself in bed with him. It's not dissimilar to the look Dane gives Lulu as his eyes follow her through the plane.

Sybil doesn't greet Lulu and me, and no one introduces us. She doesn't even look at us, so transfixed is she by Dane.

Okay, so it's not the group I would have chosen for my first, and most likely only, private flight, but I'm lucky to be included at all. I amuse myself hoping I don't like it *too* much and become spoiled and jaded about traveling my normal way, on discount coach tickets.

Pierre invites Lulu to take the seat next to him at the front of the plane. Flight attendant Joy hands him two pairs of fluffy socks in the same pale blue as the blankets, and he passes one pair to Lulu. He pulls the other pair over his feet, before handing

Lulu one of the blankets. Then he tucks his own blanket in around himself and raises his eyebrows at Lulu as if to say, Isn't this great?

I take a seat at the back, facing forward, buckle myself in, and try to relax as we take off. I want to enjoy this ride. It feels like we're going faster than the speed of light, propelled up into the dark sky wrapped in pale blue cashmere. I've brought books to read, and also the notebook that Lulu gave me. I pull that out now and jot a few notes to myself. I want to remember this experience.

Despite the cushy atmosphere, it's not easy to relax. There's the tension in the air that comes whenever two powerful men — three, if you count Dane — are gathered in a small space. Robert Bain probably has a plane of his own. If he does, I'm sure he'll find some way to work that into the conversation. Wheels up, indeed.

There's another kind of tension between Dane and Pierre, and not just because Dane can't take his eyes off Lulu. Dane still hasn't finished the works for the show opening at LaReine's Chelsea space for April. He's been painting and has lost interest in the large sculptures that will make up the new show. Apparently they're not only unfinished, they're awful. So awful that LaReine is going to have a hard time selling them. There are even doom-and-gloom reports that this show, this one overpriced, overhyped show, could be the pinprick that causes the art bubble to burst.

Once we're in the air and Joy is setting out dinner, Lulu comes back to see how I'm doing.

"I hear once you go private you never want to go back," I say, joking with her.

"This could be a problem," she says.

Both Pierre LaReine and Robert Bain follow Lulu to the back of the plane where she's standing over me. They have ideas. Bain wants to introduce her to a fashion designer. LaReine suggests she write a book.

"The life of the muse," he says. "Your name will come to mean something."

Bain thinks Lulu could design her own line of clothing if she wants to.

"Call it MUSE," he suggests.

They talk *to* her at first, then they talk about her, over her head, to each other. Lulu makes a wry face at me, as though she senses how absurd and yet funny the situation is. The two men seem to have differing views on how Lulu Finelli can be presented to the world, but both sense an opportunity — whether for her or for them, it's hard to tell.

Lulu accepts this attention stoically, as though she's resigned to it. She must be used to men reading many layers of potential opportunity into her beauty, although perhaps not exactly in this context. She listens to their ideas without committing to anything.

Throughout their exchange, Dane grows increasingly agitated, fidgeting and pulling his seat belt clasp open and shut. It clamps back down noisily, over and over, as he stares at Lulu. When he's finished clamping, he sucks at a bottle of Guinness.

Sybil simply looks disgruntled, although whether that's a permanent state for her or a reaction to Dane's itchy-toddler impersonation, it's hard to tell. She's buried herself in a thick catalog with Chinese lettering on the front. Sybil's traveling to Florence to do research, not to attend the Finelli memorial service, although it seems the real reason for her trip is to keep an eye on Dane. Perhaps their relationship is on-again.

"Did you know my uncle?" Lulu asks of the two men, Pierre and Robert.

They didn't, of course. But that doesn't stop them from sharing the stories they've heard. The commitment to painting, parties in the studio above the *salumeria,* the all-night race to Madagascar. Sure enough, Bain mentions his own plane.

"I'd really like to buy that painting of you," he says to Lulu.

She nods. "A lot of people want that painting."

"I'll help you," Pierre LaReine says. It's unclear to whom he addresses these words. I think he wants it that way, unclear, so they both believe him.

"LaReine," Dane suddenly calls from the front of the plane. He has another bottle of Guinness in hand and is starting to look drunk. He must have had a few before we made our late arrival. "Tell her the truth."

He stands and lurches toward us as the plane hits a bump.

Sybil says with a warning note in her voice, "Dane."

"Lulu deserves to know what you're really up to," Dane says. He's talking to Pierre in a joking sort of tone, as though he's only kidding around, but there's an implicit aggression underneath. "Why you're flying all of us to Florence. It's obviously not because you're broken up about a dead artist you didn't know and didn't represent. And don't try to tell us it's because you're a hopeless romantic."

"It's neither," Pierre LaReine says in the calm and patient tone of a parent. "I was flying to Florence this weekend with my client. I offered you a ride because I always take care of my artists. Especially ones who have to be ready for a show in two weeks and need to take as little time as possible to travel. I offered the lovely Lulu a ride too."

Dane scoffs at this. "You're going to Florence for one reason only. To see if there's anything in that studio. Tell her what's really going on."

Lulu looks at Dane with the same half-smile she wears in her portrait. "I know what's going on, Dane."

"Do you?" he says.

"Of course I do." Lulu deftly defuses the tension. "I might be new to the art world, but I'm not naive."

No. Naive, she's not. She seems to have a very good understanding of what motivates a man like Pierre LaReine. Lulu acts very confident that the mystery of what her uncle's studio contains is going to play out in her favor. And if Pierre LaReine can help her, she doesn't seem at all bothered by what might be motivating his generosity.

"Your uncle was a very good friend to me," Dane says to Lulu, quieter now. "I feel a responsibility to look out for you."

"That's enough," Pierre LaReine says with a light clap of his hands. "Let's eat."

There's lobster salad and spaghetti with fresh clams, steak with béarnaise sauce, and roasted artichoke hearts, and we all dig in. Everyone except Sybil drinks wine. As we fill our plates, I notice Dane watching Lulu carefully, as though he's trying to memorize how she moves.

Dane moves to sit in the middle of the plane after dinner. Robert Bain sits across from him. Sybil moves next to him, Lulu goes back to the front, across from Pierre. It's like a game of musical chairs. Only I stay put, wondering what the etiquette is about switching seats. The one rule seems to be not to take Pierre's seat.

Pierre hands around a bottle of Ambien to help everyone sleep. I manage to doze a bit and then, quickly, it's over. We're in Florence.

The light is beautiful, a pale yellow in the early morning. It will turn more gold as the day progresses. We say good-bye at the airport, awkward with each other after the intimacy of sleeping together in a relatively small space. Pierre kisses Lulu's cheek and then runs one finger along the spot he just kissed. "See you soon," he says.

Lulu and I leave the others at the airport. We're staying at a small hotel no one has ever heard of, right near Jeffrey's studio. Sybil and Dane are staying at the home of an artist friend of Dane's, a sculptor who was also a friend of Jeffrey Finelli's. Pierre and Robert Bain are staying at the Villa San Michele in Fiesole. When Simon arrives on the Continental Airlines flight through Rome, he will be staying there too, even though it's ridiculously expensive. Simon can't be seen to stay at a lesser hotel than the rest of the art world at any event, even at a memorial service. Especially at a memorial service.

Pierre sends us in our own car to the hotel and offers to send one to pick us up for the funeral. "Isn't he thoughtful?" Lulu asks me.

I want to believe he's thoughtful. I want to believe I'm his friend too. After all, I flew on his plane. Pierre LaReine is a name to drop, if you play that game. A trophy friend. There are people who would love to claim to have flown on his plane. That I'm now one of the people in possession of this claim amuses me to no end. If only he was my dealer.

"You know he's got ulterior motives," I

remind her. I'm looking out the window at the signs in Italian, the *tabaccherias* and the *bancos* and the *salumerias* and, yes, quite a few pizzerias.

"Doesn't everyone?" she asks. She sounds tired.

"Zach says if there's money to be made on your uncle's work, you can bet that LaReine is the one who's going to be making it."

Lulu shifts in her seat to face me and puts her hand on my arm. "I don't care about the money. I know that sounds phony because everyone cares about money. And we should. Care, I mean. But in this particular instance I care about that one painting that he left me. I care about what he said to me on the phone and why he said it to me. And I hope some of the answers are going to be contained in his studio. That's what I care about."

Thirteen:
Please come to a private memorial service for
Jeffrey Finelli

Jeffrey Finelli's memorial service is sad and lovely. It takes place at four in the afternoon, when the mellow light of Florence is at its most magical. A perfectly saturated gold. It's a color infused in all of Jeffrey's paintings still hanging in the gallery in New York.

"Who are all these people?" Lulu whispers as we step into the chapel and find seats in the front row. She sits between me and Pierre LaReine. Dane O'Neill is on Pierre's other side, with Sybil next to him. Simon is on my side, shooting glances at Pierre's silver head down the row, not happy that Pierre LaReine has insinuated himself into this scenario.

There is a priest, which surprises Lulu. "I thought art was his religion. Why a priest?"

"Maybe someone else decided that part," I say. Even though I gave up all things Catholic when my mom died, I find the presence of this gray figure in the white collar reassuring. His religion may offer little comfort in the face of death, but there's authority in the uniform of robes he wears and in the rituals he will perform at the simple wooden altar.

"The contessa," she says. "I have a feeling she's deciding a lot of things."

As the priest begins to speak in Italian, I become overwhelmed by emotion. I'm not even sure why, especially as I don't understand any of the words. If I had to guess, I think it's because Lulu's loss reminds me of my own. To have no family at all, this is the strange bond I share with my new friend. And there was something about Jeffrey Finelli, just as there was something in the enormous painting of Lulu that still hangs on the wall before my desk back in the gallery. Something that forced me to ask myself about my own relationship with painting. Funerals sure bring out the existentialist in people, don't they?

Tears roll down my cheeks. Simon gives me an exasperated look.

There are a few more speeches in Italian and English. And then the contessa makes her appearance.

It's quite an appearance, a dramatic entrance in a flourish of mournful organ music. She wears a tight black suit with a small peplum at the waist, her shapely legs encased in fishnet stockings. On her feet are pointy stilettos of shiny black patent leather.

If central casting sent you a contessa for your movie, this is what she'd look like. She is very beautiful, with high, pronounced cheekbones and deep-set eyes, sleek hair pulled into a neat bun and jutting collar bones that accentuate an extremely long neck and thin graceful arms. She was once a famous beauty, or so the story goes. She's still stunning, shedding elegant, discreet tears as she speaks in English with a gently rolling accent.

"We were lovers," she states, in that dramatic way that only European women can use the word *lovers* and not sound like a *Saturday Night Live* skit. "For many years, twenty years, we were in the life of the other one, hand in hand. Only I have the keys to his studio. Only I understand the difficult life of the artist. To be given this gift is a blessing from God. And also obligation."

When the contessa mentions the difficult life of the artist, Pierre takes Lulu's hand in his and holds it gently. Out of the corner of my eye I can see Dane's head shift downward, as though he's just spotted their hands.

When it's over, we all sit a minute or two. Lulu looks stunned. "I didn't even know him," she says softly, expressing her surprise at her emotional reaction.

Afterward there's a party in a courtyard down the street set with round tables covered in orange tablecloths. There is a wooden trellis overhead on which knotted vines grow. The light streams in through the vines and makes shadows on the table. There are cocktails — Bellinis with fresh peach juice.

It's beautiful and poignant and somehow romantic. I feel a pang of loneliness, wishing there was someone here to enjoy this with me. The person whose arms I envision encircling me as we gaze across the charming courtyard? Zach Roberts? I try to banish the image of him standing behind me, whispering funny comments about all the people in black milling about laughing uproariously in mourning for Jeffrey Finelli. But I have no image to replace it with, and Zach keeps coming back, like one of those annoying Internet pop-up ads.

To take my mind off the unavailable Zach, I watch Lulu. She's at the center of a circle of men, Dane, Simon, and Pierre, among others. She's talking, and they're all listening to her. When she asks a question, it seems they all answer at once, talking over each other.

When she sees me looking in their direction, Lulu breaks away from the group to come toward me, and all the men follow her with their eyes.

I'm about to ask her how she's handling it all when the contessa joins us in a smoky cloud of what smells like hash. Hash, is that possible? She has a thin hand-rolled cigarette fitted into a long ivory holder that she waves in our direction. Is the contessa a stoner?

She takes Lulu's hands. "Ah, dio mio," she says, studying Lulu's face intently. She's so melodramatic I want to laugh, but I wouldn't dare. "Such a beauty. And those eyes. Jeffrey's eyes."

"My father had them too," she says. "Everyone in the Finelli family had round gray eyes."

The contessa nods, her own eyes filling with tears. "Yes, but yours? . . ."

Her voice trails off.

"On the phone —" Lulu starts to speak, but the contessa cuts her off.

"It's obvious," she says. "You are so much like him."

"It's so sad," the contessa continues. "And

258

he couldn't know for sure."

"Know what?"

"Now," the contessa says, "let me hug you." She folds Lulu into her long thin arms, holding the cigarette holder away from her body. "I told him to go to New York. I live with the guilt."

"We all live with guilt," Lulu says, allowing herself to be embraced. "On the phone you said you had something important to tell me about Jeffrey."

The contessa takes a deep drag from the cigarette. "Did I?" She waves the smoke from in front of her face, as though she's waving away Lulu's words along with it.

Lulu glances over at me, frustration on her face. "You said you would tell me when I got here."

The contessa shakes her head. "I'm not certain," she says, still shaking her head. "I'm not certain."

"I'm eager to go to his studio," Lulu says, changing the subject as she realizes the contessa is not going to explain any more at this moment.

"First, a Bellini. The peach juice is fresh."

Lulu and I sit at one of the tables. The contessa moves toward a waiter, snapping her fingers to summon Bellinis. "This is weird," Lulu says to me. "There's something she's not telling me."

Simon quickly appears to take a seat next to Lulu, pulling the chair close. "Jeffrey would have liked this," he says. The contessa is pointing a waiter in our direction with a tray of drinks.

"We were very close," Simon is saying to Lulu. "I discovered him, you know. He would never have agreed to a gallery show if I hadn't talked him into it."

The waiter sets down Bellinis for the three of us. I notice the contessa now talking to Pierre LaReine in an animated fashion. She is gesticulating elegantly with her cigarette holder as she makes a point.

"An artist's estate has to be carefully managed," Simon says to Lulu, as though he's interviewing for a job. In a way, I suppose he is. "The work has to be placed. Museums, well-known collections. Sold to collectors with whom there's a trust. People like Robert Bain. I've told him he could buy a piece when I have something to sell him. Maybe even *Lulu Meets God*."

He pauses, allowing his announcement to sink in, as though we are both going to be ever so impressed that he has a relationship with Robert Bain. Robert Bain is quite a name to drop, for an art dealer. Simon looks disappointed by our lack of reaction. He assumes that we don't understand him. Obviously he doesn't know Robert was on the plane with us. Robert Bain is our new best friend, Simey old boy!

Dane sits himself down with us then, slumping into a chair. "This is surreal," he says. "I can't believe the old prawn's dead."

Lulu looks at him. " 'Old prawn' is not very nice," she says. She raises one eyebrow at him. I've always wanted to be able to raise one eyebrow.

"It's an endearment," Dane says. "We were very close."

She responds with weary sarcasm. "Oh, you too?"

"What?" he says.

"Oh, nothing," she says. "Mr. Simon Pryce here was just telling me how close he was to my uncle."

The contessa and Pierre LaReine join us then too, approaching the table together. She walks like a runway model, hips first, those long legs — what do they call them, gams? — snaking across the courtyard. The contessa finishes her cigarette, or joint, or whatever it is she's smoking, and leans over us to tamp it out in the ashtray at the center of the table.

"Tell me about him," Lulu says to her. "What were his days like?"

The contessa lights another cigarette before she answers. She takes a long drag and speaks through a thin plume of smoke. She looks at one of the chairs and then at LaReine, indicating without a word that he should pull it out for her. He does, and she sits close to Lulu. LaReine takes another chair for himself.

"The count, he was orderly," the contessa says, as though she's doing a voiceover for a documentary. "He liked to begin work at nine in the morning. Jeffrey was very, how do you say it? Punctual about it. He began at exactly nine, after breakfast and the newspapers. He painted from nine until lunchtime. After lunch he would work again, until four in the afternoon."

We're all focused on her, waiting for her words as she pauses to allow a waiter to serve more Bellinis to everyone. Only LaReine is distracted, scrolling his BlackBerry under the table.

"He taught classes in the evening," she continues. "Some of the time, he received visitors. He liked to talk about art. He never painted at night. He loved to eat nice food and drink wine, and the night was for these things."

"The exact opposite of me," Dane says. "I can only work at night. I start at nine at night, usually. Not that any of you asked."

The contessa laughs at this and puts her hand on Dane's. "I love artists," she says. "You're like snowflakes, all similar, and yet unique. In some ways, my Jeffrey, he was like a factory worker. He arrived on time. He kept his tools and his workplace neat and tidy. He worked until it was time to stop."

"Wasn't he very prolific?" Simon sips his drink as though he's just throwing out a casual question, though there's obviously nothing casual about any of it. We're all, the five of us at the round table with the contessa, wondering the same thing: What's in the studio?

"Process, not product," the contessa intones. "That's what the count was about."

"The count," Lulu says, as though she's trying on the word. "Was he really a count?"

The contessa nods thoughtfully. "He was to me."

"Contessa," Lulu says, with an air of diplomacy. "On the phone you said you had something important to tell me. I know you don't remember that, but I'm wondering if it had anything to do with why my uncle would say he's giving me a painting that didn't belong to him."

Fleetingly, the contessa looks guilty. Her

eyes dart away, and she takes a drag from her ivory holder before answering. "I'm not so certain he knew," she says, after a long pause. "He didn't care about finances. I took care of such things for him."

Now it's Lulu's turn to pause. "He didn't know you'd sold them?"

"Of course he did," Simon interjects.

"Yes, he knew we were selling them," the contessa says. She still looks guilty. "But he might not have paid much attention to how we sold them. Before or after the opening. He didn't care about selling them. He needed the money, of course. And he spent the money. But the real reason he did the show was to exhibit that painting of you in New York. Where you live. Where he was from. It was coming home for him. And he knew it was time to come home. Maybe somehow, he sensed his days were numbered, I don't know."

The noise of the rest of the party seems to have receded, and there is silence at our table. Even Pierre LaReine is paying attention now.

Simon speaks first. "Now, then," he says. "He was happy to sell. He needed the money."

"Because I told him so," the contessa says, looking down into her untouched peach drink. "There was no more money. My money is gone."

Lulu sighs. "So we're still not sure if he intended for me to have the painting."

"Oh, he wanted you to have it," Dane says. "That piece was made for you. There's a message in his gift to you. And it's not about actually living with the painting. I'm quite certain of that. It's about you becoming the artist you were meant to be."

The contessa is nodding. "Was meant as inspiration. For you, mostly, yes, Lulu. And for everyone who is in pain for being a failed artist."

"He said we come from a long line of them," Lulu says softly. "But I'm not an artist. I could never even draw."

We all fall silent again.

"You don't have to be good at drawing to make art," Dane says after a while. "This is what I used to tell my students. Try something else. Painting, photography, sculpture. Any way you express yourself. Contemporary art is about ideas. Get someone else to manufacture your vision if necessary."

"Do you know how many bad artists there are out there?" Pierre LaReine hasn't said anything up to this point. Now he becomes animated. "Not to mention all the awful screenwriters and guitar players and those *American Idol* wannabes. They start out with no talent, and then they don't want to do the work. Nobody wants to practice. They just want to be famous."

"Jeffrey would have agreed," says Dane. "Because what those people are looking for is the wrong thing. It's through the process that transformation occurs. And you find God."

"And that's where the doubt comes in?" Lulu asks, now sounding even more tired. It's not just jet lag, I can see.

" 'Is it art?' people ask, filled with doubt, as if they're not sure." Dane stands to make this point. " 'Is there even a God?' they ask, filled with doubt. 'Who am I?' they ask. Again with the doubt." He gestures toward Lulu. "There's always the doubt."

The contessa excuses herself, and we all watch her leave our circle. She moves through the crowd of mourners, dragging on another cigarette, trailing the smell of hash. At the rate she's going, I think she's going to pass out before we get to the studio, although she seems completely unaffected by whatever is in her smokes.

We eat gnocchi with fresh tomato and thin slices of veal. There's melon and prosciutto and fresh figs. There are platters of glistening grilled vegetables. Continuous Bellinis. And underneath it all, a combination of queasy anticipation and dread as we contemplate the visit we will make shortly, to the dead man's studio.

When the party is over, the five of us, Lulu, Dane, Simon, Pierre, and I, follow the contessa across the dusty street to the building nearby that houses the *salumeria,* her apartment, and the studio where Jeffrey lived and worked on the top floor.

The contessa is still impossibly elegant after three or four hash-laced ciggies. She leads our black-clad group, striding along on her shiny patent leather stilettos as though she's wearing Pumas.

"Come on, then, give us a taste of what we're to see," Simon says to her, stepping quickly to match her stride. "Paintings, drawings, did he ever do photographs?"

"Yes, tell us," LaReine adds.

She gives him an odd look, brandishing a huge black metal ring of keys. She doesn't say anything as she leads us to an old building covered in yellow peeling paint.

There is a metal grate pulled down over the *salumeria* and tall green shutters closed over each of the windows.

"He's on the top," she says. "I have the first two floors above the shop."

She hands Lulu a large metal key she's pulled from the ring. Lulu leads the rest of us up the flight of stairs to Jeffrey's studio. Simon is right behind her, Pierre at his heels. I follow Pierre, and Dane brings up the rear.

Lulu fits the key into the big wooden door and swings it open. We step in, one by one, each of us envisioning a studio piled high with masterpieces. All that "process," wouldn't that lead an artist to be extremely prolific?

Fourteen: Please come for a private studio tour: Jeffrey Finelli's Studio in Florence

Jeffrey's studio is one large room that takes up the whole top floor of the building. There is a separate kitchen that opens to the rest of the space, and an old-fashioned bathroom. The wood floors, wide planks mellowed with age and splattered with years of paint, are mopped clean. Through the tall windows we can see the navy sky, and I picture the perfect gold light that comes in during the day, the same gold that tinged all of Jeffrey's paintings.

There is a double bed in one corner, draped in dark brown velvet fabric. The bed is flanked by a beat-up desk and chair on one side and a small table piled with books on the other. At the far end of the space sits a long sofa and two shapeless overstuffed chairs. There is no television and no art on the walls. There are no walls, actually, as the windows surround us on every side of the building.

In the center of the far wall of windows are three easels covered with tarps. Lined up under the windows are old wooden cases that contain tubes of paints and bottles of turpentine and brushes. There is an enormous table, covered with nicks and paint drips, and underneath it are blank canvases, full of potential, ready to be used, but empty.

There are no masterpieces. There are no painted canvases leaning against the wall. There is no art at all, at least none immediately visible. The place feels scrubbed down, almost sterile.

"I'll leave you to your privacy," the contessa says.

She swings the door shut behind her. Simon looks unsure about what to do. Dane too. Pierre LaReine, the confident king of dealers, looks nervous. The studio feels airless. It's too quiet.

We look to Lulu to begin. She moves gracefully to one of the easels along the far wall and stops in front of it. She hesitates for a few seconds, then pulls at the tarp. We collectively hold our breath.

The tarp slides onto the floor to reveal . . . nothing. Just an empty wooden easel covered in drips of paint.

Lulu moves to the second easel, also covered with a tarp. Same thing, empty easel. She looks at me before pulling the third tarp off. There doesn't seem to be any other place to keep the large canvases that we're hoping to find.

She pulls the tarp off. There's nothing on the third easel. Where is Jeffrey's other work?

Pierre stands near the door, as if keeping himself ready to take flight. The rest of us look under the worktable and open the closet doors. We pull out the small oven drawer and peer into the fridge. We look in the bathtub and under the bed. We search the entire studio, and we don't find one single painting. Not even a tiny one.

No one speaks. The only sounds are the ones we make, pulling a blank canvas aside or moving a pile of cardigans in the closet to check if anything's been hidden in the back.

Lulu sits at the desk. She pulls open the drawers, one by one, although they're too tiny to contain anything but desk supplies.

Pierre goes for the door. "It must be somewhere," he says. "In storage somewhere. I'll ask her."

Lulu is still going through the tiny drawers of the desk. "What does all this mean?" she asks, not looking at any one person. It's not clear if she expects an answer.

She stands, leaving the drawers open.

Dane lays himself out on the bed and looks up at Lulu. "It means he loved you very much. That show is his life's work. An artist's whole life, tied into his relationship with his estranged family."

"We weren't estranged," she says. "Strange, yes. But not estranged. He's the one who decided to live in another country. No one told him he couldn't come back."

She moves slowly through the space, lightly touching the empty canvases. She lifts some of them and peers again at the blank ones underneath, as if we might have missed something.

Pierre returns with the contessa. He has a phone to his ear and doesn't look at Lulu. "It appears there is no other work here," he says, speaking over the phone at all of us. He makes no eye contact with anyone.

"Process, not product," the contessa says with a firm nod of her shapely head. She looks at LaReine. "He destroyed as he went along. The results can never be more important than the journey to get there. That's where God lives, in the journey, not in the result."

She sounds as though she's repeating

something Jeffrey must have said many times. Simon sighs, a long breath easing out through his teeth. "Rii-ii-ii-ght."

Pierre immediately gets busy, scrolling down his BlackBerry and claiming an emergency at his London gallery. "I have to fly there now," he says to all of us in general, and to no one in particular. With a brisk sort of salute, he is gone. No tender gaze for Lulu, no lingering kiss. Not even a good-bye. I guess this means no G-5 home.

Lulu seems to almost have expected such behavior from him, or at least that's what I read in the distracted look on her face. She seems focused only on what's going on in the studio. This surprises me less than it should; Lulu Finelli is playing a completely different game than any I'd recognize. These men, and their wants, she just seems to understand them.

Now she moves to the wooden cases where the tubes of oils are neatly organized. She pulls one out and examines the color, a cerulean blue. "You were his friend," she says to Dane. "Weren't you ever here? You must have known."

Dane sits up on the bed. He tilts his head at Lulu, thinking. "A lot of artists are secretive about their work in progress. I had no idea he destroyed his own work. We never talked about it. It seems uncharacteristically harsh, a form of infanticide."

Lulu pulls a wooden palette from a slot in the case and twists the top off the blue paint. She squirts a dollop out onto the palette and then eyes the case for other colors. No one says anything for quite a while. We watch her select colors and move on to the brushes.

"What is here in the studio is all yours," the contessa states magnanimously, as though she's the one granting the gift. "The paints, the canvases, all of it belongs to you. You can do whatever you want with it."

"But not one piece of art, not even a tiny sketch, not even a study for something," Lulu says. "Isn't that strange?"

Lulu gives the contessa a pointed look. The contessa looks away, her eyes filling with tears. "I never should have let him go to New York."

Two perfectly formed matching tears spill over from each of her dark eyes and roll slowly down her cheeks. It's quite a performance.

Her hand shakes as she pulls a cigarette from her pouch and lights it with a duplicate to the lighter Jeffrey kept in his pocket. That's when I remember. The lighter. It's still in my coat pocket. I pull it out now, holding it in my hand.

"Is that hash?" Dane asks.

The contessa doesn't answer him, just looks at each of us in turn. The tears roll neatly down her cheeks. Once she's made sure we've all received the full visual impact of her grief, she leaves, leaving behind a cloud of fragrant smoke.

"Crikey, she's stoned," Dane says.

"I wish there was something I could do," Simon says to Lulu. I think he is telling the truth for once.

"Let me buy the painting from you, Simon," Dane says. He pounds one fist against his chest and points at Lulu. "I'll give it to you."

"You don't have to do that," she says. "He's going to do the right thing. Aren't you, Simon?"

Interesting, how well she knows how to read him. Simon likes to do what he perceives to be the right thing. He's particularly talented at rationalizing his behavior.

Simon clears his throat. "Yes, I must do what's right. What's right is to sell the painting to the first person who put it on hold."

"Connie?" I spit out.

275

He looks at me like I'm an idiot. "Of course not," he says.

"Come on, mate," Dane says.

Simon pulls himself up to his full height. "I'm sorry," he says. "I can't disappoint my client."

He drops the celebrity's name, and it hangs there in the air. "If he turns it down, you can have it. But I have to give him the chance first."

Simon turns on his heel, pulling his peach scarf tightly around his neck.

When he shuts the door behind him, Dane says, "Fool."

"I think I'd like to be alone," Lulu says. She's placed one of the larger canvases on an easel.

Dane kisses her on the cheek, tucking one strand of her hair behind her ear. She holds his gaze. I watch the two of them, feeling as completely alone as one can feel in a room with two other people.

"I can help you," Dane says in a gentle tone. "With your painting. I'm a teacher. Not a very good one. But I'd be delighted to help you find your way."

"I'll think about it," she says. She kicks off her shoes.

"This is the one salve I know," he says from the door. "For the wounds of

276

disappointment. Losing oneself in the creative process. Enjoy it."

He waves good-bye, and then the studio is quiet. The energy in the space around us shifts so dramatically, it feels as though someone's just dimmed the lights. For the home of a dead man, the studio is surprisingly happy, a place you'd want to linger. I don't want to go back to the hotel, but I understand how Lulu would want to be alone here.

Before I go, I hand her the lighter I'd been clutching in my fist. "This was Jeffrey's."

"Thank you." Her eyes meet mine. "You're probably wishing you never got sucked into this."

"Are you kidding? Before last week my life was so boring I could hardly stay awake for it," I tell her. And it's true. Why else would I need so much caffeine to get through the day?

She hands me several tubes of paint and three different brushes. "Let's use these. You take that canvas. I'll do this one."

She hands me one of the smaller canvases, the same size as the one she takes. "You want to be alone," I say. "It's okay. I understand."

"I wanted them to leave. Not you," she says. "Keep me company."

"No, really," I protest.

"Please," she says. "Something strange is happening to me. And it has nothing to do with all that fuss over buying and selling my uncle's work. I feel as though I've come home somehow. But I've never been here before."

"Okay," I say. "But I'll just sit here. I don't need to paint. You try it."

"I'm scared too," she says. "I haven't done this since college. Try it with me. Have you ever painted before?"

Suddenly I'm overcome by the urge to tell her. But then I look at the blank canvas, and I'm filled with trepidation.

"Go on," she says. "Remember, process, not product."

I watch her squirt some more oils from their tubes onto a palette.

I haven't done this since college art class, painted in front of another person. It's a terrifying concept to a death-stage perfectionist. I hesitate. And then the urge just takes over. Is there anything more satisfying to the soul than an untouched canvas, brand-new boar-bristle paintbrushes in various sizes, and an assortment of colors of oils, all pristine in their new tubes?

I choose my colors carefully, a range of greens, pale heathery gray, earth tones. I don't know what I'm going to put onto the canvas, and I just let myself respond to the colors. I used to sketch for days and weeks before I would commit to the expensive paint. Now I let the dripping brush slide right onto the canvas, without real thought to what I'm going to do. I simply enjoy the feeling of the brush hitting the canvas, the way it slides so easily with that much paint on the end. I dip and brush again.

It's a sweet feeling of relief, simply getting a brush onto canvas. I feel like a fish who's been out of the water, slipping into a river. I am actually painting, not just agonizing over how bad the image on the canvas looks. Is this you, God?

We both lose track of time. We don't even stop to go to the bathroom.

After a while, inevitably, the joy seeps out of me. I can't help expecting something brilliant to emerge from all this good feeling. But the brilliance is all in my head, in a vision for something that should be great but comes out on the canvas as, well, nothing.

When I finally move, Lulu speaks to me for the first time in what feels like hours. "I understand," she says. "About meeting God. I think I can feel it. It's like someone or something is guiding me. Do you think that's it?"

I look at her. It's as though Jeffrey's painting of her has come to life. She's holding on to a dripping paintbrush, giving me the same knowing half-smile. And in her eyes, Jeffrey's eyes, that cloud of doubt. "Is this what he meant?" she asks. "The feeling of joy as you lose yourself in that zone, that purely creative place where you lose track of time and the outside world? It's spiritual, I guess."

I glance at her canvas. The painting there is far from finished, but the image taking shape is unmistakable. It's a figure of a woman who looks quite suspiciously like Lulu. A self-portrait.

The woman in the painting is standing at a canvas, a dripping brush in one hand, a look of crude ecstasy on her face. It's rough in its current state, but there's no mistaking two things. One is that the woman in the painting is her. And the second is that Lulu Finelli is un-fucking-believably talented.

It figures.

The sky is lightening when we decide to go back to the hotel. I roll the canvas I've been painting up to take it with me, not concerned that it's still wet and the colors will merge into each other. It's already nothing but a mess of muddy colors, and all I intend to do is destroy the evidence. Evidence, that's what I see here. That however intensely I may yearn to be good at this one thing, painting, God, if such a thing as God exists, did not see fit to bestow upon me the basic necessary skills to accomplish that.

I'm hoping, expecting even, that Lulu will comment on my canvas. I want her to say something complimentary. But she's distracted, focused only on her own work. She signs her painting with a flourish, just "Finelli," along the bottom right corner of the painting, exactly the way Jeffrey did on his paintings. I wonder if she's copying his signature or if it's coincidence that it looks so similar. The big *F,* the tail at the end of the *l.*

We clean our brushes at the sink. We're moving slowly now, exhausted. She leaves her canvas pinned to the easel as we move to the door. I have my canvas rolled under my arm. "Don't you want to take it with you?" I ask, pointing at hers. I could sell the thing if she doesn't want it, I think. If I cared about selling paintings.

"It's still wet," she says. "Anyway, I don't want it. I've got a long way to go."

It's only later, crammed into the coach

section of the commercial flight from Rome back to New York, that I think to question what she meant. A long way to go to get home with a canvas under one arm, as I've done? Or a long way to go as a painter?

FIFTEEN:
OPENING RECEPTION
DANE O'NEILL:
PIERRE LAREINE
GALLERY

April

The week after we return from Florence, Jeffrey Finelli's show closes. The last of the paintings, *Lulu Meets God and Doubts Him,* has been sold. Yes, to the actor. Of course. Did you really think Simon could resist such an opportunity?

Simon's sent the celebrity an invoice for $275,000. The money's been wired, and all seven of Finelli's paintings, including Lulu, are scheduled to come off the walls and be crated and shipped off to their various new owners. Do I even need to mention that Simon is feeling pretty damn proud of himself? To celebrate he's bought a new pair of handmade shoes, and he's strutting around the gallery like he's Pierre LaReine. Damn peacock.

Jeffrey's show at the Simon Pryce Gallery is closing the very same day, the first Thursday in April, that Dane O'Neill's new show is opening just down the street at the LaReine Gallery. There is something pleasingly appropriate about this timing.

The morning that the paintings are coming down, Lulu asks me to meet her for breakfast. I haven't seen her in the days since our return from Florence, although we've spoken on the phone every day.

She gives me an address in Tribeca, and I assume I'm meeting her at a restaurant. The address, however, corresponds to a building with a row of buzzers at the locked front door. I'm about to take out my phone to ask Lulu where I'm supposed to go when a woman appears at the door. I don't immediately recognize her. Then I realize it's Lulu, with short hair. She's wearing an orange sweater over her jeans and looks younger than she did with her hair long. If possible, she's even more beautiful without the hair, all cheekbones.

"Welcome to my new life," she says, laughing. "New home, new look, new job. Actually, no job."

"What are you talking about?"

"Come in, come in," she says, holding open the door for me. "Watch the stairs, we have to walk up."

I follow Lulu as she leads the way up a narrow industrial-looking staircase.

"Sorry I didn't say anything on the phone," she says over her shoulder. "I didn't want to tell anyone until it was complete. The day we got back from Florence I told my boss I wasn't coming back. I offered to work for two more weeks, but I told him I was still grieving. He took the hint and said I didn't need to return. The next day I took five bags of black and gray clothes to a church thrift store."

We get to the third floor and keep going. I'm breathless, but Lulu keeps talking. "Dane O'Neill had a friend who was going to Tokyo for a while, so he arranged for me to sublet this place. And I have a friend whose cousin was moving to New York, so he's taken over my lease. And then I cut my hair. What do you think?"

"I like it," I tell her. "I like all of it."

"Change is good," she says.

The studio is small but bright with sunshine, and Lulu has made herself at home. There's an orange Moroccan bedspread over her formerly white-clad daybed, and the easels and canvases, paints and brushes, that were in Jeffrey's studio in Florence are neatly organized.

"She sent them Federal Express," Lulu says, pointing at a stack of canvases that must have cost a fortune to mail.

I've never seen anyone transform the externals of their life so quickly and in such a dramatic fashion. The only one who came close was my now-dead aunt Ginny, who at twenty-two took her vows and went from being a punked-out rocker chick to a nun in a convent. She too cut her hair.

In Lulu, this extreme transformation makes total sense, a logical transition. Lulu Finelli in a Tribeca painter's studio seems more natural than the Wall Streeter in the tidy box. "I was miscast in my old life," she says. "It didn't fit me, the job, the apartment, the fear. Not to get too evangelical about it, but everyone should know what this feels like, to live the life you really want to be living. To be the person you believe yourself to be."

Easy for you to say, I think. "What about money?"

"I've already started painting," she says, pointing to an easel covered with a tarp. "But I can't show you. Tomorrow I'm taking my first lesson with Dane. If he's not too hungover from his opening. Although he told me he doesn't actually drink that much, only when he's out doing the art world thing, he says."

"Lulu, this is amazing." And amazed is just what I am. Amazed and, frankly, jealous.

Lulu's got money, saved from her job, and a little inherited from her parents. She's got time now to paint. And she has the encouragement that Dane's offering. Most importantly, if the painting in Jeffrey's studio was indicative, she has talent.

I wonder if the contessa sent Lulu her painting when she FedExed the rest of Jeffrey's studio contents.

"I'm determined," Lulu says. "I'm coming to my painting career late but with the zealotry of the newly converted."

Painting career. Is it just me or is that presumptuous?

After breakfast I go to work in a bleak mood. I'm alone in the gallery with Jeffrey's paintings for the last time. Although Lulu's told me how sad she is that she's never going to see her painting again except in a photograph, she was all lightness and warmth this morning. I, however, am overwhelmed with sadness to think of that painting getting crated up and shipped off to California, where the actor will probably hang it in his pool house.

I spend most of the morning playing on my computer, printing out the jpeg of *Lulu Meets God* onto photo paper, fiddling with the tints and hues and cropping of the printed digital image. I make two copies, one for Lulu and one for me.

Sadness at the fate of this painting is not the only thing affecting my mood this morning. That night in Jeffrey's studio in Florence was a cold jolt of reality for me. Lulu's talent, so much more developed than that of any of my school friends, made it all too obvious to me that I'm going to need another plan. Because being the painter I dream of being is not going to happen.

The large image of Lulu on the wall stares down at me as though she understands. I'm ready for the painting to come down. Right now all that inspiration is a little much for my fragile creative soul.

The art handlers have packed up the last of the smaller pieces and are ready to move on to the big Lulu painting when Lulu herself appears at the gallery in the late afternoon.

"I came to say good-bye to the painting," she says. "Is that weird?"

"No. I did it too."

She takes a position she's taken many times in the past month, standing before her painting in the center of the gallery, her back to me.

"It's like an endorphin rush," she says. "As though God could be present, the way you feel when you're in that creative zone."

I remember that feeling. I don't want to tell her what happens to it over time. Let her go on thinking it always feels this good. Maybe for her it will. For someone with that kind of talent, maybe the suffering is minimal.

"Something tells me this isn't the last I'm going to see of this painting," she says.

"Maybe not," I say. "Zach says collectors only borrow works of art. They can never really own them. Maybe this one will come back when this guy's done borrowing it." I don't really believe this. The painting is going to the other end of the country. All the way to Hollywood. These walls will be rehung with more art tomorrow. Large color photographs of cemeteries at night by an artist named Carlos Peres. Editions of six and one Artist's Print. Simon's already sold a few, in the rush of his newfound popularity fueled by the interest in Finelli.

"Good-bye, young me," Lulu says to the painting on the wall.

"Good-bye," I add.

If attendance at an opening is any indicator of the power of the art, Dane O'Neill's show is a blockbuster. There are crowds lining the sidewalk, almost all the way to Tenth

Avenue. A burly bouncer in dark sunglasses manages the chaos from behind a velvet rope, just like at a nightclub.

Alexis and the other pretty women and thick-haired men who work for LaReine stand behind the rope and pull recognizable collectors and people they know past the crowd. People they don't know they look right through. Alexis waves Lulu and me in.

I might as well say that it does give me a small amount of pleasure to be waved past the unconnected masses of people who are content to stand on line, a very long line, for the privilege of entering the gallery on the night this brand-name show opens.

Doesn't the crowd know that there is no advantage to seeing the show this evening? The works have all sold — we're still in the bubble, remember? Despite the doom-and-gloom reports predicting the demise of the market, every one of Dane O'Neill's purportedly unfinished installations is gone. It's not a party. There will be no food or drinks served in the gallery. The people lingering on line until the bouncer determines that enough of the crowd inside the gallery has cleared out to let them in are not invited to dinner with the artist. And yet they wait. They wait simply for the privilege to see the art.

Construction detritus, this is what Dane's new show of untitled works consists of. It's a metaphor, certainly. But for what? Life? Death? Sex? I should know this. When in doubt, always opt for sex. Yes, that must be it. The works are large installations, made from the debris that is cleared from building projects. There are stacks of old wood with nails jutting out. Piles of powdery white dust and glass bottles of assorted shapes and sizes filled with dirt are stacked on shelves of distressed painted wood.

Nobody seems to know what to make of them. But that could just be my observation of the crowd milling about the enormous LaReine Gallery. Maybe they all understand the sex metaphor.

Sybil Worthington finds the work genius. She offers this to Lulu and me without any sort of greeting. She seems incapable of greeting, as though she's missing the hello gene. She's missing something, all right.

"It's genius," she barks at us, as though defying us to disagree. "He's finally dealing with the political situation in his homeland."

Lulu asks, "How is this related to Irish politics?"

Sybil puts both hands on her hips as if Lulu's trying to pull her leg. "Can't you see it?"

We shake our heads no.

"The religious conflict. The confinement, the trap that is the religious backdrop in his country?"

"It's wood," Lulu says. "And I don't even think he finished them."

"They're about sex," I add.

Sybil glares at each of us in turn. "They're brilliant. And all he can talk about is giving this up for figurative painting." She spits out the words *figurative* and *painting* as if they were toxic.

"Don't you think it's the mark of a mature artist to work in many mediums?" I ask her.

She ignores me, eyeballing Lulu. "He's taken with you."

"It's a purely professional relationship," Lulu says. "He's my teacher."

Sybil folds her arms over her concave chest. "I suppose you've become his muse. Isn't that special?"

Sybil's right. Dane's motives in offering to teach Lulu are not purely altruistic, of course. He wants to paint her. In homage to Jeffrey, or so he's told her.

"Let me ask you something," Lulu says to Sybil. "If you didn't know these things were done by a name artist and people were paying, what, a few hundred thousand dollars for the privilege of owning them, would you think they were any good?"

Sybil seems to view the question as impertinent, and she wrinkles her nose as she moves away from us. Lulu and I head into the larger space at the back of the LaReine Gallery. I take note of the babies, two so far, drooling on their parents' chests.

"There he is," I tell Lulu, pointing to the silver-haired Pierre LaReine. He has a brunette almost as beautiful as Lulu on his arm.

"Let me ask *you* a question," Lulu says, nonplussed at the sight of the handsome dealer. "Do you think you can fall in love with an artist if you don't like his work?"

I pause in front of one of the enormous cabinets of distressed bits of wood and hammered tin. "I'll assume you're talking about Dane O'Neill?"

She laughs. "Assume nothing but a purely hypothetical question."

I pause, because I'm not sure whether to tell the truth. I'm thinking about Zach and what he does for a living when I say, "Yes, I do believe you can."

"I hate this stuff," she says, gesturing around us. "By the way, Zach Roberts is over there, and he hasn't taken his eyes off you since we walked in."

I turn to see what she's talking about.

Zach is looking at me intently from the other side of an interior velvet rope that separates the public areas of the gallery from the private areas. He's talking to two of LaReine's junior sales guys, with Alexis hovering in the background. When my eye catches his, a slow smile breaks across his face. He waves at me to come over.

I turn away. "Don't be absurd," I say to Lulu. "He's with Alexis."

And then he's there, the man of the hour, Dane O'Neill, in a *Caddyshack* plaid blazer worn, I suppose, for ironic effect. He greets me and then Lulu with kisses on our cheeks, and when he kisses Lulu a photographer takes a picture.

"Does this work have anything to do with the political situation in Ireland?" Lulu asks him.

He looks surprised. Then he laughs. "Crikey. You're a funny girl."

He's pulled away then, and he draws Lulu with him. She lets herself go along, giving me a little wave. Pierre LaReine stops the two of them and bows over Lulu's hand in greeting. In such a situation I'm sure I'd be idiotically embarrassed, but Lulu is much too cool for that. She greets LaReine as though nothing ever happened between them.

I watch the two men lean into her in proprietary fashion. As I'm looking in their direction Zach catches my eye again, from a conversation with a collector who looks extremely enthusiastic about the show.

I see him say good-bye and head toward me. I turn, trying to find someone else to talk to, but he catches me alone.

"McMurray," he says. "You haven't answered my e-mails."

This is true. He's e-mailed me a few times since Florence, and I haven't responded. I'm sure he already knows the Lulu painting's been sold, and I'm sure he's heard about the empty studio. Alexis has much better information than I do; let him get the poop from her.

"I've been busy," I tell him. "The Finelli show's come down."

Zach pauses, as though he's assessing whether I'm telling the truth or not. "What happened with the Lulu painting?"

"Like you don't know."

"I don't know," he says, with a laugh. "My client still thinks it's hers. Although she wants a discount."

And there she is. Simon is standing just to the right of Zach and me, and it seems this is the direction Connie is heading. She's going right for Simon, and behind her is

Lulu, pulled now not by Dane but by Connie, who seems to be enlisting her in an attack on Simon. "What kind of low-rent operation are you running over there?" Connie's voice is a shrill squeak, so high she can hardly get the words out.

Lulu hangs back as Connie gets right up into Simon's face. "You sold that painting out from under both of us."

It's sort of admirable, to see Connie engage in this kind of mano a mano battle, toughing it out face-to-face rather than hiding behind Zach or communicating via scathing e-mail. It's savvy of her to recruit Lulu to back her up.

Lulu looks horrified to find herself in the role of Connie's ally. "It's okay," she says to her. "It's over."

Connie turns on Lulu now, vicious. It's hard not to make a Chihuahua comparison as she tilts her head up at the much taller Lulu. "Easy for you to say. It wasn't yours to begin with. I was the one who bought it."

"Now, now," Simon says, popping candy into his mouth nonchalantly. "No need for a catfight."

A catfight? Oh, Simon.

"I'll sue you," Connie says to Simon. "Litigation excites me."

Simon shrugs. He's got a mouthful of Smarties. "Buy one of the other ones. Apparently Mr. Finelli was quite prolific. He simply neglected to tell me so."

"There are no other ones," she says. "You know that."

Simon makes a bitter face. "That's not what Pierre LaReine is suddenly saying. Or so I hear. Apparently there were under-the-table negotiations to which I was not privy. Certain other works, works no one knew about, appearing in locations other than the poor dead man's studio."

We're all stunned by this news, delivered in Simon's most jaded fashion.

"Is this true?" Lulu asks him.

He shrugs again. "It's a rumor. But I knew there was something sneaky about that Italian woman. And I'll tell you another thing, I don't for a minute believe she is actually a countess."

Connie says, "Mark my words. That painting is going to be mine one day."

Mark my words, Lulu mouths in my direction from behind her.

I move away from all of them, ready to get out of the crowded gallery. As I'm nearly at the door, Simon catches up with me.

"Were you invited to the dinner?" he asks, suspicious.

I nod.

"I obviously was not invited," he says with a sniff. He tosses his pale green cashmere scarf over his shoulder. He actually cares, I realize. Why would he, a rival dealer — although calling him a rival of LaReine is being generous — be invited to a dinner for Dane O'Neill?

"What do you think? Of the show," I ask, to take his mind off his lack of dinner options.

"It's sold out. Bully for LaReine. He could sell ice to an Eskimo."

"Why so petulant?" It feels good to be bold. "You got what you wanted."

"Martin Better's furious with me," Simon says, still feeling sorry for himself. "Now he tells me he wanted the painting all along. Says he had it on hold."

"I thought he was going cold turkey. He said he was giving up art."

Simon scoffs at this idea. "He couldn't do it," he says.

Simon likes to pretend he's sympathetic to the artist's plight. He's an artist too, he wants to believe. And come on, isn't it obvious by the way he's paired a lavender tie with the navy Brioni shirt that he's a colorist? Now he says, not very sympathetically, "This show is bloody awful.

I'm going home."

I'm about to leave too when Alexis Belkin taps me on the shoulder with a jabbing motion. I spin around, avoiding a long slab of oak that sticks out from the piece behind me.

"So, is it true?" She squints at me, defying me to withhold the truth. Julia and Meredith gather to hear my answer. They line up, the three of them, each striking the same pose; one hand on a tilted hip.

"Is what true?"

Alexis rolls her eyes impatiently, indicating that I'd better not play dumb with her. Not after she waved me past the velvet rope onto her turf. The other two roll their eyes in sympathy.

"Simon sold the Lulu painting." Alexis states this as fact. It *is* fact.

Meredith looks at me suspiciously. "It was Martin Better, right?" She says this with a know-it-all tone that doesn't really suit her.

"No way, Marty wouldn't buy it. I wouldn't let him," Alexis says, flaunting her access to and influence on such a big collector.

"You're so right. I can't believe anyone would buy it," Julia says. "It's terrible."

"So, who did?" Alexis is impatient now. "He didn't give it to the niece."

"Dane O'Neill offered to buy it for her," I say, knowing they'll like this. "Simon wouldn't sell it to him."

"That's so romantic," Meredith says, clasping her hands together.

"What about his girlfriend?" Alexis asks. "Sybil." She pronounces it with a mocking sibilant hiss.

"As she says, he's pretty taken with Lulu," I say. I present all this in a matter-of-fact way, more forthcoming with information than I usually am with the Weird Sisters. "He wants to paint her portrait, in homage to his friend Jeffrey. And he's teaching her."

Julia giggles. "Is that what they're calling it these days?"

I drop the actor's name. Plop. Not a ripple. I'm getting better at this. "The piece went out today. Going to Hollywood."

"HE bought it?" Alexis looks shocked at the name I've so skillfully plunked down. "That's strange. He's just given us some stuff to sell, all paintings. He said he's exclusively into video art now. He's all about the moving image, he says, and if it's not video art he doesn't even want to see it."

I'd heard nothing about a new direction for the actor's collection, but that's not out of the ordinary. I never have the poop. I know Simon must not have had it either, because he's not stupid enough to sell the piece to anyone who might just turn around and flip it to another dealer. No one is that much of a starfucker.

"There's my friend Marty," Alexis says with the sort of squeal that doesn't come naturally to her. She dances toward Martin Better in his leather jacket. We all watch as she puts both her hands over his eyes from behind, playing cute. He turns and gives her a hug, wrapping both arms around her tightly and lifting her up. He certainly doesn't seem to think the cute act is unnatural.

As we watch, Zach approaches them. Alexis kisses him. I turn away, exhausted now. I might not have feelings for Zach, or so I'm still trying to convince myself, but that doesn't mean I want to watch him and Alexis canoodling in front of me.

"They're so sweet together," Julia says.

"Did she tell you they're going into business?" Meredith says in a fawning tone.

"I wish I could meet someone who understands what I do," Julia says. "But Zach is the only normal guy in the art world."

"I wouldn't trust any of them," I say, more vehemently than the conversation warrants.

Okay, I'll admit it; it's irking me to see Zach and Alexis together. Yes, irking, that's the word I'd choose, because anything stronger would imply that I care, and I don't. I really don't.

My vehemence causes Julia and Meredith to give me matching curious stares. Nosy, these two.

"You like him, don't you?" Meredith says, nodding her head toward Zach. Her blue eyes drill into me.

"Who? Zach? Are you kidding?" I protest too much. I can feel the heat spreading across my cheeks as I blush. I hate blushing.

"Meredith, you're so right. She does like him," Julia says, watching me carefully.

"No," I lie. "Not at all."

As I head for the door, I see Zach coming in my direction. I turn away, moving quickly. I don't want to get stuck having to play it cool. I'm really no good at cool. There happens to be an empty taxi in front of the gallery, and I slide in. As we pull away, I see that Zach's followed me out the door.

He stops my cab and pulls open the door. "Are you mad at me about something?"

I allow my eyes to meet his. Big mistake. I pause, not sure what to say. This is what I come up with: "There's such a thing as lying by omission."

This causes him to look perplexed. What I meant to say was Yes, I am mad at him. Very mad. I'm crazy mad that he didn't tell me he and Alexis were together when I was allowing myself to fall a tiny bit in love with him.

"I've never lied to you," he says.

I don't answer. I look away.

"Talk to me. I'm going to be gone most of the next month," he says. "Beijing, then Tokyo, a week in London, and then Berlin, Amsterdam, Rome, and Paris."

"I'm sure Alexis will miss you," I say, very prim. I lean forward to talk to the taxi driver. "You can go."

Zach steps back as we pull away. I try not to look back, but I can't help myself. Zach is watching the taxi drive off. I feel a tug at my chest in the vicinity of my heart.

I decide not to go to the dinner for the artist. Later I will learn it's a good one. Dane O'Neill gets naked.

Sixteen:
Noon Service, Saint Sebastian's Church

End of April

If there is a God, He — or She — must have a great sense of humor. At the very least, a well-developed sense of irony. Because really, let's face it, there's no one more ironic than God. Only a God with a sense of humor could have come up with the unlikely circumstances in which I find myself in the dark month of April with the fittingly bleak Peres cemetery photographs lining the walls that surround my desk at the gallery.

Only a God who enjoys a chuckle or two could have conceived the particular irony of this month as Lulu Finelli, the beautiful muse and now emerging artist, lives out my personal fantasy down to the tiniest details, while I contemplate abandoning my lifelong ambition, my identity, the only self I know.

Only a God with a fully developed sense of irony would have made unlikely friends of Lulu and me, affording me, the invisible girl behind the desk with secret pathetic artistic aspirations, a close-up on Lulu's life as she plays the lead role in a dream I thought so personal and private to me.

Actually, that's not even true. My own imagination is too limited to have come up with this dream. I could never have fleshed out the fantasy in the way it's playing out for Lulu. It's not just the talent. And the money. She also has a famous artist taking her on as his protégée. She has access to his well-staffed, brightly lit two-story enterprise as well as her own studio. All the canvas, paint, and expensive bristle brushes she could possibly wish for. And how about the encouragement? I could never have dreamed of the encouragement Dane is giving Lulu, constrained as I am by the censorious mutterings of my inner perfectionist.

So am I jealous? I don't think that's it. I suppose I'm incredulous. Yes, *incredulous* is the word. I'd never believed anything like this could really happen, despite all those nights reading *The Artist's Way* as though it were written expressly for me.

Incredulous. But not all that surprised. Somehow in Lulu it makes sense. She has a way of making her transformation seem the only logical next step, as though all smart

305

artists would spend eight years on Wall Street before undergoing a sudden and intense metamorphosis into a fully formed creative being, changing everything to become an artist.

By the end of April the Carlos Peres show is all sold. Every single piece. The day before the show is to close, Lulu stops in to see me, as she often does. This time she's with Dane. She's wearing an orange jacket the color of a Caribbean sunset and a hot pink cap, and she looks like she's on a fashion shoot, stylish and cool. Now the thumb ring that seemed so out of context when she was a Wall Street financial whiz makes sense.

Dane holds the door open for her. They're both laughing as they come into the gallery.

"I told you I always win my bets," Dane says. He turns to me. "Hullo, lovely Mia." *Loovly.*

"You won't believe what Dane's heard," Lulu says. "There are two paintings in a gallery in Germany with Jeffrey Finelli signatures on them."

"I made a bet there'd be more," he says. "Either fakes, or someone's got their hands on early work."

"Someone like the hash brownie contessa," Lulu says. She moves into the gallery to look at the Carlos Peres photographs. She's seen the show a few times, stopping in to pick me up or to pay a quick visit, and she likes these images. I like them too, particularly for the way they complement my mood.

"So, what are you going to do?" I ask Lulu. "About these paintings? They should be yours."

"I don't know yet," she says. "We're not sure they're real. Dane heard about them from someone at LaReine. This person thought your friend Zach might have something to do with them."

"Zach? He's just an adviser," I tell them, annoyed at the way my heart skips a beat at the mere mention of his name. God, that's irritating. "This doesn't sound right."

"I don't know, but I'll bet they're real," Dane says. "And I'll wager there's more."

"I'm not betting with you anymore," Lulu says, pointing a finger at him flirtatiously. She's told me their relationship is purely platonic, teacher and student, but there seems to be a lot of what she calls chemistry going on here. She sees him most afternoons, after she's spent the mornings in her own studio. When she's there, they paint together on the second floor of his three-story studio space while assistants work the phones and the computers downstairs, managing the details of a global artist's career.

"Let's ring this Zach Roberts. Get to the bottom of it," Dane says.

"I'll call him," I offer.

"These are good," Dane says, of the Peres photographs on the wall. "I'm surprised LaReine hasn't gotten a hold of him."

"You said he doesn't like any artists until their work can command the big numbers," Lulu says.

"That's right. Then they're genius," Dane says with a sardonic laugh. "Like Dane O'Neill."

"Dane's having lunch with LaReine," Lulu says to me. She removes the cap and shakes out her cropped hair. "And I'm taking you out."

I mumble something about needing to stay in the gallery. Simon really doesn't like it when I go out, and I'm not in the mood for his petulance today. And also, I said I was going to call Zach, and now I'm eager to hear his voice.

"It's too gorgeous," Lulu says. Her warmth is infectious. "I insist. It's a day for champagne at an outdoor table."

Champagne sounds good. Although what am I celebrating? I watch the two of them as they stand before the photograph of a cemetery that fills the wall space where the Lulu painting hung last month. Two artists, connecting through their shared passion for their work. Yup, that was part of the fantasy for me too. In fact, I remind myself, there was no part of the dream that involved an art adviser, even one as charming as Zach Roberts.

Lulu's told me how the two of them can get so lost in their work together that they often forget to eat until late in the day. "Then Dane will call down to one of the assistants and order up whatever we're craving." "We almost always agree immediately, deeming it a Chinese dumpling day, or jonesing for guacamole at the same time."

See, I could never have gotten the fantasy to that level of detail, down to the food. And guacamole is practically a religion for me.

"Come on," Lulu says to me now. "You look like you could use a break."

"I'll check with Simon," I say. I could use a break, yes. I need to get out of this gallery. And I'm not entirely sure how much longer my friendship with Lulu can last, at least on the level of spontaneous lunches, because something tells me she's on a path to becoming the thing that I've dreamed of for a very long time: a publicly adulated artist.

She waves her hand in the direction of Simon's office. "Don't check with him. Tell him."

Before I get across the gallery, though, Simon comes through the door. He's on his way to lunch. Or so he says.

"I'm taking Mia out," Lulu announces to him. She makes it sweet, hard to resist, even for him.

He tries to say no, with a quick shake of his head. "I'm meeting a client."

"Lock up for an hour," Dane suggests.

Simon pauses. "All right then," he says, but only because it's Dane O'Neill, famous artist.

"Did you hear the news?" Dane asks him. He looks like he's enjoying himself, sensing how dealers in general, and Simon in particular, hate to be the last to hear the poop. Especially about their own artists, the talents who provide them with a meal ticket through life.

Simon frowns at me, blaming me for there being news he doesn't know. As if I'm the gatekeeper of all the good stories.

"Two Jeffrey Finelli paintings have turned up in Berlin," Dane announces.

Simon's hand goes immediately to his hair, a defensive reflex he resorts to hundreds of times a day. "What d'you want me to do about it? I've no claim on my artist's other work."

He gives Lulu a pointed glare, as though she could have done something about that.

"Apparently I have no claim on them either," she says. "The terms of his will stated I was to inherit the contents of the studio. That was it."

"As far as I'm concerned, there is no further Finelli business to be conducted," Simon says.

"Ha!" Dane says, as he heads for the door and lunch with a much more influential dealer than poor old Simon. Simon seems to be feeling the weight of such a comparison as he too makes for the door, shoulders slumped. Even his hair looks a bit deflated. Hey, I know how you feel, Simey.

Once I've locked the door to the gallery I turn to Lulu. "Thank you. I do need a break."

She points down the street at Simon's back, retreating from us. He walks slowly, looking depressed. "Where's he going?"

"Not to meet a client," I say, locking the door behind us. "He lies about everything."

"Why would he lie about what he's doing?"

"Exactly," I say.

We start moving down the block in the

same direction as Simon, toward Eleventh Avenue.

"Let's trail him," she says, and she takes my arm, her face animated now as we start moving more quickly.

Simon walks with intent, like he needs to get somewhere on time. We follow, staying about a half block behind him.

I'm nervous. What if he turns around? "I don't know if this is a good idea."

"Aren't you curious?"

And suddenly I am. It's always irked me, the way he lies. "I feel like Nancy Drew. The Case of the Mendacious Art Dealer."

We pick up the pace, narrowing the gap between us and Simon. I'm not nervous anymore, moving along next to Lulu. Now it's an adventure.

"You know," she says, "I can't really blame him for selling my painting."

"I can," I say.

"I'm over it," she says. "Yes, it would have been nice. But as Dane says, it's object fetish. I don't need the actual painting to have gotten the benefit of the message."

We walk in silence for a bit.

"Still," she adds, "it would have been fucking nice to have it."

"It should have been yours," I say. "And the other ones too, whatever they are."

"I'm going to find out," she says. "I knew it was too weird that there were no other paintings in his studio. The contessa probably stashed them all in a closet in her place."

"It's strange, because he's probably still unknown in Europe," I say, moving as fast as I can to keep up with her. "If the contessa does have more work, I'd think she'd give it to LaReine or someone like him to sell here in New York, where there's more of a market for the artist."

"How do we know she's not going to do that?"

Simon turns left at the corner, and we trail him. He seems to be moving more quickly now, heading downtown.

"Where's Simon going? There are no restaurants he'd go to this way," I say.

"Maybe he goes to a brothel," Lulu says with a laugh.

"Maybe he gets his hair highlighted," I offer.

"Good one," Lulu says. "He's vain about that, isn't he?"

"He could be going to a voice coach," I say. "To work on his accent."

"His accent? You think he's hiding his lower-class roots, maybe he's really all cockney?"

"I'm not really sure he's even British," I say, to which she laughs.

We follow him for about four and a half blocks. Then he disappears into a nondescript building. When we get to the building, I'm disappointed to realize our escapade has gotten us nowhere.

There's nothing to tell us what's inside. Just a row of buzzers.

On one, there's a small sign. Saint Sebastian's Church. I don't assume that's where he's gone, of course. I just find it amusing that the building into which he disappears for something questionable should house a church.

Lulu points to the buzzer. "He goes to church?"

"There must be something else in the building," I say.

"Let's try the buzzer," she says.

I'm about to say no, but she presses the button. We're immediately buzzed into the lobby, without having to declare ourselves. At the far end of the space there is a door with a plaque on it. Saint Sebastian's Church.

We pull open the door and peer inside at the church, if you use the term loosely. I possess the lapsed Catholic's fascination with such places, churches, especially the ones with lots of pomp and circumstance. Stained glass and incense and candles, these things invoke memories of my childhood as an awed believer. But this place doesn't look anything like my idea of a church.

It's simply a large open space like a gallery but filled with folding chairs. It's the kind of space that probably houses Weight Watchers meetings in the evenings. There is nothing on the white walls. At the far end a man in a gray suit sits in one of the folding chairs on a dais, one leg crossed over the other. We see the backs of a few heads. And one particularly large head, a familiar sight. Simon.

We pause for a moment at the door. When one of the heads turns to look at us, we turn to go.

As we walk to Pastis for lunch, we ponder the question. Lulu says it out loud. "Does Simon believe in God?"

I'm not as surprised as I would have expected to learn that Simon finds his path to God through church. It seems fitting, actually, that he would meet his God in a formal setting. "I suspect he does. Believe, that is. Plus, he likes to do the right thing. And church is the right thing."

"There could be an angle," Lulu suggests. "You know how agents in L.A. go to AA meetings to find clients? Maybe there are collectors here. Or artists. Ones he could poach."

As we walk toward Fourteenth Street, I wonder. What does Simon pray for? Maybe I should try it.

It's a little windy on the outdoor terrace at Pastis, but we get a table in the sun and order champagne.

"What's wrong?" Lulu asks. "You're not yourself."

"If only I knew who that was," I joke. I take a sip of the champagne and decide not to darken our lunch on this pretty day with my identity crisis.

"To new beginnings," I say, raising my glass. And right there, I decide, although I don't say anything out loud. I'm giving it up. That box of paints under my bed, the unfinished canvas on the easel, this ambition to be an artist? I'm getting rid of all of it.

This is what I do; I go home to my apartment that night, and I take a long look at the self-portrait I've been fussing with for the last three and a half years. I try to imagine this half-baked painting going out into the world representing my artistic vision and realize I'd rather die than reveal my appalling lack of talent to anyone who might see this.

As I place the box of paints and brushes on top of the metal garbage cans in front of my building, I imagine that an artist, someone younger and less cynical than me, will find them and put them to good use. I pause for a moment on the quiet dark street, breathing in the newly warm spring air. Just as I'm contemplating God's possible involvement in my moment of self-discovery, a car alarm goes off. God, is that you?

Seventeen:
Oxana Verklanski:
Simon Pryce
Gallery

May

Every month the gallery is transformed. An artist's vision takes hold of the white cube, and the space becomes something else. As April turns to May, Carlos Peres's photographs of cemeteries in Mexico come down and Oxana Verklanski's delicate sculptures of lace and beads and fragile white linen go up on our walls. These works are quiet and feminine and introspective. It so happens that this is exactly how I feel these days.

I've decided to call Zach Roberts. My excuse is finding out about the Finelli paintings in Europe for Lulu. I admit this is just an excuse. Truthfully I just want to talk to him, hear his voice.

I dial his cell phone number, wondering what country I might find him in. Is this the Berlin week, or is he still in London?

Isn't he supposed to be back in New York soon?

After three rings a female voice answers Zach's cell phone. "Zach Roberts, art magnate," she says into the receiver. It sounds like Alexis Belkin. "Want an art collection? He can get it for you. (Laugh)."

It *is* Alexis Belkin. What is she doing there? Wherever *there* is.

"Know nothing about art?" she continues on the other end of the line. "Don't worry, as long as you have the cash. (Laugh) For the right amount of money, he'll make you a connoisseur."

This is delivered into Zach's phone through giggles and squeals, as though Alexis is holding the phone away from him. "Who's calling, please?" she says.

I decide to hang up. Obviously.

"Oh, I can see it right here on the caller ID. Hi, Mia McMurray," she says. Alexis emphasizes my name loudly, as though for the benefit of her audience.

"Hey, Mia." I hear someone who sounds like Julia in the background.

"We're all in London. Everyone's in London this week," Alexis says. "Why aren't you here?"

Um, because I wasn't invited?

"Mia McMurray wants to talk to you,

319

Zach." I hear Meredith say this in a jokey tone, all laughs and implications. Someone should smack that girl.

"What is the nature of your call?" Alexis wants to know, imitating a snooty British accent. "Mia McMurray from the Simon Pryce Gallery, that fine bastion of mediocrity. You must have something to sell."

"She has something to sell, all right." There goes Meredith.

I'm about to hang up when Zach comes on the line. "McMurray," he says. "How are you?"

Now I feel like an idiot, of course, but I ask my question. "Do you know anything about some Finellis in Europe?"

"First, hello," he says. "Sorry about that."

"Very professional, that was," I say. Why do I say this? It sounds all wrong. Stiff. As if I care.

He laughs. "LaReine would not have been amused if it had been him on the other end. How *are* you?"

There's that loaded question. But this is a business call, remember. "What about these Finellis? Rumor has it you've got something to do with them."

"Me? I just heard about them today," he says, talking softly into the phone. "This is what I know. The Italian countess has ten paintings she's going to sell, not all at once. She put two of them out there, to gauge the market as she works out a deal with La-Reine. She's driving a hard bargain."

"She told Lulu he destroyed everything," I say, wondering if he's standing there in front of Alexis and friends. "Are the Weird Sisters still listening in?"

"I came outside," he says. "Finelli did destroy a lot. Apparently she siphoned off a few for herself along the way. Rent, gifts, payments on loans. I hear they're pretty great. LaReine is wetting his pants."

"Who told you that, Alexis?"

"I don't reveal my sources," he says, teasing. "I've missed you, McMurray."

"Everyone says you and Alexis are going into business together."

"Everyone," he says, "or just Alexis herself?"

I don't respond.

"Are you there?" he asks. "I'm going to Rome next. Why don't you meet me? I'll send you a ticket."

What does he mean by that? "That's inappropriate," I say. Although, Rome? I've always wanted to go to Rome. The airport on the way home from Florence doesn't count.

"Why, because we're in the same business?"

"No. Well, there's that. But how about because you have a girlfriend," I say. I sound petulant. Is Simon rubbing off on me?

The phone is going staticky. "Come to Rome," he says, as though he hasn't heard me.

I intend to say I've got plans, something involving a date with someone very impressive and important and, by the way, handsome. It comes out as "No . . . thanks."

I know what you're thinking. Sassy, Mia.

EIGHTEEN:
THE MUSEUM GALA
BENEFIT

May

In May, the streets of Chelsea are jammed with people. Every night, it seems, there are openings, parties, museum shows, galas, installations, performances. Every other day, there's a new gallery opening, filled with more art. As we head into auction week, everywhere I go, every magazine I open, every blog I read, all anyone seems to be talking or writing about is contemporary art. Frankly, it's tiresome. But that could be because I seem to be the only person in New York who is not either making art, collecting it, or talking about it.

Yet another magazine about art is launched this month. On the cover? Dane O'Neill and Lulu Finelli. And inside, a ten-page story entitled "Artists and Muses" featuring the two of them, the teacher and the student artist, the friend and the muse, in a variety of outfits. Lulu justifies it as promotion for Dane's new paintings, one of which is the portrait of her, and for the paintings she hopes one day to show and sell.

"It's building a brand," she explains. "I'm getting my name out there, and for Dane, he's planting the idea of the paintings before he shows them."

It's strange to see Lulu and Dane posing this way, like frivolous socialites on glossy magazine paper. Especially the shots in the studio. It's kind of undignified. But boy, are they photogenic.

Stranger still is the proposal Connie brings to Simon as we're getting our inventory ready to ship to Art Basel. She wants to go into business with him. The loss of the Finelli painting has so affected her, or so she tells him, that she can't go through the trauma again. "We could be partners," she proposes to him in a series of closed-door meetings. Actually I think what she says is, "I'm tired of getting fucked over by the art world," or something equally pornographic.

At first Simon claims to find the idea ridiculous. "Bloody hell," he says to me when he tells me about it. "Partners? With the likes of her?"

But he quickly warms to the notion when the sum of money she has in mind is divulged to be in the neighborhood of several hundred thousand dollars. A loan, she tells him, against future purchases. All he has to do is give her the right of first refusal on any work he's showing in the gallery.

Connie's smart, yes. But shortsighted. She's already a pariah in the gallery world, and this "partnership" ensures that no other dealers will want to sell to her. The collection of her dreams will come expensively and in a limited way, only through auctions and the few artists Simon can convince to show with him. But more than for a collection, I'm starting to realize, Connie's been searching for an identity.

Simon agrees to the proposal, and Connie starts to hang around the gallery like she belongs there, giving out the phone number so I have to answer calls from her Pilates teacher and the salesman at Bergdorf. A few blocks downtown my friend Lulu fields calls from magazine editors wanting to write stories about her and photograph her in fall's hottest looks and call her an emerging artist, when she hasn't even shown anyone her work. Jealous? Me? Not at all.

To celebrate the new partnership, Connie's taken a table at a benefit gala for her beloved museum on the Monday night that begins auction week. She's still hoping for a board position, poor dear. She buys one of the most expensive tables, and commands that Simon produce the photogenic Lulu Finelli and Dane O'Neill to occupy it.

"You're her friend," he says to me, leaning over my counter with his dripping tea bag. "Beg. Plead. Promise something. Just get them to come."

"Won't Dane O'Neill be sitting with his own dealer?"

He purses his lips at the mention of Pierre LaReine. "Throw this out for me," he says, handing me his tea bag.

"Please come," I say to Lulu on the phone. "And bring Dane."

"He hates those things," she says.

"Of course he does. He's supposed to hate them," I tell her. "We want him to hate them. But I'm sure you can get him to come."

"For you, my friend, of course. Are we sitting with you?"

"Not me. I wasn't invited," I say. "Thankfully."

"I don't want to go if you're not going to be there," she says.

"It's got to be names," I tell her. "Simon's bringing a date, a well-known divorced socialite. There seem to be a lot of those these days. But she is one of the really pretty ones."

"Who else?" Lulu wants to know.

"Carlos Peres and his wife, who doesn't speak English. And Connie's seizing the social-climbing opportunity. She's invited Robert and Jenna Bain to sit at her table."

"This sounds like the worst torture."

"It's a good opportunity for you," I tell her, half teasing. "Establish yourself as a presence in the art world on Dane's famous arm. Then when you show your work you'll already have name recognition."

"You're getting back at me, aren't you?" Lulu laughs. "Just because I did that shameless self-promoting magazine thing."

I'm thrilled that I don't have to go. I know there are people who enjoy getting dressed up and assembling with large crowds in support of causes they deem important. But I can't stand these kinds of big events. Ratfucks, they're called here in New York. I don't know who coined that term, but it seems appropriate enough.

Instead of the museum gala, I plan to go out with Azalea and Joey and some other friends that night and have some fun, something I seem to rarely do these days. I'm thinking Mexican and margaritas and an evening talking about anything and everything except the contemporary art world.

Simon comes in late the morning of the museum event. He stops at my desk on his way in with his tea. "You'd better wear something nice tonight. It's a black-and-white theme."

"To the museum? I wasn't invited."

"Of course you were." He puts the tea on the counter and drops his umbrella, fishing around in his pocket for his tube of candy. One of these days I'm going to tell him he looks like a pervert doing that, like he's playing with himself.

"What about the Bains?" I ask, certain he must be wrong.

"For Connie Kantor? Is that a joke?"

My shoulders slump. There's no time I feel more alone than at a black-tie party without a date. I really don't want to go. "I thought she invited them."

"She very well did. They're not available," he says, making quotation marks with his fingers to indicate what he thinks of their excuse.

My protest is halfhearted. I already know the response. "I had plans."

"You'll have to break them," he says,

gathering his things. He makes it sound like he's doing me a favor.

"Who's the tenth person?" I ask his back as he returns to his office.

He doesn't turn around. "Don't know. Someone available." He makes the quotation marks again.

I wear a vintage dress I bought a few years ago. At that time I was so distressed at the thought of attending a black-tie party that I considered quitting my job. I didn't even know what black tie meant; was I supposed to wear a tie? I exaggerate, of course, but I did know that whatever might be considered appropriate black-tie attire did not exist in my closet. Events that benefited something were not part of my sartorial vernacular.

Then I found this long black dress in a vintage shop. It's very simple, black silk, cut on the bias, and always appropriate. Even Azalea approves of this dress. I've worn it at least thirty times.

I've learned to make a point of skimming *Artforum* the afternoon before an event. That way I can always ask the person next to me if they'd read it as a way of starting a conversation with someone I'd inevitably have nothing in common with. Simon and I would always be in the cheap seats, and the men at my sides would usually be the cousin of one of the honorees or the lawyer who worked on the deal or some other low-rent gallerist. None of them has ever read *Artforum,* so I usually end up summarizing, and this passes the time for all of us.

I have to tell Azalea I can't go out for margaritas. She offers to bring the margaritas to my place to help me dress, because that's the kind of friend she is.

"I don't need help dressing," I tell her. "I only have the one choice, remember?"

"That old thing, how could I forget," she says. "I'll bring accessories. Maybe a Turkish shawl and prayer beads."

There's a backed-up line of people dressed in black and/or white trying to get to the entrance of the museum. The photographers are creating the traffic jam by having stopped someone whose picture they know they can sell to one of the magazines that cover these sorts of events. The publicists are all aflutter, trying to make sure their clients are discreetly pushed forward for a photo op.

I take a spot at the end of the line and follow the people slowly snaking past the photographers. As I get closer, the crowd shifts, and I can see the person who's causing the flurry of flashbulbs. It's Lulu, spectacular, in a frothy melon dress. With Dane O'Neill at her side, she's the money shot, even more so for daringly disregarding the suggested theme attire. No one who wanted to ensure their appearance in a photo spread on the event would dare not wear black and white, in deference to editorial coherence. But Lulu seems not to care whether her picture is taken.

"Lulu, over here." "Look this way." "Can we get one more, alone?"

She handles the attention of the press smoothly, no longer the reserved person who rubbed her hand against the letters of Jeffrey Finelli's name that first day in the gallery. One foot in front of the other like a trained model, she poses. She wears a shy smile on her face, chin down, as she turns this way and then the other, holding her dress out to show it off. I sense the melon dress is not a mistake. The photographers love it.

Then, suddenly, Connie appears between Lulu and Dane. She pulls them toward her on each side, waiting for the photographers to snap a shot of the three of them. But the photographers are done. They wave them along.

"Thank you," Lulu sings out.

She hugs me and whispers in my ear. "That woman Connie freaks me out. She keeps calling me. When I don't call her back, she calls again. Then she leaves messages like we're old friends and she can't believe I haven't called."

"She's just trying to connect," I say, in a pang of sympathy for poor lumpy Connie, in her unflattering black-and-white sequined dress. I watch her greet Simon with what looks like an inappropriately intimate kiss on the lips. I close my eyes to this vision, certain I haven't seen what I've just seen.

"She's hostile," Lulu continues. "I've never met anyone like this. She sends me e-mails wanting to know where I buy my clothes, what I like to eat, if I go to the gym. She asked me for diet tips. And then she gets angry when I don't respond."

Everyone wants to talk to Dane and the beautiful girl at his side. People circle around us, closing in on them, and I'm trapped. It's claustrophobic in the middle of the pile, especially when no one is talking to me.

"Are you his muse?" one collector asks of Lulu, pointing to Dane.

Lulu laughs. "I'm a painter," she says.

Oh, I admire how easily those words flow from her tongue. There's no stammer, no hesitation. Just a matter-of-fact tone, I'm a painter.

"Who represents you?"

"No one," she says. Again, no apparent embarrassment at this admission. "Yet."

I extricate myself from the collectors and dealers and trustees surrounding Dane and Lulu and get some air. The two of them are still at the center of a large group as the rest of us allow ourselves to be herded upstairs to dinner.

When I get to the table, I find my name on a place card, certain I'll be seated next to the wife who speaks no English. I'm correct on this one, of course. But there's a surprise on my other side. Zach Roberts.

That figures. Just as the sting has faded. And yet I feel a pull. I'm glad to see his name.

The president of the museum, a smooth sort with slicked-back hair and dapper patent leather shoes, gives several impassioned pleas over the microphone to get everyone to sit down.

Zach appears at my side, just as I've taken my chair. "McMurray."

"Hey," I say, aiming to sound like his girlfriend Alexis, frosty and disinterested.

"Don't say I never invited you anywhere," he teases, like a husband to a complaining wife. "Rome was gorgeous."

"Where's Alexis? Why aren't you sitting together?"

He gives me a curious look. "She's sitting with Martin Better."

"You weren't invited to join the big table?" It comes out more snide than I'd like.

"Connie insisted," he says. "Besides, I wanted to sit with you."

"I'm sure your girlfriend would appreciate that," I say. This time, I think it comes out right. Not snide.

He looks amused. "Which one?"

Just to show him I don't care whether he has one girlfriend or twenty, I turn to Carlos Peres's wife. "Are you having a nice time in New York?"

"Sí," she says.

So much for that conversational tactic. As the first course, a seafood salad, is placed before us, Zach leans into me. I breathe in his scent, fresh laundry and something else, like clean skin. I like the way he smells. "Did you hear the latest?" he says.

I try to resist getting pulled in by those words. I'm certain that whatever the latest is, I haven't heard it. "What?"

"LaReine's bringing *Lulu meets God* to Basel."

"It's being flipped?"

He gestures toward Lulu. "This could be her chance, if she really wants it. LaReine's doing a Finelli booth. With the other pieces that have mysteriously appeared on the scene."

"A whole booth? What other pieces?"

"Some of the contessa's closet stash, according to Alexis," he says.

After more imploring from the president, all five hundred guests at the museum's spring gala are seated and eating their seafood salad. These evenings always seem to involve many awards of some sort, and tonight there are enough that the program begins with the first course.

There's an award for philanthropy to the arts. That's nice. This award gets the big-money honoree and his friends to take many expensive tables.

And there's an award for lifetime achievement. That's smart too. A brand-name artist, adored by his public. More table sales. Then there's my favorite — the award for best new young artist. Collectors like this one because they feel they're getting inside information. Everyone always wants to know who the best new young artist is. Especially if they happen to own some of the work or can get their hands on some. Tonight's best new young artist is a nervous Chinese man who doesn't look very young at all.

During a break in speeches for the main course to be served, Simon comes to my side of the table to talk to Zach. He's quite dapper tonight, in his sharply cut Italian tuxedo and velvet slippers with skulls embroidered on them. There are skulls everywhere these days, it seems, on lots of paintings and on sweaters and shoes and hats. Even baby clothes, but only the cool babies being dragged to openings wear those.

"Mia McMurray," Simon whispers nastily. "That old frock again?"

Obviously he hasn't noticed my Turkish accessorizing. "Nice to see you too."

Simon puts one hand on the table and leans his narrow torso in between Zach and me so his back is rudely in my face.

When Simon leaves, I whisper to Zach, "Does he know about the LaReine booth?"

Zach shakes his head. His hair's gotten long, and a piece of it falls endearingly across his forehead. I resist the impulse to push it aside.

I watch Simon. He's standing on the other side of our table now, greeting Martin Better with a clamp of a hand on the shoulder. I wonder if Martin's still angry about losing out on the Finelli.

"Simon's going to have a fit when he finds out," I say to Zach.

All of a sudden Simon's face goes crimson. He begins to gesticulate, arms above his head like a monkey's. I've never seen him look so agitated. He must be choking on the tapenade toast that's being passed around.

Martin Better is just standing there, wearing a cat-got-the-canary look. Why doesn't he call 911? I push my seat back to check if Simon wants me to get an ambulance, perform the Heimlich, or fetch him a gin and tonic.

Simon opens his mouth. I expect to see a Thai shrimp or the tapenade toast come flying out.

Instead, it's a flood of obscenities, sounding suspiciously un-British, except for a few well-placed "bloody hell"s. "That bloody bullshit artist. Bloody hell. I'll fucking tear his arms out. I'll kill him."

So that's it. My prediction was right. He's having a fit.

Simon pulls at his hair as though he's going to tear it off. Wouldn't that be funny? If it turned out he was wearing a rug this whole time?

Simon clutches his heart and sinks to the floor.

"Clear some room," Martin Better shouts. "Clear some room."

Simon looks to be break-dancing. He leans on one hand on the polished floor, the other hand rubbing his chest. "Bloody hell, I'm having a heart attack."

I call 911 from my cell phone. As I give the dispatcher the information, I hear Connie say to Andrew, "I want that painting."

Simon slowly drops to the floor. A crowd has gathered. Simon peers up at the faces surrounding him. "What's it supposed to feel like?"

"Is your arm tingling?" someone calls out.

He nods, and then leans forward and puts his head in his hands. "I'm going to die."

At this, the crowd gets unruly. There is pushing as people try to get close enough to see what's happening. Someone shouts, "This is crazy." Someone else cries out in a panic, "Where's the ambulance?"

A doctor comes forward and puts his hand on Simon's chest. He's a plastic surgeon, not a heart specialist, but his presence seems to calm everyone down. Including Simon. "I think I'm okay," Simon says. He's not dying. He's simply allowing himself to feel. And what he feels is very, very angry.

The paramedics arrive. They insist on taking him to the hospital.

"I'm fine," Simon says, agitated now that they're going to interrupt his evening. But they're persuasive, and they load him onto a gurney and strap him down.

"My Smarties, get my Smarties," he yells in my direction as they take him away.

Connie says we can't leave. "There would be an empty table right at the front."

Andrew's already digging into the filet mignon before him. "Let's eat," he mumbles through a mouthful of rare meat.

"This is a fifty-thousand-dollar table," Connie hisses, noting hesitation from the rest of us. "Sit down."

"Do you want to go to the hospital?" Zach asks me. He gestures toward the pretty divorcée who was Simon's date, now chomping on her filet mignon. "She doesn't look like she's going anywhere."

"Do you think I should?" I can't hide my lack of enthusiasm.

"It wasn't a heart attack," he says. "But Simon might find comfort in having you with him."

"I'm the last person Simon would want to have with him," I say, cutting into my beef.

Zach says, "Connie tells me you two are

really close."

I look over to Connie, seated between Carlos and Dane, neither of whom talk to her. Carlos talks to his wife because he's the only one who can. Dane whispers into Lulu's ear, one hand playing with her hair. Connie watches Lulu, staring rudely, like she's taking mental notes.

"She says you've been together since you started working there," Zach says with a grin.

"Together? Like, sleeping together?" God, that's a gross thought.

He nods. "Not true?"

Do I imagine that's relief I see? "Not true," I say. "Absolutely not true."

"I didn't think so," he says. "But she told me to stay away from you."

And you listened, I want to say. But it comes out as, "Maybe she's fishing. You know, wanting to get you to find out if it's true."

"I think she's jealous of you," he says.

"Jealous of me? Trust me, no one is jealous of me. Especially not Connie Kantor." I don't really want to delve into Connie's psyche.

He gives me an odd look. "Well, I'm glad to hear it's not true. You deserve someone really nice. Someone who appreciates you."

"Someone single," I add.

"Single helps," he says.

Later, he offers to take me home. I almost say yes. After two glasses of wine, I've forgotten about his job and his girlfriend and the fact that I'm never letting myself get hurt by anyone in the art world again. After two glasses of wine, I want to kiss him. But I give myself a stern talking-to and, very prim and polite, I say, "No, thank you."

He looks surprised. And disappointed. Or it could just be the light.

I stop at the ladies' room before heading out. There's a long line, of course. So I'm surprised, by the time I get outside, to see that Zach is still there, in front of the museum, looking for a taxi. He's alone. I consider taking him up on his offer of a ride downtown.

I'm about to walk over to him when Alexis rushes over to him from a cluster of women.

"Zach," she calls out. She grabs his arm and whispers into his ear.

I turn away, disappointed. I start to walk in the other direction, thinking I'll find a cab on a less crowded corner.

"McMurray." It's Zach, from a taxi window. "Come on," he says. "A bunch of people are coming down to my place."

Alexis pokes her head around him. "Don't be a stick-in-the-mud. Everyone's coming."

I hesitate.

"Hop in," he says, pushing open the door. I climb in. Oh, why not?

He slides down so he's in the middle, sandwiched between Alexis and me. I can feel the warmth of his leg pressed up against mine. Okay. This is awkward.

The two of them don't seem to notice any awkwardness. They chat amicably about a restaurant Zach went to with some German collectors when he was in Berlin, and that leads to talk about other restaurant meals and a chicken vindaloo that Zach says was the best thing he's ever tasted in his life.

There are already about twenty people in Zach's apartment when we arrive. Half the faces are familiar, belonging to the young art crowd. Gallery staff, baby collectors, some not-yet-emerging artists. There are drinks on the kitchen counter, and someone's turned on the music.

Behind us, more people come through the door. They all seem to adore Zach, calling out his name. There are a lot of hugs and loud exclamations. "Yo, dude." "This place rocks." "What're we drinking?" "Sick crib."

I accept a glass of wine. I'm greeted by a few friendly faces, and I'm happy to be pulled into the group. Every once in a while I pretend I'm an extrovert.

I'm aware of Zach's presence, across the crowded room, but I mingle. Every few minutes my gaze is drawn to Zach, there to my right, or then just to my left. I can't help but seek him out with my eyes, even as I concentrate on the person before me.

Later, Lulu and Dane arrive together just as I'm moving toward a door on the far side of the kitchen that looks like it might lead to a bathroom. "Dane O'Neill," the crowd seems to announce in a clamor at the sight of him.

Lulu follows me toward the door, looking for the bathroom too.

"Did you hear about Pierre LaReine?" I ask, although I'm sure she's heard. She's more connected in the art world than I'll ever be. "He's doing a Finelli booth. Five paintings, including, get this, *Lulu Meets God and Doubts Him*."

Lulu's face shows her surprise. "The guy who bought it is selling it already?"

"He's collecting video art."

There's no answer on the door. I push it open, thinking it leads to the bathroom, but we're in Zach's bedroom. It gives me a sudden small thrill to be there, looking at his bed. It's king-size, with four crisp white pillows at the head and a brown-and-white comforter. There's a chair in one corner and more black-and-white photographs on the walls. Now I recognize two of them as Zach's own works. He's got an interesting eye for quirky images that have a sense of humor.

"Nice room," Lulu says, taking it in.

"The bathroom must be through there," I say, pointing.

"Why wouldn't he have given my painting back to Simon to sell?" Lulu asks, still admiring one of the pictures on the wall.

"Probably because LaReine has better video artists. And a gallery in L.A."

"The other stuff must be paintings the contessa was hiding, right?"

"I guess so. You go first," I say, pointing toward the bathroom.

She goes into Zach's bathroom first, and I wait, looking around the warmly lit room where Zach sleeps. Yes, it *is* a nice room.

When Lulu comes out of the bathroom, I go in. It's late, almost one, and I have to work tomorrow, so I should be getting home.

As I move through Zach's bedroom on my way back to the party, I'm stopped by a stack of photographs piled loosely on the bedside table. The stack is held in place by a small clock, and I probably would not have noticed it but for a flash of a pattern. It's a gray and brown and beige swirl on a sweater that I keep at the gallery to combat the chill.

The pattern catches my eye, and I look at the picture on the top of the stack. It's an image of a smiling girl who looks familiar. She has one hand outstretched. That's me, I suddenly realize.

I pick up the print and examine it. Zach Roberts has a photo of me at his bedside?

This is how Zach finds me, when he comes into the room then: standing at his bed holding the photograph of me.

"Hey, you," he says, his features softening as he smiles at me.

I hold up the picture. "From that day in the gallery?"

He nods. "Do you like it?"

Someone comes through the open door behind him then. It's a guy I'd heard referred to as one of three "college buddies" of Zach's who were at the party "to meet hot art chicks," according to the one who was introduced to me earlier.

"Art boy," this one calls out. "Oh, sorry." He stops in the doorway. "There's a dude dancing on the table. He's got no fucking clothes on."

You know you're at a good party when Dane O'Neill gets naked.

Nineteen: Mira Tokuno: New Work, Simon Pryce Gallery

June

At the beginning of June Mira Tokuno's watercolors on enamel bring an entirely different mood to the gallery, belying the hectic energy that surrounds us as we prepare for the Basel art fair.

It's not a very good show, but the soft watercolors suit the new Simon. Let's call this the postmodern Simon, a kinder, gentler version of the old Simon, although just as peculiar. Ever since his faux heart attack, he's taken to being almost nice. He's calling me "darling" and "sweetie" and sometimes — this one scares me the most — "sweetie darling," like he's a character on *Ab Fab.* And twice he's complimented me on my outfit. It's a white blouse with a gray A-line skirt, not exactly fashion-forward, but he must like something about it, as he would never have done that before.

The Keeping-It-Real collector with the

orange sneakers gets Simon to take up yoga. This means Simon buys himself a special mat and one of those silly little carriers to transport it. He takes to drinking green tea instead of Earl Grey and asks me to pick up some spelt bread to keep in the gallery kitchenette.

Even the news that Carlos Peres is leaving him to seek new representation doesn't cause Simon too much stress. Carlos is dumping him for . . . you guessed it, Pierre LaReine, and he informs Simon of this by a terse note faxed to the gallery at three o'clock one morning. And yet Simon's attitude was calm and accepting. He shrugged it off easily.

This new attitude worries me. I'd gotten very comfortable with the way he treated me, a patronizing combination of familiarity and disdain. I'm afraid this new kindness means he's going to fire me. I seem to spend an inordinate amount of time worrying about being fired from a job I now realize I don't want. This is the sort of person I have become.

The morning of the Tokuno opening, Simon lingers at my desk, waxing philosophic over his cup of Tazo Zen. This has become something of a habit, ever since the apoplectic fit that turned out to be a release of built-up internalized rage rather than a brush with death. "I've been dealt a hand of perspective," he says, repeating something I've heard him say to anyone who will listen. "Given the gift of clarity."

This is how he explains that he's not unhappy that LaReine is controlling the Finelli estate. I suspect he lies to himself, and everyone around him, when he claims not to be resentful, saying, "Life is too bloody short to be lived in the petty."

This morning he's lamenting his lack of legacy. "Mia, who is going to inherit all this?" he asks of me, as though the gallery is a global enterprise. "I work and work and then, at the end of the day? What will happen to my business? If I die, it's just over."

"Maybe you should get married," I suggest, although this is a terrible idea. Simon could never be a husband.

He shakes his head as though acknowledging that he'd be a terrible husband; getting married is not the solution.

"Have children," I add, another awful suggestion.

Simon seems to realize these are bad ideas. He ignores me and moves on to another favorite topic, grumbling about the position of his booth at the Basel art fair.

He's forgotten, I think, that it's part of the fun to grumble about the position of one's booth. Grumbling is a luxury afforded only to those dealers invited to participate in Art Basel, and Simon is lucky to be included at all.

"All the way in the back on the second floor, we'll be lucky if anyone finds us. Only if they're desperate for a toilet will they happen upon us."

And he's worried about the pieces he's bringing. Too many paintings, when collectors want installations, or too many photographs, when taste is shifting back to painting. He only has one video.

"These days people want video art, Mia," he declares, with the world-weary tone of a philosopher who understands that the most fundamental thing about the human condition is that it will never be understood. "Even if it's hard to live with."

When he finishes his tea, he leaves the cup on my counter and walks slowly through the gallery, lost in thought. He leaves me in charge of pretty much everything. The hanging of the Tokuno show, the packing of the inventory for Basel, the phones. There are ten art handlers in the gallery awaiting my instruction as Simon locks himself in his office.

Needless to say, I'm feeling particularly frazzled when I check my cell phone voice mail. The message goes like this: "I'm doing a story on up-and-coming women in the Chelsea gallery world."

If you must know, I'm flattered. I know, I know. I have no interest in actually being such a thing, an "up-and-coming woman in the gallery world." But still, it's nice to be acknowledged as such. And if I'm going to be totally honest, I might as well recognize that my feelings might be slightly influenced by the press attention Lulu Finelli's been enjoying. I've never gotten a call from a writer before.

"I got your name from Alexis Belkin at LaReine Gallery," a man named Michael Genner says to my voice mail system. "I've talked to Julia Di Matteo and Meredith Long already."

He speaks in a friendly tone, and there's an implication; Alexis, Julia, and Meredith are attached to the piece. This makes it sound like all the gallery girls who matter are going to be in it. If this is a portrait of the contemporary gallery world as it exists right now, who wants to be left out? Not me.

Does this mean there's a possibility I really am an up-and-coming woman in the

Chelsea gallery world? Maybe this is how it happens. You start out wanting to be an artist. Like Simon. Then you realize no one is going to push you there. So the shift begins. You take on another role, working with artists rather than being one yourself. You let go of the dream, and help others find theirs.

I decide not to return the call.

Simon leaves the gallery at lunchtime, claiming to be taking a client to Pastis. Connie has popped in, a nasty habit she's gotten into since she's become Simon's silent partner. When she hears Simon say he's going to lunch, she jumps at him. "Who? Who're you having lunch with? I should be there. Shouldn't I be there?"

Give it up, I want to tell her. He's going to church. But I can't let him know I know. It's not out of respect for his privacy; it's just that I would never admit that I cared enough to spy on him.

Lulu stops by to say hello after they leave.

"I called her," she says, sounding breathless. "The contessa. I wanted to know what she did with the canvas I left in my uncle's studio in Florence. And I asked her how she got these paintings."

"What did she say?"

"She said these were her paintings. They weren't *in* the studio." As she talks, Lulu looks over at the first of the watercolors now hanging on the walls, ready to be revealed to the public this evening. "Nice," she says. "These are good."

Since the Finelli show, Simon's begun to be considered a more established dealer. I've noticed that visitors to the gallery are more inclined to like the works on our walls now. The Carlos Peres show was a good example of that. Even Lulu seems to view Simon's name as a sort of Good Housekeeping Seal of Approval now that he's become known for having discovered Count Jeffrey Finelli in the studio above a *salumeria* in Florence.

"What did the contessa say about your painting?" I ask her. "The one you left behind?"

"She did her mysterious routine. You can't know before you know, or something like that. I asked her to send me the canvas. She said, I'll do something better than that. She almost sounded as though she felt bad, although she's a pretty good actress." Lulu talks to me from the center of the gallery, still looking at the Tokuno paintings.

"She was adamant that I go to Basel for the art fair. She says she has something to tell me. I told her she said that the last time. She said now she knows for sure."

"Are you going?"

Lulu drifts back toward my desk as she answers my question. "Here's the thing. There is something so unseemly about fighting over the things the dead leave behind. But *Lulu Meets God and Doubts Him,* that was a kind of inheritance from my uncle. Even if he didn't intend for me to own it. He wanted to pass something on to me. And I want it."

"I understand," I say.

Lulu leans on the counter over my desk. "Do you? Because I don't even understand it myself. Why do people want to *own* pieces of art?"

"Well, for you, I imagine it feels like a connection. To your family. To some of the mysteries that families contain."

"Maybe that's why anyone collects anything," Lulu says, with a deep sigh. She looks out the glass wall, as though searching for something. "To feel a connection."

We both go quiet then, thinking.

Suddenly Lulu brightens. "How much will LaReine ask for it?"

"I don't know," I say. "And who knows if he's already sold it? Martin Better still wanted it. And if not to him, LaReine will have sold it to anyone on a long list of potential collectors."

"Why would Pierre LaReine bring a piece of art to an art fair to sell if it was already sold?"

"To show that he has it," I say.

"But isn't the whole point of an art fair to sell art? Why have it if the work's already sold?"

"Most of the stuff at the fair is sold before it gets there," I explain. This is a question I needed to have answered myself, back when I first started. "But the dealers still want to have a respectable booth that represents a vision. Otherwise they won't get invited back."

After she leaves the gallery, I play the story back from the beginning, starting when Jeffrey Finelli came through the door with his cheese. Then there was the fight with Simon and his use of the word *leech.* Then Finelli's death the night of the opening, and the sudden interest that generated. The niece who inherited his artistic talent but not the painting he made of her. The wily contessa manipulating the market for the work that she owns. And now, the painting reappearing in Basel only three months later.

As I'm recalling the first time I saw the

painting of Lulu and the way it's changed me over the past months, I feel my creative juices begin to flow. It feels the way it used to feel when I would get excited about a painting I'd want to make. It's a high unlike any I've ever been able to re-create artificially.

I dial the reporter's number. I do have a story for him. As I punch the numbers into my phone, I warm to the idea of myself as the person he described. "Up-and-coming." By the time the phone begins to ring, I'm pretty convinced by the idea of myself as the next Marian Goodman. I can be easily persuaded. Especially by me.

"Have I got a story for you," I tell the reporter when he answers. Certainly a brash up-and-coming gallery girl talks like this, telling the story behind the painting. I can feel the creative urge taking hold of me. The story behind the painting, that's the kind of story I like.

"Hold on," he says. "Let me get a pen."

When he comes back on the phone, I become completely caught up in the opportunity. I vaguely realize that tossing my usual restraint in the presence of a reporter probably isn't a great idea, but something seems to have come untethered inside me. The nervousness passes as soon as I start talking.

"My story begins as a good story should," I tell him, crafting the beginning of the tale. "With a dead man."

I dig down deep into my creative soul and pull up a persona to offer this reporter. The up-and-coming gallery girl. Someone who always knows the poop. The girl behind the concrete-and-metal desk who is always, always watching.

"His death is suspicious," I say. Like too rich or too thin, I don't believe there is such a thing as too creative.

"The dealer is British, or so he claims. His accent is suspiciously erratic. He's straight. Or gay. No one knows for sure. But he's very well dressed."

"Simon Pryce, your boss," the reporter clarifies. "How long have you worked there?"

"Over five years," I say. "But they're like dog years."

"So thirty-five years," he says. He sounds like he's enjoying my story.

I take up where I left off. "The police don't sense any foul play."

"You think there are hedge-fund speculators involved?" the writer asks eagerly.

"No." I'm emphatic. I'm working the idea

of dealer as villain here. "I blame the dealer."

I'm warming up. I like myself as a storyteller. I tell him about the sudden demand for the paintings, especially *Lulu Meets God,* and how it's all part of the dealer's nefarious plan. "Everyone agrees. It's a crazy painting. It has intense powers of inspiration."

"Now here's the strangest part," I whisper into the phone. "Simon paid for the paintings up front."

"Really," the reporter says. "That's not how it normally works."

"Exactly. And there's a problem," I say. "The artist gave the painting to his long-lost niece," I say. "The girl in the picture. She has his eyes. And his talent."

I go on to tell him about Lulu and the surprise phone call. "There's even a devious contessa. She tells the young muse there is nothing of her uncle's work for her to inherit. But the contessa has been hiding paintings."

I relay how many people were hoping to live with this one painting. "Not just collectors. Dane O'Neill was in it too. And then Pierre LaReine got involved. The more expensive it got, the more everyone wanted it."

The reporter asks me a lot of questions about Simon and LaReine and also about me. His questions seem vague, but my responses are pointed. I guess I become kind of besotted with my new notion of myself as an art world commentator, because my answers get more and more colorful.

It's only when I've talked for too long that the nervousness I felt before I started talking comes back. Suddenly it hits me. "You're not writing about Chelsea gallery girls."

Silence on the other end of the phone. But so brief, I could almost imagine it didn't happen. "I'm interviewing a lot of people, trying to get a real insider's look at the contemporary art scene in New York. We're in the middle of a bubble, you know."

"It's not a profile, then?"

"More of a pastiche," he says.

I take "pastiche" to mean I'm not an up-and-coming girl in the Chelsea gallery world after all. This comes as a relief.

The reporter is explaining about how the art market has changed with all the new money being pumped into it, blah, blah, blah, when Zach comes into the gallery. I turn so I'm not facing the door. I don't really want to see him. I mean, I do want to see him, but not now. Not in this context.

I cover my ear so I can listen to Michael Geller on the phone. Zach leans over my desk and takes a piece of notepaper. I feel his presence in the area of my heart. Forget sassy — I resolve to be friendly and businesslike. That's it. Be still, foolish heart.

On the paper he writes, *Burger tonight?*

Busy, I scrawl underneath his words. It's not a lie. I'm going out with Azalea and friends after the opening. Geller is saying something predictable about hedge-fund managers and what they've done to blow up the art bubble, and I try to concentrate.

Tomorrow night, Zach writes.

BUSY. This too is not a lie. Tomorrow night I'm meeting Lulu for Chinese and backgammon, a weekly event. I slide the notepaper toward him and turn fully around in my chair so my back is to him. I'm trying to listen to the reporter. I think Zach should just leave.

"Call me if you think of anything you want to add," the reporter says before hanging up. "I'm looking for collectors I could talk to who go to graduate student shows."

I click the phone shut, but I don't turn around right away. First, I take a deep breath. I thought I'd gotten over Zach. As usual, I was wrong.

"Thursday night, then," Zach says as I turn around. He's moved to the middle of the gallery, inspecting one of the watercolors.

"I'm busy," I say. I'm not about to go out with him again just so he can find out what I know about the other Finellis. If he wants to know what Lulu is up to, he can call her himself.

"Saturday, July seventeenth," he throws out at me, joking.

"I'm sure I'll be busy," I tell him, feeling awfully proud of myself.

And then the words just come flowing out of me. "I don't see how you can keep asking me out when you're going out with her." Not friendly. Definitely not businesslike.

"Her, who?" he says as a slow grin spreads across his face.

"You know who," I say. I'm getting heated up. What's he doing, smiling at me like that?

"McMurray," Zach says through his grin. "I never took you for the jealous type."

"Jealous?" I'm sputtering with indignation. "This has nothing to do with jealous. It has to do with ethics. It was wrong of you to invite me to dinner when you have a girlfriend."

He laughs now. It's infectious, yes, as always, but I don't let it infect me. "I don't have a girlfriend," he says.

"Now you're going to lie about it? Last I heard, you and Alexis Belkin were getting married at the LaReine Gallery in the fall."

"Where are you getting your information?" he asks, still in that teasing tone. He comes back toward my desk. "You've got to get some better sources. You'll never get anywhere in the art world if you don't have access to good information."

I stand to face him as he comes around the counter. He's much taller, and I feel almost dainty as I look up at him. "Who says I want to get anywhere in the art world?"

"Alexis and I are friends. Colleagues," he says. "That's it."

"That's not what I've heard," I say. I sound petulant, wanting it to be true.

He reaches out and lifts my chin with one finger. "Is that why you've been so weird?"

"You're the one who was weird. I don't go out with anyone who is attached to someone else."

"I'm not attached," he says. "Yet."

We hold there for a few seconds, his hand under my chin, our eyes locked.

"Hey, are you going to Venice?" he asks, dropping his hand and looking away.

"Of course."

"I'm leaving the day after tomorrow," he says, looking back down at me. "I'm going with a client to Korea and then Tokyo. Can we meet in Venice? Can we have dinner together there?"

I nod. He kisses me gently on the cheek. It's just a slight brush of his lips against my skin, but it burns with electricity.

At the opening that evening I've got a bounce in my step. Even Simon notices my cheery mood. "Mingle, mingle," he says. "Watercolors agree with you, sexy them up."

I do my best, make the Keeping-It-Real collector feel like a champion for being one of the first Finelli buyers. I'm about to suggest he continue his winning streak with one of the Tokuno paintings when Meredith, Julia, and Alexis file into the gallery. They're all wearing the same dress, or a variation of it, a strappy black column.

They gather around me, ignoring Orange Sneakers until I tell them he's a hot new collector. "He was smart enough to get in on the Finelli action early," I tell them. "He's building a great collection."

In no time, Alexis has deftly pulled him aside.

"Why did you tell me she was going out with Zach?" I ask Meredith and Julia as soon as Alexis is out of earshot. I've asked too quickly. Meredith and Julia both eyeball me, nosy. Why the interest? Why, indeed.

"They were just friends," Meredith says. She waves her hand dismissively, like this is old news.

"You said she was planning a wedding," I remind her.

Julia lets out a ladylike snort. "She was. He wasn't."

"She was hoping it would turn into something more," Meredith explains, still watching me carefully.

"She's all about something more," Julia says, surprisingly catty. She points to Alexis. "And some guys offer more MORE than others. Even if they're inconveniently married."

Meredith peers into my eyes intently, the interrogator. "You interested?"

"Of course not." I protest. Too much again. "I'd never go out with anyone in the art world."

"You're so right. Me neither," Julia adds.

Meredith says nothing. She's sleeping with a married dealer. What's she going to say?

"I thought they were going into business together," I say. That was the part that made it seem so logical.

"Wishful thinking, on her part," Meredith

says. "She wanted him to put up some money so she could get involved. Trouble is, he doesn't have any."

"Once she realized he doesn't have money, she knew he wasn't for her," Julia adds, unnecessarily. "Poor Zach."

That night I allow myself to indulge in a romantic fantasy involving Zach and me in a gondola in Venice, riding along the Grand Canal. The gondola part is cheesy, so I try to replace it with one where he tosses me onto the bed. I like that one too, especially the part where, in the morning, wrapped in nothing but our sheets, we throw open the shutters and have breakfast on the terrace overlooking the canal. I've fallen for him, I realize, stupidly. That I seem to have had no say in the matter is vexing, to say the least. But I can't stop thinking about him.

To put him out of my mind, I take out the notebook Lulu gave me. The creative urges that were stirred in me that morning haven't settled back down. I start to write, letting my hand flow over the pages. It feels good. It used to feel this good when I put brush to canvas for the first time in a while, like that night at Jeffrey's studio in Florence. For now, I delude myself into thinking it always feels like this.

TWENTY:
THE VENICE
BIENNALE
VENICE, ITALY

Every other year in early June the international art scene travels to Venice for the Biennale. Participating countries are given pavilions in the Giardini where art is displayed, and over the course of the summer and into the fall thousands of people come from all over the world to view the works. For the dealers and collectors and museum staff and trustees and critics who comprise what might be termed the "art crowd," there is only one time to visit the Venice Biennale, and that's for the opening. The opening takes place, conveniently, the week before Art Basel.

This year, Simon has us staying at the ultra-luxurious Danieli hotel where Connie Kantor has taken a suite without her husband. I'm so excited to see Zach, I wouldn't mind if we were staying in a youth hostel. I'm just happy to be there. Simon is happy to be there too. For once, he feels like he belongs.

I check into the hotel the day before the opening. I'm fully expecting to have a message or several from Zach waiting for me. And frankly, I wouldn't have been shocked to find some kind of flower delivery in my room. A bottle of champagne, perhaps. Chocolates, even. But there is nothing waiting for me. I check that my BlackBerry is working. It is.

I check with the Italian telephone operator again. "Are you sure, no messages for Mia McMurray?"

There's a pause. "Oh, yes, signora. Here is one. I'm so sorry. Shall I send it to your room?"

Ah, I think. Of course. "Just read it to me."

"Is from a Signora Connie Kantor. Don't be late for dinner tonight. Nine o'clock. Harry's Bar."

Okay then. Perhaps his flight was delayed. I'm sure I'll see him at dinner.

I take extra care getting dressed that evening. I've brought three dresses, chosen with Azalea's help. I try them all on multiple times. I finally settle on the lavender one, although it seems too colorful. Very mother-of-the-bride, I think, as I check the mirror again.

I'm early. Connie's invited fourteen people

to dinner, and all of them arrive late. Even Simon is late. As each person comes into the crowded restaurant I look up, expecting to see Zach. There's an empty place next to me the whole night. But he never shows up.

Connie and the new Simon are getting along extremely well down at the other end of the table as I sit through what seems an endless dinner. Connie giggles and flirts. And Simon? Simon seems to find her adorable. It's enough to make a girl lose her appetite entirely. This is one way to lose five pounds.

Back at the hotel, there are no messages. No e-mails. No text messages. No voice mail on my cell phone. Nothing.

I convince myself he must have had a problem with a flight and take an Ambien to fall asleep. I'm certain I'll see him in the morning.

The next day I check my e-mail before I even fully wake up. Nothing from Zach. I go to the opening of the Biennale and wander the pavilions alone. I don't see any of the art. I'm only looking for Zach.

That evening, there is still no word from him. Now I start to get worried. Even if he had been leading me on with no intention of taking me to dinner, he wouldn't miss

Venice. He couldn't miss Venice. This is his livelihood. Something must have happened to him.

As I get dressed for a party Simon's insisting I attend with him, I start to get angry. Something had better have happened to him. There's no excuse for no communication.

That night I run into Ricardo, the dealer from Milan who was the last guy I let myself fall for.

"Cara Mia," he says to me, as though he didn't ever use the words "I love you" as a euphemism.

"Hello?" I say, as if I can't quite recall his name.

"You don't remember me?" He looks disappointed.

I remember all too well.

In the morning, as I'm leaving for the airport, I check my e-mail one more time. I've looked at it so many times I don't expect to actually see Zach's name in my in-box. But there it is. With one word in the subject box: *Sorry.*

"Too complicated to explain. See you in Basel," he writes.

That's it?

On the short plane ride my notebook gives

me solace. It was a small gift, a nice gesture probably conceived in a quick moment of thoughtfulness without regard for any wider implications, but somehow it's turning into something more meaningful. I lose myself in my words, trying to capture my feelings . . . humiliation? Disappointment? Shame? Yet underneath all of that is a lingering sense of hope.

Twenty-One:
Art Basel
First Choice:
BY INVITATION OF THE GALLERIES
Basel, Switzerland

June

I've been to Basel three times — not including three trips to Miami for Art Basel Miami, the sister fair that occurs in December — and my favorite thing about it is the sausage they sell in the center courtyard of the convention center. Otherwise, it's simply exhausting.

Art fairs mean grueling hours on my feet in high heels. Whether in Switzerland or London or South Beach, it doesn't matter, because I hardly see the outside. We do well at the fairs, selling Simon's random selection of artists to third-rate collectors and people who either want souvenirs or just stuff to hang on their walls. Even if we didn't do well, we'd still have to go to Basel. You can't not go to Basel.

I used to feel resentful at fairs. I wanted

to be the one with the work on the walls, not the one trying to sell it. But now, who am I to complain? I have a job, for one thing. And it's a job that involves glamorous-sounding travel to foreign countries. Even if it is in the company of a dyspeptic Brit who continues to ponder the question of really, why do American women have such large bums.

I unpack and take a shower before I meet Simon at the convention center to start installing our booth. We have two days before the VIP opening preview to get it right, and Simon is always extremely disorganized and insecure about his choices of where to hang things. He needs my help.

I show my exhibitor's badge to the Swiss German security boss at the entrance to the convention center where the fair takes place. He scrutinizes my face, comparing it with my badge a few times before nodding and letting me pass. In the past collectors have been known to sneak into the fair before the opening, using badges handed along by sly gallery staff, but now the Swiss are getting strict.

Every year there are a couple of stories about known collectors or advisers attempting to disguise themselves in wool caps and old shoes, only to be thrown out.

If they don't get caught, they buy up the most desirable pieces before the fair opens, and this makes everyone else cranky, including the fair directors. This year I hear one of the consultants who was tossed last year has hired a theatrical hair and makeup person to completely disguise him.

The Swiss guard waves me in, but I'm stopped again just as I move into the fair space. There she is at the very first booth on the first floor, the most prominent booth in the fair. This booth belongs to . . . the LaReine Gallery. The rest of the Finellis are still crated, but leaning against the wall, unwrapped and waiting to be hung, is the young painted Lulu in *Lulu Meets God and Doubts Him.* She's propped against the most prominent spot in the double-wide LaReine booth, and her eyes meet mine as I come into the convention center.

I wonder if she's been sold. Is it possible that the painting is available? Might Lulu herself stand a chance to do business with LaReine? I doubt it, no pun intended. A lot of the more well known work in Basel is spoken for by now, dealers having e-mailed jpegs around the world in an anticipatory flurry, building excitement and generating a hush-hush kind of buzz that gets louder and louder in the days leading up to the opening of the fair.

I head upstairs. The Simon Pryce Gallery booth is tucked away at the back of the second floor, near the bathrooms. It's a terrible location. Simon was right to complain.

"Sweetie, darling," Simon greets me when I get to the booth. "Finally you're here."

We work together into the afternoon, arguing in an amiable sort of way about placement. At the end of the day I realize I haven't eaten, and I head outside with a sausage and a Diet Coke, or "coca light," as they call it here. I sit on a low wall in front of the convention center, feeling jet-lagged.

When I spot Zach loping across the plaza with his long, graceful stride, my heart skips a beat. I'm angry at him, I have to remind myself.

When he sees me, his whole face lights up. "McMurray," he says, moving in my direction. "I'm so sorry I didn't make it to Venice."

"Oh, you weren't there?" As though I hadn't noticed. That's good, Mia. Cold and disinterested.

He looks hurt. "You weren't worried about me?"

"Not at all," I lie. "I didn't realize you weren't there."

"You're lying," he says. "Admit it, you were worried."

"Why would I have been worried?"

"You weren't expecting to see me there?"

Now I really lay it on thick. "I guess if I'd thought about it, yes. But I'm not one to keep tabs."

He looks incredulous. And angry too. "Keep tabs? We were supposed to have dinner."

"Were we?"

I've rendered him speechless, I see with satisfaction. He stares at me, and I return the stare. His eyes search my face, checking to see if I'm telling the truth. Just when it seems he's going to make a move and either walk away or kiss me, we're distracted by a familiar voice.

"I'm an exhibitor, dammit, not a criminal!"

We turn at the same time to see Connie Kantor being escorted out of Art Basel by two of the Swiss security personnel. They have her by the arms.

"I work in a gallery," she screams, kicking at one of the guards.

They unceremoniously drop her arms, and she stumbles to the ground. The guards speak to her in Swiss German, probably telling her to keep out of the fair until it's open.

Connie catches sight of the two of us watching her. "You could have warned me," she says, pointing at Zach. "You said everyone sneaks in."

"Only the most recognizable collectors get kicked out," Zach tells her. "So congratulations. You've arrived."

"That damn piece better not be sold by the time I get in there tomorrow," she says. "I can't get anyone at LaReine to call me back." She stands and smoothes down her too-tight jeans, self-consciously dusting herself off.

"There's a whole fair. Two full floors of art," Zach says. "You'll find something to buy."

"I want the Finelli that was stolen from me," she says, glaring at me to remind me of my role in this.

She stomps off, and Zach turns back to me. "Now, where were we?" he says, and before I can answer he's wrapped his arms around me and leaned me back on the wall. He kisses me. It's a deep and passionate kiss that lasts a long time. Nothing has ever felt more right.

When we come up for air, he says, "I've been wanting to do that for a long time."

"What took you so long?"

"Come on," he says, taking me by the hand and helping me down from the wall. "I was with Samuel Fong. We were on his plane, and then there was a problem with one of the wheels." He goes on about the plane trouble and no cell service in the remote town where they'd landed and his BlackBerry locked away in the back of the plane. It doesn't matter, I want to tell him. I'm just enjoying matching his stride as he leads me across the plaza to the Swissotel where we're both staying.

"You're in room 212," he says.

"How do you know?"

"Give me your key," he says as we get into the elevator.

He opens the door to my room and swings it open, allowing me to step into the room first. The entire room is filled with white flowers. There are roses and calla lilies and peonies everywhere, on every surface of my small room. The smell is intoxicating.

"Sorry," he says. And I realize he's nervous too. "Is it like a funeral? I thought all white for you. Minimal."

"It's beautiful."

He gives me a sweet sheepish grin. "Is it goofy? It is, isn't it? Sorry."

"Stop saying sorry."

That's when he throws me down on the bed. Our kiss quickly erases any doubt I might have had about whether this was a good idea. The first time we make love, it's rushed. The second time we take it slow. I've never known anything to feel this good.

We spend the rest of the night in my bed. I try to commit Zach's body with its long limbs and pale skin to memory. He makes me laugh. I think I'm in love.

In the morning I'm a little sore, but I've become one of Them, those annoying happy cheerful people you see around sometimes. Cheerful? I'm ecstatic.

At eleven o'clock the fair opens for "First Choice." This is the VIP advance-viewing time for collectors who hold special passes, allowing them access before the two o'clock preview. It's a group that includes any and all persons vaguely able to claim even the slightest interest in contemporary art, a horde that will cram the corridors and jam the booths, unwilling to wait until the following day when the fair will be less crowded because then they will no longer be a Very Important Person. Besides, everything will be sold.

When I walk into the convention center in the morning, I'm stopped by what I see. On the most prominent wall, enjoying pride of place, is *Lulu Meets God and Doubts Him.* Her smile seems to take in the rest of the booth as though she's in on the joke. There *is* some kind of joke going on. To the left of the Lulu painting is another one. Yes, another Lulu painting. Also signed with a Finelli flourish. But this one is the canvas Lulu painted herself and left behind in the studio in Florence. Unfinished. And Untitled.

The painting is still rough. But the canvas has been mounted like the other paintings, and in the context of these other Finellis it almost fits. It looks like very early work, a less evolved product of the same artist. I'm shocked to see it there. But the painting itself doesn't look shockingly out of place.

There are also two portraits of the contessa, one vertical and dark, the other a horizontal nude. They're gorgeous. The first is called *The Contessa in Conflict.* The other, *Woman Thinking Pure Thoughts.* Rich, saturated colors. Haunting images. They're sure to sell. There is one beautiful scene of a blond woman in a kitchen, *Memories Can Be Deceiving.* And one of Jeffrey's enveloping interiors, this one an interesting blend of colors, magenta and blue and lavender.

I'm standing there, incredulous, when Alexis comes out of the small office that's been fashioned out of one side of the extra-large LaReine booth. She greets me with her usual sneer. From her, this passes as friendly. I wonder if she'll care about Zach and me. I doubt it.

"How much do we hate Basel?" she says, by way of greeting.

"It's not like LaReine to do a themed booth," I say.

"You see this?" she says, gesturing at the Finellis surrounding us. "Sold. Sold. Sold. Such dumb work. I hate it. But everyone loves it. I almost wasn't able to hold on to this one for Marty."

She's pointing at *Lulu Meets God and Doubts Him.* Sold. So much for Marty going cold turkey. "He bought it?" I'm half laughing. "He could have had it at the opening. For an awful lot less."

"Martin says he likes it more at this price," she says. "Isn't that funny? He says he went to the 'Pay More' School of Life. It's a more interesting painting for him now."

"What was the price?" I ask.

"I think six seventy-five," she says. She makes a face to indicate her opinion of the work and its price.

I point at Lulu's own untitled painting. "And this one?"

"We just got that. Dreadful, isn't it?"

I shrug. "I like it."

"It's available. Only because Pierre hasn't had time to sell it yet."

"How much?"

Now it's her turn to shrug. "You think I know? Probably a half a million."

It's almost time for the hordes to be let in. I've got to get up to my spot in the booth. Simon greets me cheerily. "What did you do last night?" he asks me.

I give him a sharp look. Does he know I spent the night with Zach? Yes, the whole night. We never left my flower-scented room, not even to eat. "Nothing," I lie.

He doesn't seem to find anything unusual about this. "I went out with the young chaps. That was a mistake. I've got the mother of all hangovers."

Just after eleven, before any of the crowds have made it up to our lonely spot at the back of the second floor, Simon says, "Fetch me a Coca-Cola, would you, luv? I'm in pain."

He hands me some Swiss francs. "And see what's happening with the Finellis."

I head downstairs, against the crowd. This

is not easy when the crowd is made up of the world's most intense art collectors jonesing for a fix. I get knocked in the head with a Louis Vuitton Murakami bag.

I reach the LaReine booth just as Connie does. She's moving as fast as her stacked sandals can carry her. "There it is," she says to Andrew, who isn't anywhere near hearing distance of her. He's still down the corridor on the CrackBerry. Connie points up at the large painting before her. The Lulu in *Lulu Meets God* greets both of us with a familiar smile.

"You'd better not say it's sold," she says, shaking a finger at Alexis.

"It's sold," Alexis says, obviously enjoying herself.

Connie stomps her foot. It's very dramatic, in the way that five-year-olds can be dramatic. "I don't believe this."

Her voice goes screechy, as it tends to do when she forgets to breathe. "It's because I'm a woman, playing a man's game. They'll never let me win."

A small crowd gathers, watching Connie. Art lovers do enjoy a spot of drama.

Pierre LaReine sees that Connie is making a scene in his booth and says, to no one in particular, "Voilà. Zis is why I hate fairs."

"Calm down," Alexis says to Connie. "It's

only a painting."

"Only a painting!" Connie retorts. "That piece belongs to me."

LaReine waves Connie wearily toward him. "I think we can work something out."

"On a Finelli?" Her voice is still whiny, but she can't hide her interest.

They disappear into the office.

"You think he's going to sell her something?" I ask Alexis.

She points at the other Lulu painting, Lulu's version. The self-portrait with its Finelli signature, almost exactly the same signature as on all the other paintings, the sold paintings in the booth. "Maybe that one."

By the end of the day, I've sold eighty thousand dollars' worth of art — not bad, considering that aside from Jeffrey Finelli, Simon is not very good at finding the kind of artists international collectors want to buy. He's not exactly a finger-on-the-pulse sort of fellow, my boss, but don't tell him I said that.

When the fair closes, Simon's already gone. He's having drinks with his yoga buddy. I've taken off my shoes and am rubbing my feet when Zach appears, holding a cold bottle of water. He hands it to me.

Just a bottle of water. But the fact that he thought about how thirsty I would be after a very long afternoon of talking, talking, talking, makes me want to cry in my exhausted state.

He cups my face in both hands. "How was your day?"

And then he kisses me.

"I couldn't concentrate all day," he says.

"Me neither."

He kisses me again.

Everyone is gone from the convention center by the time Zach and I head out, hand in hand. It feels so different, to walk through now-quiet corridors with someone at my side, rather than alone. And not just someone. Zach.

There is so much art. Sculptures and photographs and installations and videos and paintings, one booth after another. Endless rows of art, plenty of stuff to buy, despite collectors' complaints that "everything is sold." Jeffrey Finelli's oeuvre, his life's work, seems insignificant here in this massive concentration of product for sale.

Zach's hand holds mine lightly. It fits just so. As we make our way to the escalator, we're stopped by a piece on a large flat-panel LCD screen that hangs on the front wall of the booth of a German gallery. It's an unfamiliar name.

Ominous music blares from the speakers at either side of the screen, their volume obviously set for the decibel level of the crowded fair rather than the evening quiet once the hordes have gone on to the parties and dinners to which they've presumably been invited.

The screen shows a tight shot of a body on a rainy street. At first glance it seems like a still image. The music stops us, and we watch the screen, waiting for something to happen. There is something subliminally familiar to me about the image, but I assume that it's because the work is derivative of some other artist whose name eludes me.

We watch as the rain beats down on the body. Suddenly the camera pulls way, way back in a jerky handheld style. And it hits me. I know what we're watching. This is the video of Jeffrey's body on the street that guy was shooting that night when he yelled out in his own defense, "Hey, man, this is art."

The way the shot is framed, you can't see that the body is Jeffrey's. You see people walking into the gallery, and through a trick of perspective, or through digital manipulation, it looks as though they are stepping callously right over him as they move into the gallery.

Then the action speeds up, and there is mayhem. The music gets faster and an ambulance pulls up and people are everywhere, but the digital film has been tinted and blurred, so you don't actually see who the people are. You see outlines of bodies, shadows moving around the body and the ambulance, and you hear a siren. The music gets slower and slower and the mayhem quiets and the movement disappears. The camera zooms back in on the form on the street. And we're back to the initial tight shot of the body, with the ominous music blaring around us.

Honestly? I don't get it. There are nicely framed images, but don't ask me what it's all supposed to mean. I'm sure this guy didn't know Jeffrey and has no claim to his death. Why would he make this work?

As I stand there with my hand in Zach's, I can't help thinking about how much everything has changed since that night. My whole perspective on life has shifted, as though I'm painting the same scene, but from an entirely new angle. I'm a failed artist, as Jeffrey might have put it, but my point of view has gone from a narrow focus to a wide-open lens.

Twenty-Two:
Please Come to Dinner at Restaurant Hirschen, Bus Departs at 8:00 p.m. Opposite the Messeplatz Don't Forget Your Passport

Most of the fun of art fairs is to be found at the parties. The traveling international art scene is basically a year-long fiesta with certain set stops along the way. Contemporary collectors and dealers and even curators enjoy vacationing and drinking and socializing with like-minded artsy souls. Some particularly enjoy the satisfaction of attending the party that on any given night feels like the right one. Only that's where it gets complicated. On any of the three or four or five nights around any fair or at any destination there could be three or four or five events with the potential of being "the right one."

It can be very stressful. The collectors either want to be invited and aren't, or they have to try to squeeze it all in. They don't want to miss anything. It's even worse for the dealers if they're hosting a party. They might have to turn away important collectors who haven't been quick to respond if the venue they've chosen can't accommodate any more people. Cue sound track: Queen, "Under Pressure."

Tonight the right party appears to be one being thrown by a group of dealers at a restaurant over the border in Germany, where the elusive white asparagus is in season for only a short time that happens to coincide with Art Basel. It certainly seems like all the high-profile international players are doing this one, including New Yorkers Robert and Jenna Bain. Even Pierre La-Reine is coming, according to Alexis, who's thrilled to accompany her new best-friend-slash-client Martin Better.

The hosts have arranged for buses to take their guests to the restaurant. It's a short ride from Basel, Switzerland, but we have to bring our passports.

Even though my feet are in such agony I would cut them off if I thought it would help, and I'm not really a fan of white asparagus, I can't help catching the contagiously buoyant mood in the bus to Germany with Zach at my side. He whispers a witty commentary about the rest of our bus mates the whole ride that keeps me laughing out loud. It doesn't seem so tough to be in Basel as part of the dealer community instead of as an artist, with Zach to keep me company.

He takes my hand, and a bolt of electricity runs down my arm. "Be gentle with me, McMurray," he says.

"I should say the same to you," I whisper into his ear.

"I hear you've left a trail of broken hearts."

"Where are you getting your information? You've got to get better sources if you're going to get anywhere in the art world." I'm kidding, but I don't think this is a good time for us to relay our dating histories. I change the subject. "Did Connie buy anything today at the fair?"

"I'm sure she did," he says. "I heard her bragging about getting thrown out."

The restaurant is only about a half hour away, even on a cautious Swiss bus, but there are border guards and purported passport controls to make it exciting, and there is something very festive about boarding a bus to another country for dinner. It seems like only minutes before we're pulling into the garden where we'll be eating.

Lulu and Dane are in the garden when we arrive. Flutes of champagne are proffered by frauleins in frilly aprons as Zach and I greet them.

"Did you see it?" Lulu asks me, pulling me aside.

"Your painting? It was hard to miss."

"The contessa sent it. She said she was doing me a favor," she says. "But I don't know if she told LaReine or not. She says she told him it was mine. But he could have understood that to mean he thought I owned it and was selling it, through him, as part of the whole deal."

Before I can respond, Connie comes at us, clinging to Simon's arm as though she will fall down if she lets go. She looks like she's already had a few glasses of the bubbly stuff.

"I bought a Finelli today" she says, lifting her champagne glass and clinking it to the one in Lulu's hand. "From Pierre LaReine."

She takes a big gulp and finishes what's in her glass. "Early work," she says. But mark my words, if Martin Better ever sells *Lulu Meets God,* I'm buying it. I don't care what it costs."

She burps quietly. "Mark my words," she says to Lulu.

Lulu and I exchange looks as Connie waves her glass toward Simon. "Simey," she calls. "Refill."

She steps away from us to hand her glass to Simon and, at the same time, lick his ear. She nuzzles up to him and then looks backward toward the four of us, Zach, Lulu, Dane, and me, gaping at the two of them.

"What happens in Basel," she says loudly, "STAYS in Basel." Then, breaking into a fit of giggles, she pulls Simon's head toward her and plants her lips on his.

"I think I'm going to throw up," Zach says, in all seriousness.

"I've lost what little appetite I had for asparagus," Dane says.

"I've got something to tell you all," Lulu says quietly, a small smile playing at her lips.

She pulls the three of us from the crowd that is being herded toward the tables to sit for dinner. "It's actually kind of funny."

"What is?" Zach asks.

Dane points at Simon and Connie. "What, those two?"

"This kind of thing happens all the time in Basel," Zach says. He looks at me, and then quickly adds, "or so I've heard."

"Please to find your seating now." A German waitress gestures toward the garden where most of the party is already seated.

"She bought a Finelli," Lulu says to the four of us. "A Lulu painting, all right. It's one I painted. I left it in the studio the night of the funeral. I'm not sure LaReine knows it. And from the sound of it Connie definitely doesn't know it. She called it early work. But it's a fake. It's my work, not my uncle's."

"Crikey, you're a funny girl," Dane says.

Zach laughs. "It's not your fault. It's that countess. She's the one selling the fake."

At that moment Pierre LaReine appears at the top of the steps down to the garden where the crowd of dinner guests is gathered. With him is a very beautiful woman in a long red dress. The contessa. The four of us stare at the two of them. The whole garden full of people stare at the two of them.

They pause, as though posing, even though there are no cameras here tonight. The contessa is impossibly elegant, more dramatically graceful than I remember. She has one of her rolled cigarettes in an ivory holder in one hand and the other hand draped gracefully at her hip. LaReine holds a small package, wrapped in brown parcel wrap and tied with a string. He doesn't seem at all bothered by the red dress and the dramatic red lipstick she wears.

The conversational buzz dies down as we all stare rudely. It's hard not to look at such a couple. Even the people who don't know about Jeffrey Finelli — where've they been? under a rock? — can't help being struck by the visual image of these two together.

"You have the package?" the contessa says to LaReine. The chatter in the garden has gone so quiet we can all hear her.

Pierre LaReine is not in the habit of carrying packages, even his own. Of that I'm quite certain. But he looks perfectly comfortable clutching hers. There are at least seventy people seated in the garden ignoring the asparagus and straining to hear as we watch the contessa come toward our table.

"I brought a gift for you," she says to Lulu, gesturing at Pierre LaReine as if he's someone's houseboy.

LaReine hands over the wrapped package to Lulu. She stares at the contessa as if trying to decide how to play this. I can't tell if she's angry or confused or just amused, as she wears a look similar to the one in the painting of her at nine. Lulu opens her mouth as though she will say something.

Then she closes it and pulls the wrapper off the package in her hand.

Underneath the brown paper and twine is a small painting. There is only one artist who could have painted this piece, a figure of a woman reclining on an orange sofa. The colors are very similar to the ones in the Lulu painting, and the woman resembles the real-life Lulu, although older.

Lulu lets out a tiny gasp. "My mom."

"Is my gift to you," the contessa says. "Jeffrey would want you to have it."

Lulu fixes her round gray eyes on the woman before her. "For a man who destroyed all his work, my uncle seems to have been awfully prolific."

The contessa holds her gaze steadily.

"Why didn't you tell me when I was there?" Lulu continues. "You could have showed me these works. Even if I didn't inherit them. You said everything was destroyed."

"Everything in the studio *was* destroyed, yes. The count, he liked to work on something for a long time, and then . . . *Basta.*" She makes a gesture, like she's putting a fist through a canvas. The ash from her hash-scented cigarette falls. "Is all I have of him. I make this gift for you. Is worth a lot, I know." She waves the cigarette toward

Pierre LaReine. "My friend here tells me this."

Pierre LaReine seems to read this as a cue to leave, and he moves toward the bar at the far end of the garden.

"What about the painting in the booth?" Lulu says. "Did you tell LaReine I painted that?"

The contessa takes a deep drag and lets it drift out of her mouth slowly. "I make you more than one gift. The count would have wanted this. And I tell you why."

The contessa looks at me, then Dane, then Zach and Pierre. "In private?" she asks. "Or you want them to hear?"

It seems everyone in the garden is listening. Or trying to. I spot one white-haired Belgian leaning so far in our direction he practically falls off his chair.

"They can hear," Lulu says, indicating Zach, Dane, and me. "These are my friends."

The contessa blows smoke away from us. "Are you ready?"

"Of course," Lulu says, looking around at the rest of us.

The contessa pauses. "He was your father."

We all lean closer, as if we couldn't have heard her right.

"What?" Lulu says.

The contessa nods. "He wasn't sure. But I've never been more *certo*. Once I saw the canvas you painted. And your signature. Just like his. Certain."

"If he was my father," Lulu says slowly, like she's having a hard time processing what the contessa's just said, "then who is that man who was married to my mother?"

"His brother. They had an affair. Very brief. Very forbidden. After the marriage. Your mother was, how you say, confused. She'd made a terrible mistake. She married the wrong man. She didn't love him. When she met Jeffrey, it was the *coup de foudre,* in French. Instant mad love."

"Oh, my God," Lulu says. "I think I'm going to be sick."

"Here," Dane says, handing her a glass of water.

"When she became pregnant, she wasn't sure who could be the father. It became too complicated. She went a little crazy."

"She went a lot crazy," Lulu says.

"Her husband never knew. At least Jeffrey didn't think so. Jeffrey loved you, but as you got older he realized how difficult it would be to remain part of your life."

"Oh, my God," Lulu says, over and over. "My mother never said anything. Even after my father died. Even when she was dying."

The contessa lights another cigarette, fitting this one into the long white holder, and I watch her, the woman who was part of Jeffrey's life for twenty years, so close to him that he became known as the count to her countess.

She speaks as though this is a story she knows intimately. She's a pretty good storyteller, this wily old countess. "He could see it in your eyes. He knew. But what could he do?"

She breathes out a long plume of smoke. "They didn't have all that, what do you call it, DNA testing? So they could never have known for certain. But your mother, she would not have chosen that anyway. She wanted to forget she'd ever been unfaithful. She couldn't live with the guilt. She was Catholic, you know."

"I can't believe she *was* ever unfaithful. It seems so out of character," Lulu says.

The contessa looks at each of us, me, Zach, Dane, in turn. "So she completely cut him. *Basta,* out, no more. She put him out of her mind. And he did the same. He had no choice."

"She was miserable for the rest of her life," Lulu says, thoughtfully rubbing her cheek. "Why did he paint me? And then say he was giving me the painting, after he'd sold it to a dealer in New York?"

"It isn't obvious?"

"Obvious? No, it's not obvious," Lulu says. "It makes no sense at all."

The contessa takes a long, deep breath, lifting her foot and stubbing her cigarette out on the bottom of her elegant pointy black pump.

"He couldn't be sure, you see. He thought he was right, but he didn't know. There was a longing he felt, for the family he couldn't have and for you, the daughter he didn't know. It became, what's the term? A spiritual quest. To find his home, he called it, to find God. And this he found through his art."

"Why didn't he get in touch with me?"

"He wanted to show you the painting. That was how he would explain. He wanted you to understand what he wanted for you. You were the end of the line, he said. A long line of failed artists, he called it. He thought you would be the one who would be the success. How you say it? A legacy. That was his message to you."

"Me? Why not him? He wasn't a failed artist anymore."

"He didn't know that," she says. "Is why he went to New York. I'm sorry. I should

399

have told you in Florence. I was very sad that day. And I became unsure. It seemed too, difficult. For you to know, when really, it didn't matter."

The contessa reaches our her arms. Lulu pauses briefly. Then she allows herself to be embraced.

"Does Pierre LaReine know that I painted that painting? Or does he think it was Jeffrey's? My father's?"

"Let's ask him," the contessa says, waving at LaReine across the garden. She takes Lulu by the arm.

"Please to find your seats," one of the frauleins says, even more insistently now. Zach and I take the closest available seats and watch across the garden as Lulu talks to Pierre LaReine.

We see her point in the direction of Connie, sitting with Simon at a table of French people, all speaking a language she doesn't understand.

Zach and I taste the asparagus as we watch Pierre LaReine approach Connie's table. She looks up at him with glee, proud to have the famous art dealer come to her. She can now claim to be a client of his. Maybe one day she'll get invited on his plane.

We watch as Pierre kneels at Connie's

side, talking into her ear. She listens intently. The Birkin bag at Connie's feet? Ten thousand dollars. The diamond hanging off her finger, what's that? A hundred thousand or so? The look on Connie's face when she learns she's bought a Lulu Finelli painting instead of a Jeffrey Finelli? Priceless.

Her thin lips seem to freeze in rigor mortis as Pierre LaReine's words take shape inside her brain. When he finishes talking, she doesn't respond immediately. Her gaze shifts in our direction. Zach and I both pretend to turn our attention to the asparagus.

There's a moment when it seems Connie is going to want her money back. A half a million dollars, if Alexis was right. Connie stands and gestures toward Lulu, who is at the other end of the garden with Dane and the contessa. We brace ourselves for a good show of drama, screaming, perhaps even a tossed glass of champagne. But Connie simply smiles, the stiffness in her face loosening.

She doesn't seem bothered by the news that she's just spent a half a million dollars on a painting by an unknown — sorry, emerging — artist. Pierre LaReine must have convinced her he was representing Lulu now. And that is exactly what he'll go on to do, promising a show of new work the following spring.

Zach and I spend our second night together in his room at the Swissotel. There are no white roses this time, but the sex is good. Very good. Not that you asked.

"Can I tell you that I love you?" he asks, leaning over me on the bed when it's over and we're catching our breath.

"Only if you mean it."

"I loved you from the minute I met you," he says, kissing my forehead before he flops down next to me and pulls my head onto his chest.

"We're going to have to work on that story," I say. "When people ask us how we met, I don't want the first time to be something I don't remember."

"It was love at first sight," he says, laughing. "At the Simon Pryce Gallery. That's my story, and I'm sticking to it."

"But it took eight months for you to do anything about it," I say. "And I'm certain we met at auction."

"Actually, it was closer to nine months," he says. "It's eight months since the auction. The day when I walked into the gallery and you sneered at me, that was the day my heart stopped for the first time."

"That could not have been me," I protest. "I never sneer. I'm friendly. People tell me I have a nice smile."

"You have a great smile," he says with a laugh. "But I didn't see it until I plied you with martinis and got you so drunk you couldn't see straight. I always did feel bad about that."

And that, my friend, seems to be how the story ends. Lulu doesn't get the painting she wanted, but she does get what the artist, her father, intended her to get from it. And she has another Finelli to take home. So does Connie. And so do three other collectors on Pierre LaReine's list, who all got the early call on the contessa's Finellis. Martin Better goes home with the masterpiece, *Lulu Meets God and Doubts Him.*

Just like the asparagus, Finelli season is over. Or so it seems.

Twenty-Three:
Fall Postwar and Contemporary Auction
Monday 7:00 p.m.

November

The story doesn't end there. There's the bit about the article for which I agreed to be interviewed in a fit of creative expression that led to me finding myself as a writer rather than a visual artist. Remember that? The magazine article comes out soon after we all come home from Basel. And let's just say Simon never appreciated me for my creative genius. He fires me immediately.

I don't think it's the part where I accuse him of murder that gets him mad. I don't even think it's anything I say about his unethical business practices. But he really doesn't appreciate my implications about his accent.

Getting fired from the gallery is the best thing to happen to me. Zach helps me get a job cataloging a collection for a lovely Japanese woman. This leaves me a lot of free time to work on this, my . . . well, I'm not really sure what to call it. It's not a roman à clef, is it? And it's certainly not a memoir. I didn't have a miserable childhood, after all, or any traumatic dental work without anesthetic.

This is just a story about a painting that inspired a lot of people. It's a story about "the goods," as Simon might say. By September, after a wonderful summer of writing and Zach, I'm at the part where we find out Jeffrey is actually Lulu's father. I'm about to let Zach read my manuscript when he learns that Jeffrey Finelli's portrait of Lulu is coming up for sale once again.

As the word goes, Martin Better is bored with art. Bored!? This rumor sends a cold chill up and down the Chelsea streets, as though all the collectors in the world are going to grow bored and follow in Marty's footsteps, selling off their collections and moving on. This is the bursting of the bubble. It will be like the nineties, people are saying, dread lacing their words. Prices have just gotten too high, they say, like during the tulip craze. It will be a relief, some add, to go through a correction.

Of course there's a lot of negative talk about Martin Better, because art dealers and curators and historians have a tendency to imbue decisions about a collector's art purchases and sales with character qualities or flaws. The talk disparages Martin Better as both a collector and as a person. But the truth is, Marty's not really bored. He's getting divorced.

Alexis Belkin is on her way to trading one cliché for another, from obnoxious gallery girl to an even more prevalent type, the former gallery girl turned wife. She'll be Martin Better's third wife eventually, if all goes according to plan. She's left Pierre LaReine to become the curator of Martin Better's art collection, and now she's helping him edit the pieces she doesn't like, the ones she's happy for him to lose in what will be a relatively large settlement of cash onto his second wife.

When I hear the painting is coming up for sale in November, I realize I can't finish my written version of the story until I know what happens to it at auction. So I wait. In the meantime, Zach and I celebrate the first of our two anniversaries. In October, right before he leaves for London and the Frieze Art Fair, a year after the date he insists he saw me in the gallery for the first time, Zach fills my room with white flowers (again!) and asks me to give up my apartment to move in with him.

"Twist my arm," I tell him. And then yes.

By the second week in November, when the first of the fall auctions takes place, I'm living in what is now *our* apartment with a fireplace. Zach has a meeting with a client before the sale, but he's gotten me a pass for the standing section and asks me to find him by the door to the sale room when it's over. "No slipping out early," he says in reference to the length of the sale, some seventy-eight lots.

I'm nervous heading to the auction. I haven't seen Simon since he fired me, and I'd prefer to avoid having tonight be our first meeting. He could choose such a moment to express a lifetime of pent-up British rage at me.

The spot that I take in the sale room, just to the right of the large column, allows me to see someone slide in, unnoticed at the back. It's Lulu. I'm not entirely shocked to see her, although I *am* surprised to see her attempt at disguise, in a black hat and big black glasses. What is she doing? I think I'm the only one who recognizes her; no one else in the room seems to even look in her direction. I am surprised at the outfit, the hat like something out of Grandma's closet, big tacky sunglasses, but I'm astonished to see her holding a paddle. I knew she had some Wall Street money, but not art-auction kind of money. This is what we call funny money, and even Lulu with all her good fortune doesn't have funny money.

Yet when lot 22 comes up on the block, there she goes. Bidding up the piece. Bidding over and over and over. Yes, the mystery bidder at the back of the room is none other than Lulu Finelli herself.

Is she planning on taking home her painting, or is she just trying to bid it up? And what the hell is she going to do if Connie stops at three and a half million, forcing Lulu to come up with that kind of money for her painting?

I can't believe my eyes when I see her continue to bid. But Lulu seems to know what I know too, what everyone in the room seems to sense. Connie won't stop. She can't stop. There's a voraciousness to Connie's appetite that can't be fed, even with a world-renowned collection of contemporary art.

I still don't know why Lulu was there. I never ask if she went simply to bid the piece up, or if she really intended to take it home with her. And if so, how she would have paid for it. I don't want to know. All I know is anyone who says this sale wasn't exciting is lying.

■ ■ ■ ■

A funny thing happens after the auction. Simon introduces me to his mother. I didn't think Simon had a mother. But yes, he does, and she is a very lovely woman, with a large mane of artfully highlighted blond hair, windswept off a lined brown face, whom he introduces me to as his mum.

She wears a smart Chanel-type suit and a strand of pearls. "Hullo," she says, in an unmistakably British accent. "Lovely to meet you."

"Mum," he says, friendly now. "This is Mia, she used to work for me."

"I don't know how you did it," she says to me with a warm smile.

As Zach and I leave the building together, Martin Better is outside in front of the auction house. His soon-to-be ex-wife is not with him, but Alexis is. "Strong sale," Alexis is saying as we pass them. "This market just keeps going up and up."

But Martin is feeling seller's remorse. "I should've kept that painting."

ABOUT THE AUTHOR

Danielle Ganek lives in New York City with her husband, three children, and some inspiring art. Her favorite paintings are the ones her kids bring home from school. This is her first book.

www.danielleganek.com

The employees of Thorndike Press hope you have enjoyed this Large Print book. All our Thorndike and Wheeler Large Print titles are designed for easy reading, and all our books are made to last. Other Thorndike Press Large Print books are available at your library, through selected bookstores, or directly from us.

For information about titles, please call:
  (800) 223-1244

or visit our Web site at:
  www.gale.com/thorndike
  www.gale.com/wheeler

To share your comments, please write:
  Publisher
  Thorndike Press
  295 Kennedy Memorial Drive
  Waterville, ME 04901